"I am *virtuous!*" Her cheeks p…
"And you are wrong."

"Am I?"

Her annoyed gaze locked with his. "Yes."

"Hmm. That's interesting." He observed her anew, liking her courage. "I bet you wish you'd left when you'd had the chance."

He felt a smile sneak onto his face and was dumbfounded by it. It couldn't be that he was *enjoying* her company, could it?

It seemed it could, Griffin marveled, and smiled afresh. He couldn't remember the last time he'd smiled twice in one day.

His pleasure only appeared to gall her further. "I wish I'd clobbered you with your breakfast tray. *That's* what I wish!"

He offered a tsk-tsk of sham politeness. "Come, now. That's hardly the exemplary service the Lorndorff is known for."

An unintelligible sound of frustration came from her. Oddly enough, Griffin liked it. He liked seeing her ladylike facade crumble. He liked knowing he could affect her. He liked...*her.*

The realization made Griffin falter.

* * *

Notorious in the West
Harlequin® Historical #1183—May 2014

Author Note

Thank you for reading *Notorious in the West!* I'm delighted to return to the Arizona Territory, and I'm thrilled to share Olivia and Griffin's story with you. If you had fun reading about them (and I hope you did!), please try another book in my Morrow Creek series. It includes *The Honor-Bound Gambler, Mail-Order Groom, The Bride Raffle* and several others (including some short stories and an ebook exclusive), all set in and around my favorite Old West town.

If you'd like to try a few sample chapters, you can find complete first-chapter excerpts from all my books at my website, www.lisaplumley.com. While you're there, you can also download an up-to-date booklist, sign up for new-book alerts, read sneak previews of upcoming books, request reader freebies and more. I hope you'll stop by today!

As always, I'd love to hear from you! You can follow me on Twitter, @LisaPlumley, "friend" me on Facebook, at www.facebook.com/LisaPlumleyBooks, send an email to lisa@lisaplumley.com, or visit me online at www.community.harlequin.com.

Best wishes till next time.

LISA PLUMLEY

—

NOTORIOUS IN THE WEST

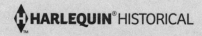

Recycling programs
for this product may
not exist in your area.

ISBN-13: 978-0-373-29783-2

NOTORIOUS IN THE WEST

Printed in U.S.A.

**Did you know that these novels are also
available as ebooks? Visit www.Harlequin.com.**

To John, with all my love,
now and forever.

LISA PLUMLEY

When she found herself living in modern-day Arizona Territory, Lisa Plumley decided to take advantage of it—by immersing herself in the state's fascinating history, visiting ghost towns and historical sites and finding inspiration in the desert and mountains surrounding her. It didn't take long before she got busy creating light-hearted romances like this one, featuring strong-willed women, ruggedly intelligent men and the unexpected situations that bring them together.

When she's not writing Lisa loves to spend time with her husband and two children, traveling, hiking, watching classic movies, reading and defending her trivia-game championship. She enjoys hearing from readers, and invites you to contact her via email at lisa@lisaplumley.com, or visit her website at www.lisaplumley.com.

Chapter One

March 1872, Boston, Massachusetts

Even at the age of fourteen, Griffin Turner always knew when one of his mother's "bad times" was coming on. First she'd quit cleaning the meager four rooms they shared. Dust would pile up. Dirty pans and plates would accumulate. Rats would saunter across the gritty floors, as bold as you please—as bold as they tended to be in the tenement building Griffin and his mother had moved into After Their Circumstances Changed—and chew their way into the few remaining foodstuffs in the kitchen. A good swat with a broom got rid of them, Griffin had learned, but he hated the way that smacking their furry bodies made his skin crawl.

He also hated how weak it made him feel to admit that. After their circumstances changed, Griffin had become the man of the house. The man of the house could not be weak. He knew that.

When he failed to remember it, his mother reminded him.

A day or so after she stopped cleaning up, his mother would pull all the tatty draperies tightly shut, so that not even the tiniest sliver of wintertime sunlight could penetrate their home's dank interior. Then she would abandon whatever piecework job she'd grudgingly taken on. Finally, she would take to her bed.

Griffin wasn't sure how that was supposed to help anything. After all, nothing happened in bed except dreaming. Dreaming didn't exactly put food on the table and kindling in the fireplace. But he knew better than to say so.

At least he knew better than to say so twice.

Most of the time, Griffin managed his mother's bad times without too much hardship. He learned how to dust and sweep. He figured out how to light the stove and how to inveigle a few grocery items from their care-worn neighbors when things got desperate. He learned to leave crackers by his mother's bedside while she was asleep, but never to mention having done so the next day. He learned the precise time to bring a bracing cup of coffee into his mother's room. He learned that doing so made her smile at him…but only if he got the timing right. So he learned well.

During the bad times, Griffin tiptoed a lot.

Overall, he didn't think about his mother's moody spells much. They came like the weather; they went for reasons that were as inexplicable and as evergreen as springtime in the city. They were a fact of life— like his growing body, his work tending the fiery furnaces at the glass factory and his knowledge that the only way to get by was to toil until sweet oblivion took him at the end of the day. Sleep was good, even if he didn't remember having any dreams of his own. Work was good. He earned money to support his mother and himself. He kept busy. He had every Sunday off to do as he pleased—which *wasn't,* by the age of fourteen, to attend Sunday church services alone, as his mother believed he did. It was to revisit their old town house, which still stood in the neighborhood where they'd lived before their circumstances changed, and try to figure out how to get it back.

Generally, life was shambolic but manageable. As long as you didn't count on anything, Griffin knew, you would be fine.

Sometimes, though, enough time passed between bouts of tidying and tiptoeing—and treating his mother with the same care that the glassblowers at the factory handled their bottles and pitchers and glasshouse whimsies—that Griffin forgot about the bad times. *That* was dangerous. That was when he was blindsided.

He came home on one such day, full of verve and vinegar, puffed up on the thrill of having spent his Sunday with a girl he liked—a girl who worked at the glass factory as a sweeper. He'd met her after church. They'd spent all day roaming around the city, going to Griffin's old neighborhood and sharing a single precious gooseberry tonic at the soda fountain. The girl—Mary was her name—had taken Griffin home to meet her parents. They'd invited him in for some Irish stew and brown bread. They'd sent him home high, with a freshly barbered head of hair—courtesy of Mary's mama—and a care package of leftover stew.

He hadn't wanted to think why they'd given it to him. He knew he was thin, on account of the meals he missed or gave to his mother, but he was also tall and broad shouldered. He didn't look sickly enough to warrant a gift of potato-filled stew.

But they gave it to him kindly, so Griffin didn't refuse. He was carrying it when he breezed into the tenement building and clomped up the rickety staircase—

daydreaming about Mary's winsome face, mentally placing her in the fancy town house he meant to own someday, dressing her in finery fit for a carriage ride—and came inside to find all the draperies drawn.

Too happy to abide the gloom, Griffin opened them.

"Leave them shut," his mother snapped from her chair.

But this time, Griffin didn't want to. He'd had a nice day. He'd felt *content.* He didn't want his mother to ruin that.

"Are you hungry?" Deliberately leaving the window curtains as they were, Griffin strode through the beams of sunlight and presented the care package—wrapped in newspaper and secured with butcher's twine—to his mother. "I brought you some stew."

Suspiciously, his mother squinted. "Where have you been? I've been here on my own all day long. The fire went out."

Her peevish wave indicated the woodstove. Undaunted, Griffin set aside the stew. He took off his coat, went through the practiced motions of laying a blaze then dragged his mother's favorite quilt from a nearby chair. He laid it on her.

She clutched it, frowning. "Only the most *selfish* boy leaves his mother alone on the Lord's day. You should be ashamed of yourself! Sauntering in here, flaunting your friends and your strength and your stupid, *stupid* stew." She cast it a disgusted glance. "It smells like Irish slop. *I* wouldn't want that."

He knew his mother still considered herself above the life they had in the tenement building. He knew she didn't mean to offend. This was the point where, ordinarily, Griffin would have apologized. That was what worked best to keep the peace. But today, with Mary,

Griffin had glimpsed a brighter future—a future that didn't involve endless toil and smacking rats and accepting handouts from neighbors. A future that held the promise of laughter and plenty…and genuine smiles that didn't need to be coaxed into being but happened all on their own.

He wanted that future. His mother couldn't stop that.

"Maybe you'll want it later." He picked up the stew, wended his way past a pile of unfinished mending— piecework was all his mother could manage, owing to her continual "nervous strain"—and started an enamelware pot of coffee in the kitchen. Keeping his voice even, Griffin called into the other room, "Coffee?"

"Men don't make coffee," his mother grumbled. "*Men* don't."

He offered her a cup all the same. He was used to her abuse. He knew she didn't mean it. Not when she was like this.

"Drink it," he urged. "You'll feel better if you do."

"Humph. You're getting older. Bigger." Her accusatory gaze moved from his shoulders to his face. "You don't need me."

He knew how to answer that. "You're all I have."

But instead of the smile he yearned for—instead of the reward he wanted for holding inside the rebuke that kicked to break free—his mother gave him a disapproving finger wag. "You're getting ready to leave! That's why you were gone all day—why you're gone every day. I see it all over your face!"

Griffin was "gone every day" because he was working. Because he was trying his hardest to keep them in baked beans and brown bread, eaten in their own home instead of in a charity ward. But he didn't want to say so. That would only rile his mother. Everything got worse when he riled his mother.

Besides, he loved her. Despite…everything.

He set down the coffee nearby. "I'm not going anyplace."

"That's what *he* said, too. But you and he—you're the same kind." Another critical look. "You've got the same mark on you that he did—the same sign that tells me you're *rotten* inside."

Griffin tried to ignore that, too, the same way he'd ignored her command to close the curtains. But he was only one boy—a boy of fourteen, at that. He was old enough to work but not to shield himself against the vitriol in his mother's expression. He was, as she'd pointed out, not a man. Not yet.

"It makes me *sick* to look at you," she went on. *"Sick!"*

Her scathing tone dug deeply. Griffin flinched.

"It makes me sick to have birthed you into this world." His mother's voice trembled with emotion. "You're going to wreak havoc on it, just like *he* did, and it will be my fault."

Griffin knew what to say to that, too.

"It's not your fault. It never was." He kept his voice low, his hands steady, his manner patient. He'd practiced this part. He knew what to say. He knew how to say it. "You did all you could for him. You were a good wife. You're a good—"

Mother, he meant to say, but suddenly he wasn't so sure.

Was she a good mother? Mary's mother was a kind woman. She was gentle. She never would have said such harsh things to her own child. All at once, Griffin was sure of it. He straightened.

"Good *what?*" his mother demanded. "I'm a good *what?*"

He could tell by the wounded sheen in her eyes that she knew the praise he was withholding. At the same moment, Griffin realized he meant to keep right on withholding it. There was no way he'd give in. Not even to make her feel better. Not this time. If that made him as rotten as she'd said—

It did make him as rotten as she'd said, he understood just then, and felt despair rush through him. Of course his mother was right about him. She was his mother! She knew him, inside out.

"You can't say it because you're *evil,* like *him.*" Her voice cut into his self-condemnation, scattering his thoughts like the hot embers he shoveled all day at the glass factory. Her gaze pinned him in place, making him listen—making him endure the way she scowled at him, from his scruffy boots to his newly shorn dark hair. "You're cruel," she judged. "*That's* the mark of it, right there on your face. *Everyone* can see it. Especially me."

"No. I'm not marked." Somehow, Griffin found the strength to raise his chin. "There's nothing wrong with my face."

But even as he said it, his voice quavered. His throat closed up. It ached, just like his hands did. He'd clenched his fists, he saw, without realizing it. Because he knew his mother was telling the truth. After all, people had stared at him his whole life. They'd pointed and whispered. They'd laughed.

They'd turned away. Away from *him.*

Even at the glass factory, where he'd earned some respect, they'd nicknamed him Hook. *Hook Turner.* Griffin hadn't blamed them for that. His oversize hook of a nose *was* conspicuous. The nickname had begged to be given. But now he wondered...

Did *everyone* see what his mother did when they looked at him? Did everyone see his lack of character, his lack of strength, his lack of *goodness?*

You're evil, he heard her say again, so callously and calmly. *You're rotten inside. You're cruel. Everyone can see it.*

Reliving those words, Griffin felt a hot rush of shame. There was no point sidestepping the truth. Ever since his voice had deepened and his shoulders had widened, his features had matured, too. He'd definitely inherited his father's nose.

And with it, it seemed, his father's wicked nature.

All Griffin could remember now of his father was his husky laughter and—hazily—his face, with its similarly prominent hawklike nose and incongruously merry eyes. Edward Turner had been scarred by the same disfigurement that now marked Griffin.

He'd been made uglier by it, even to his wife.

Of course he had. After all, everyone knew that having a good moral character was what made someone nice to look at. Virtuous women were beautiful. Decent men were handsome. That was why they were admired. Griffin didn't know how he'd let himself overlook that fact. Maybe he'd just needed to. Until now.

"*That's* the inheritance of the Turner men," his mother went on. "I'd hoped you'd be spared. Now I can see you were not. You're *rotten,* through and through." She gave him a punishing look, confirming it. "It's as plain as the nose on your face."

If that was meant to be a joke, it wasn't funny.

From somewhere, though, Griffin found a glimmer of defiance. Maybe this *didn't* have to be the end of him—the end of hope for him. It was whispered that, someplace in the city, Edward Turner was prospering. That he'd made good, despite his glaring nasal defect. Maybe Griffin could do the same.

Not that his father's success meant much to his starving and abandoned family. To them, he might as well have been dead.

Maybe he hadn't been able to bear the sight of his son....

Griffin fixed his spine. "It doesn't matter. I'll work." *I'll work like my father did.* "I'll overcome it."

At that, his mother burst out in unpleasant laughter. "You can't overcome *that,* boy!" She pointed. "It's ludicrous to try."

But Griffin knew that he could. He had to. What other choice was there? He couldn't go through life with his hated defect being all that people saw when they looked at him.

It was bad enough that he was helpless to hide it. He couldn't wear a bandito's bandanna, like a desperado from a dime novel. His only hat wasn't big enough to obscure his face. And now, with his hair cropped so closely, his nose was even more noticeable. No wonder his mother had chosen today to tell him these things. Doubtless, she'd taken one look at his protruding feature and been overcome. *That* was why she'd been so cruel.

She hadn't been able to help herself.

It had been for his own good, he reckoned.

He had to make up for his flaw somehow, Griffin knew. He had to amass *other* things, things that would compensate for his appearance. Things that would make him wealthy, make him whole, make him a real man—a real man who *wasn't* afraid of rats, *didn't* make coffee for the womenfolk and refused to be called Hook

Turner by those knucks at the glass factory. Whatever it took, Griffin vowed, he would remake himself into someone stronger.

He couldn't remake himself into someone *better*. He knew that now. Given his birthright, he couldn't be good. So he would have to settle for being strong. Being hard. Being tough.

He would have to settle for being invulnerable.

As a first step, Griffin schooled his face into an impassive mask. It was sorely difficult, but he did it. Then he drew in a deep breath. He looked squarely at his mother.

"Someday," he said, "you'll know you were wrong about me."

She gave him a dubious look. Pointedly, she glanced away.

"Someday," he added, pushed by her obvious skepticism, "you'll be *proud* to call me your son."

His mother's obstinate expression didn't change. Neither did her refusal to acknowledge his promise. But Griffin didn't care. He couldn't allow himself to care. He *wouldn't*.

What he lacked in other ways—what he longed for and couldn't have—he could make up for with single-mindedness, Griffin reasoned. His mother might be stubborn—too stubborn, even, to love him—but he was stubborn, too. Stubborn and smart and ready to work his fingers to the bone to earn his success. Whatever it took to change his life, he would do it.

"You *will* be proud of me," he repeated. "I swear it."

Then, without waiting for his mother to answer him, Griffin left her with her cold coffee and her charity Irish stew and went to figure out how he could most quickly make his fortune.

Because everything started with money, he knew… and ended with him forcing the world to admit it was wrong about Griffin Turner *and* what he was capable of—hawklike nose and all.

Chapter Two

June 1872, Morrow Creek, northern Arizona Territory

As a girl who had never experienced neuralgia, lassitude *or* vexing biliousness, Olivia Mouton should not have felt drawn to the traveling medicine show that came to town on the Sunday after her thirteenth birthday. But there was something about the peddler's intriguing medicinal claims that pulled her nearer.

"This latest miracle elixir will end nervous troubles and colonic maladies alike. It will restore youth and vigor!" The charming peddler, finely dressed in a woolen suit with a fancy waistcoat, held aloft a full glass bottle. Its label was typeset with an impressively diverse list of the ailments it purported to achieve a remedy for. The man wasted no time explaining his wares' efficacy. "Wise lore from the savage! Grandmother's soothing tinctures! Scrupulous scientific approaches! All are represented here!" He gave a graceful gesture, then grinned invitingly at the crowd. "Step right up and see for yourselves."

Interestingly, Olivia examined the wares he'd arrayed in tidy rows atop his wagon's hinged backboard.

There were brown and green bottles full of distillations, cork-stoppered vials of fascinating tonics and flat tins of curative powders. There were jars of creams and ointments, sachets of dried herbs and boxes of exotic-smelling teas printed with celestial characters. There was even a selection of preserved exotic fruits, which—according to their labels—could improve "stamina." Olivia knew it was unlikely that the medicine show's merchandise could accomplish even half the things the peddler promised in his spiel, but that hadn't stopped an eager crowd from forming.

After all, his arrival was the single most exciting occurrence in sleepy Morrow Creek township since the circuit judge had rode in a week or so ago…and promptly gotten too drunk on mescal to hear any cases or cast any judgments on wrongdoers.

Most days, nothing much happened in her tiny territorial hometown. Miners trudged off to their claims in the surrounding mountainside. Rail workers toiled on the incoming rail spur, felling the obstructive ponderosa pines and laying track past the burbling namesake creek. Wives and laundresses went about their chores and tended their children with dusty equanimity.

Someday, perhaps, Morrow Creek would be a bustling place, full of vigor and industry and stirring intellectual societies. At the moment, though, Olivia's rough-hewn hometown lacked everything from a decent mercantile or a completed rail depot to a proper schoolhouse. Lessons were sporadic and held outdoors. The town leaders were attempting to woo an instructor from the East to educate the youth of Morrow Creek. Given their current rate of progress, such a teacher's potential students would have long gray beards before that teacher's hiring was complete.

It was fortunate for Olivia that her father was so brilliant. Without Henry Mouton's tutoring and encouragement—and willingness to barter with the J. G. O'Malley & Sons traveling book agent who occasionally came through town—Olivia would have been in quite a fix herself. As it was, she spent less time studying, though, than she did helping with the day-to-day duties of running her beloved father's nascent hotel business. At the moment, The Lorndorff Hotel was not much more than a few nailed-together timbers for beams, an array of canvas for walls and several lumpy beds. But someday, Olivia knew, the hotel would define Morrow Creek as a place for sophisticated and educated folk to gather, converse and entertain socially.

The collecting crowd was *right* to be interested, Olivia reasoned as the peddler's avowals grew ever more animated and persuasive. At least *some* of the claims the man was making had to be true. This was the nineteenth century after all! Miraculous scientific achievements had taken place.

Some of those achievements had been made by women, too. Olivia knew that because she *loved* to read. She'd learned about Mary Fairfax Somerville's experiments with magnetism and about Maria Mitchell's astronomical discovery of her new comet. Olivia had daydreamed about creating and publishing botanical photograms like Anna Atkins or unearthing a *Plesiosaurus* fossil like Mary Anning. She'd thrilled to periodical accounts of Lady Augusta Ada Byron's invention of the analytical engine. Of course, she also idolized pioneering medical professionals such as the physician Elizabeth Blackwell and the tireless nurse

Florence Nightingale. To Olivia, those women were true heroines.

While her best friend Annie's oak bureau held hairbrushes and pearled pins and precious scraps of scented soap, Olivia's makeshift crate-turned-nightstand held *Familiar Lecturers on Natural Philosophy* by the intellectual Almira Hart Lincoln Phelps. The work was somewhat dated, but it was fascinating—as was *The Mechanism of the Heavens* by Mary Somerville, another of her favorites. Naturally, Olivia also treasured her well-thumbed copies of texts by authors such as Charles Darwin and Jean-Baptiste Lamarck, but she preferred reading the work of female scientists and scholars. Somehow *their* achievements felt all the closer to her own life…and all the more real for it.

Even if those women *didn't* live in a single-street Western town with not much more to brag of than a church, a popular saloon and more tobacco spittoons than were strictly reasonable.

As far as Olivia was concerned, anything was possible. The lives of the great women she'd studied proved it. They'd all asked questions, encountered important turning points in their lives and let their curiosity guide them on to greatness.

Maybe this encounter with the peddler's scientific wonders was her *own* call to greatness, Olivia fancied. So, fully ready to begin her own quest for enlightenment, she stepped a little nearer. She picked up one of the bottles for closer study.

As she did, though, someone jostled her. Startled, Olivia held tight and glanced to the side…only to see a familiar and dispiriting sight. Old Mr. Richter, one of the railway foremen, was staring at her with a contemplative expression on his face.

He tipped his hat. "Afternoon, Miss Mouton."

In time with his greeting, his gaze dropped to her skirts. He peered at their simple calico folds as though hoping to penetrate them, then moved on to her high-buttoned bodice…and lingered. His attention took a *very* meandering path back to her face, leaving her feeling fidgety and uncomfortable in its wake.

Ugh. Why did men have to ogle her? She'd noticed this happening more often as she grew taller and more mature. Her father insisted the townspeople were merely being friendly. Olivia had her doubts. The leers she garnered didn't *feel* like simple neighborliness. But without a mother to rely upon for advice—her own poor mama had died during the journey westward—Olivia was on her own, swimming in a sea of adult interactions she wasn't entirely prepared for and certainly did not want.

Politely, she inclined her head. "Hello, Mr. Richter."

With that accomplished, Olivia directed her attention back to the patent remedy in her hand. Studiously, she examined its label. It purported to use bottled extractive magnetism as a curative. *That* was an innovative approach that Olivia had never heard of before. According to Mary Fairfax Somerville's work—

Before she could consider the scientific implications further, Mr. Richter's brusque voice intruded on her thoughts.

"Did your pa talk to you about my prop'sition?"

Oh, no. The railway foreman had to be referring to his facetious offer—made at her father's tent hotel over cups of Old Orchard whiskey late one night—to "get that girl's head outta them books and into some wifely duties, where it belongs!"

"I thought you were joking." Reluctantly, Olivia postponed her examination of the magnetism-based curative. She gave him a direct look—one she hoped he'd perceive. "If you *were* joking, Mr. Richter, that would save us both from embarrassment."

He did *not* recognize her attempts to sidestep the issue. Instead, Mr. Richter merely scratched himself absently while the medicine-show man began making sales and collecting coin.

"Ain't nothin' embarrassing about getting hitched to a beautiful woman." He spat tobacco juice. "No, ma'am."

"Mr. Richter!" This time it was Olivia's turn to gawk. And likely to blush, as well. "I am thirteen years of age!"

He shrugged. "That's old enough, if your pa agrees."

"My father will *not* agree."

"Then I'll bide my time." Plainly unperturbed *and* undeterred, Mr. Richter tipped his hat. "I can be patient." He cast a glance at the peddler's preserved exotic fruits, raised an eyebrow at their scandalous promises to bestow "bull-like stamina" then sauntered away without purchasing anything.

Irked to have had her stimulating outing interrupted for such a nonsensical reason, Olivia turned toward the medicine show's wagon—only to come face-to-face with the alert gaze of a dark-haired, lean-looking Romany man. She recognized him, having glimpsed him earlier, as the medicine show's driver and bagman.

Evidently, he'd overheard her conversation with Mr. Richter, because he aimed a disgusted glance at the foreman.

"Some men, eh? They have no finesse." The bagman leaned confidingly nearer, his warmth compelling in the cool mountain air. "A girl like you deserves better.

You are—" he gave an elegant wave "—*special*. Very special. I saw that right away."

Olivia couldn't help feeling vindicated by his perceptiveness—and a little thrilled, too. "Well," she said, "that puts you one boot ahead of Mr. Richter, doesn't it?"

"No."

"Oh. Well. I'm sorry. What I meant was—"

"I am at least *two* boots ahead of him," the bagman corrected her with a teasing grin. "Give me time. I will show you this." Convivially, his gaze dipped to the remedy bottle in her hand. "You are interested in curatives? In perhaps traveling far and wide, like me, and seeing all the wonders of the countryside?"

"I am!" At least this man hadn't tried undressing her with his eyes, Olivia reflected. He obviously— *amiably*—appreciated her intellectual curiosity, too. "Most people in Morrow Creek don't think much about what's outside it. But I do. All the time!"

The bagman gave a wise nod. "That is two of us, then. But you do not need any remedies of this kind." Gently, he touched the bottle in her hand. "This one is for—" he paused, offered a few words in an accented dialect she didn't understand then translated "—old people. *You* are not old. You are…magnificent!"

He kissed his fingertips as he said it, then flung his showy kiss to the territorial skies in a grand, gallant gesture. His dark eyes sparkled with good humor and attentiveness. Olivia couldn't help liking him—or being intrigued by him. His close-trimmed beard lent him a keenly romantic air. His tattered finery and unfamiliar European inflection gave him an exoticism that felt far too exciting for staid Morrow Creek.

Finally. Here was someone who'd speak seriously

to her. Someone who'd respect her curiosity and her bookishness alike.

Heaven knew, most people in Morrow Creek couldn't fathom either of those qualities. Annie expected Olivia to gush over dressmaking illustrations in *Godey's*. Her father expected her to be helpful be quiet, and be in bed by ten. Nothing more.

"Thank you," Olivia said, quickly dispensing with the bagman's flattery. "Now. This nostrum," she said eagerly, raising the remedy bottle again. "Can you explain how the magnetic properties survived the bottling process? Surely they're too volatile to withstand boiling?"

The man laughed. "Ah! You *are* delightful!"

Delightful? "Thank you, but I truly am interested in the process," Olivia explained, "and in magnetism in general." Didn't he realize *that was w*hat made her "special" in his eyes? "You see, Miss Fairfax Somerville's experiments proved that—"

He startled her by clasping his hand, warm and weathered, atop hers. "There is no need for this pretense. I am here! You have captured my attention." Like magic, the bagman deftly withdrew the curative she'd held. "You do not care about this."

Momentarily captivated by the sleight of hand he'd performed, Olivia stared. Then she blinked. "Yes, I do."

His wave dismissed her. "Women do not think of such things. You were pretending, to make me see you. And I do see you."

With a charming manner, he gave her a bow to prove it. But this time, Olivia belatedly noticed he was using that chivalrous gesture to sneak a peek at her ankles. The rogue!

"Never mind. I'll ask your employer for the information."

Staunchly, Olivia marched to the peddler's wagon and the circle of townspeople. She waited, feeling—and ignoring—the bagman's flirtatious gaze on her all the while. When finally the peddler turned his attention to her, she was prepared.

"Good afternoon," Olivia said firmly. "I do not want a proposal or a proposition from you. All I want to know is—"

"Yes!" The peddler widened his eyes. *"You!"*

"—how your curative with the bottled extractive magnetism was created. Are you the inventor? Or did someone else—"

But the peddler only cast out his arm to silence the waiting crowd. He stared raptly at her. He nodded.

"You are perfect!" he cried dramatically. "Perfect!"

Fully out of patience now, Olivia put her hands on her hips. "Unless you mean I'm perfect at asking questions you can't wait to answer, I honestly don't see what that has to do with—"

"You must agree to pose for me," the peddler interrupted. He stepped nearer, then chuckled. "I mean, for a lithographer, of course. I need a model to grace the bottles of my forthcoming Milky White Complexion Beautifier and Youthful Enhancement Tonic. With your face on the label, I'll sell thousands!"

She stared at him, astonished. A model? *Her?*

Rudely, he reached for her jaw. He turned her face to the sunshine. He gave an evaluating sound, then turned her face in the opposite direction. He laughed with outright glee.

Olivia jerked away her face. "Sir! I am not a horse."

"Well, you *are* a mighty fine filly."

She frowned. "And *you* are a rude man. I will not—"

"I'll pay you," he persisted, annoying her further by talking right on top of her. "I only need a few sketches."

Olivia crossed her arms, feeling frustrated. Could *no one* see that she had a mind as well as a face and figure? Could no one understand that there was more to Olivia Mouton than frilly skirts, blue eyes and embarrassingly burgeoning bosoms?

She was accustomed by now to miners and railway men leering at her. But those men were outliers. They scarcely saw another living soul for weeks at a time while they were working. They could be forgiven for their resulting lack of social graces.

But *this* had been her chance—this medicine show and these well-traveled, experienced men—to be recognized as a kindred spirit, as a person who was interested in scientific progress, miraculous medicine and the world beyond her own small town.

"I'll pay you handsomely," the peddler persisted. "All I want is your likeness." He spread his hands in the air as though envisioning rows of labeled bottles, an enraptured expression on his face. "In my line of work, a beautiful girl is…priceless."

"If that's the case, then you can't afford me, can you?"

For the first time, the peddler seemed exasperated.

Olivia didn't care. "I don't think you know what's in your remedies. I don't think you are a man of science at all."

The peddler frowned. "Watch your mouth, girl."

"I was trying to give you the benefit of the doubt," Olivia went on, refusing to be cowed. "But the truth is, Mary Fairfax Somerville's published work proves that magnetism cannot be used in extractive form. It cannot be bottled. So your remedy—"

The peddler stepped nearer, appearing ready to spit nails.

"—is nothing more than sheer *quackery,* sir!" Olivia finished bravely, fired up now. "And I would rather *die* than allow my image to grace bottles of your do-nothing 'cures.'"

The crowd of her friends and neighbors gasped. But Olivia finally felt satisfied. She'd said her piece. She'd made sure the people of Morrow Creek would pay attention to her *mind* for once, instead of her face and figure. She was proud of that.

After all, she could have done worse—especially on a day when she'd been presented, at the tender age of thirteen, with one unwanted marriage proposal, one illicit flirtation and one tawdry offer to reduce herself to a mere *image* to sell nostrums.

Proudly, Olivia turned to make a triumphant exit.

Instead, she almost ran smack into her father. Henry Mouton had obviously come to fetch her. His kindly, knowing expression said that he'd expected to find her there. In the least proper place to be. Doing the least ladylike thing possible. Again.

To her dismay, he shook his head in disappointment.

Olivia's heart sank. She *so* wanted her father to be proud of her. But however she turned, she seemed to misstep.

Swiftly, she reassessed the situation. She took in her father's beloved face, his world-weary stance and the handful of posted bills he held in his grasp. He'd plainly been to the post office before coming here and had found several additions to their overall indebtedness waiting there for him.

They could use any money she could bring in, Olivia knew. Running their tent hotel wasn't particularly lucrative. Theirs was a hand-to-mouth existence. Although her father had been seeking investors in The Lorndorff's future, so far there had been no takers. As far as Olivia knew, they were on their own.

A windfall for having her likeness lithographed would go a long way toward paying their bills. Olivia had her pride. But compared with her love for her father, everything else paled.

"Unless..." she called to the peddler as he turned away, "you could assure me that your new remedy works?"

Obviously heartened, he grinned. "Of *course* it works!"

Belatedly, Olivia realized that the man wasn't actually assuring *her*. He was assuring her father. Because everyone knew that a small-town girl like her didn't have the mental capacity to understand scientific principles. Wasn't that correct?

Gritting her teeth, Olivia made herself smile back at him. If downplaying her intellect was what it took to salvage this situation, then that was exactly what she'd do. For her father.

"Very well! If my father agrees— " here, she cast a cautious glance at him "—I'll simply choose my prettiest dress and pose!"

At that, the peddler and the townspeople surrounding him released a collective pent-up breath. It was, Olivia discerned, as if they'd all been made wholly uncomfortable by her outburst. Including her father. Now, though, even he appeared relieved.

That was all the assurance Olivia needed. From here on, she vowed to herself, she'd never give him another reason to feel disappointed in her. She'd be prim. She'd be proper. She'd finance a piece of their future with her face and feel happy about it. Because she wanted to please her father. She wanted to know that their friends and neighbors approved of her. She wanted to *belong* somewhere. It was clear now that the only path to those goals was paved with ruffles and lace and rosewater perfume. It was overlaid with delicate fainting spells and crowned with an avowed interest in needlework. It stomped on her books and ignored her curiosity. It squashed her spirits.

The respect Olivia craved felt entirely out of reach.

Maybe it always would dangle beyond her grasp.

But at least she could choose another path for herself, she reasoned. At least she could step deliberately and wholeheartedly into her future. At least she could do that.

So that was how, on the day when she'd dreamed of being welcomed into intellectual and scientific society—however dubiously framed by a medicine show wagon and a saucy Romany driver—instead Olivia Mouton found herself being inducted into the ranks of the verifiably beautiful. For better or worse, *beauty* was her sole oeuvre now. No matter how much she loathed its fripperies, she'd simply have to get used to it.

Without her so-called beauty, it was clear to Olivia now, she was no one at all. And that was something she could not bear. So she put on a smile, raised her skirts and went to assume her unwanted role as the prettiest girl in Morrow Creek.

Chapter Three

June 1883, Morrow Creek, northern Arizona Territory

Shrouded by darkness, Griffin Turner stood alone on the train depot platform, surrounded by muddy planks and ponderosa pines and unlimited star-spangled skies, watching the westbound train that had brought him churn its way into the distance.

For the first time in a long while, no one rushed to help him, to kowtow to him or to take his baggage. No one hurried to curry his favor or to ask him to invest in one foolhardy venture or another. No one cared who he was or why he'd arrived.

For now, that was exactly the way Griffin liked it. He'd chosen this rusticated town with a drunken dart toss at a map of his acquisitions and holdings. From the looks of the place, he'd chosen correctly. No one would bother him here. No one would look at his face and laugh, the way *she* had.

You thought I would actually marry you? Oh, Griffin...

At least she'd called him Griffin, he reflected dourly as he shouldered his rucksack and adjusted his single valise. She could have called him much worse. She could have rejected his proposal with one of those detestable nicknames the press had bestowed on him—the ones they used in their scandalous stories.

The Tycoon Terror. The Business Brute. The Boston Beast.

He'd earned those nicknames, Griffin guessed. He'd earned them through years of scraping and fighting and doing his utmost to raise himself from his hardscrabble beginnings to his current position of success. His only mistake had been in believing that not everyone trusted what they read in the tabloids—in believing that *she,* most of all, wouldn't swallow his legend whole.

It was ironic, really, Griffin decided as he surveyed the sleepy, shuttered town below through gritty-feeling eyes. Part of his fortune was based in publishing—in printing stories about disreputable figures just like himself. He'd recognized early on that people loved mudslinging. They loved gawking at strangeness. They loved feeling superior…to people like him.

To people like Hook Turner.

With the publishing arm of his business interests, Griffin gave them that. He gave them supremacy and entertainment and a break from tedium. In return, the press had given him a notoriety that bothered him not a whit. Griffin liked being notorious. He liked being hard. He like being intimidating. He liked knowing that—even though he'd assembled a profitable empire in manufacturing, real estate, publishing and various entrepreneurial ventures—his competitors still saw him as an eye-blackening scrapper from the tenements…as a man who'd give his all to win, because he didn't have anything to lose.

The punch of it was, Griffin *had* had something to

lose. Finally, he'd had something to lose, and he'd lost it. He'd lost it when he'd arrived on Mary's doorstep and proposed to her in her family's humble parlor and seen his longtime dreams dashed.

Oh, Griffin...

The pity in her voice had gutted him. He'd thought he'd finally had enough—enough to impress Mary with, enough to make up for his shortcomings with, enough to prove himself with.

Instead, he'd learned that he could never have enough. He'd gotten it through his thick Hook Turner head that he could never *be* enough, despite all he'd accomplished. So he'd drowned himself in whiskey. He'd thrown that fateful dart. He'd boarded a train westward with not much more than the clothes on his back, and he'd escaped from a life of hoping for more.

From here on, all Griffin wanted was to be left alone.

Alone to brood. Alone to forget. Alone to enjoy the luxuries he'd worked so hard to attain...and now had no one to share with. Not that he needed anyone to share them with, Griffin told himself. He did better alone. He always had.

He crossed the platform with his boots ringing against the lonesome sound of wind whooshing through the pines, then stopped at the crest of the hill leading to the single road to town. Morrow Creek lay before him, forewarned of his arrival with a telegram but nothing else, ready to welcome him with open arms.

At that sap-headed thought, Griffin gave a wry headshake. He'd *never* been welcomed by anyone except Mary and her family—and later, more grudgingly, his father—so he had no idea why such a sentimental notion would pop into his mind.

If given the chance, he knew, the people of Morrow Creek would turn their backs on him. Assuredly, they'd first find the wherewithal to point and snigger, but they'd turn on him all the same. The trick was, Griffin understood now, to not care.

Here, he'd be left alone. If he wasn't, he swore as he strode toward town, he'd use his considerable leverage to change that. After all, he owned at least half the property that Morrow Creek's citizens had built their saloons and shops and stables and houses on. Until now, Griffin had been a genial absentee landlord, but that could change overnight. His new neighbors would give him what he wanted. He intended to make sure of that.

The Boston Beast had arrived. Soon everyone would know it—beginning with the staff of The Lorndorff Hotel, his first and last destination, where Griffin meant to make his home for the foreseeable future. If he had to, he'd take over the place.

He hoped it wouldn't come to that. But as a pair of ragged miners saw him coming down the street, gave a yelp of surprise when they saw his face then scurried to the side to avoid him, Griffin changed his mind. Suddenly, he felt in the mood to crush anything or anyone that displeased him…and he felt like starting now. Grimly, he shook out his wild, dark hair, pulled his flat-brimmed hat low over his eyes and took himself off to The Lorndorff Hotel, where—if they knew what was good for them—everyone from the merest maid to the most autocratic manager would be on their toes. Otherwise, he'd know the reason.

In retrospect, Olivia Mouton knew she should have realized something was amiss from the moment she finished breakfast in the sunny dining room of her father's

Lorndorff Hotel and heard the bellman chin wagging with the desk clerk as she passed by.

"I heard he's the terror of Boston," the bellman was saying in a scandalized tone, "with eyes like the devil and a fancy dark coat that drags along on the ground when he stomps by—prob'ly on his way to put some orphans on a chain gang or some such."

"Pshaw. The way I heard tell, he could put grown men on that chain gang of his and get no guff," the clerk replied with an offhanded wave hello to Olivia. "I ain't the one who saw him, mind, but the night clerk told me he was about seven feet tall—"

"*Seven* feet? Holy moly!"

"—with a fully loaded gun belt and knives strapped to both legs. Dressed all in black, he was. Couldn't scarcely see his face, 'specially with all that hair. Like a mountain man—"

"I heard he brung a huge ole bag of money with him."

"—only fancier," the clerk said with a nod, "but with that same no-good attitude. As if he'd sooner sock you than say hello. I heard he commandeered the train that brung him. Forced 'em to turn off their track and go his way to Morrow Creek."

At that, the bellman whistled, apparently impressed. "Do you reckon he's *really* him? I know Mr. Mouton got that telegram yesterday, but I thought Griffin Turner was practically a ghost."

"Nobody's ever seen him," the clerk agreed, "so I'd say—"

Olivia cleared her throat. "Gentlemen," she said gently, "you know we're not supposed to gossip about our guests. This *is* a guest of the hotel you're discussing, I assume?"

Both men met her inquiry with disbelieving stares.

"You haven't heard?" the bellman asked. "I heard about him even afore I got to the hotel for work! The whole town's abuzz."

This did not enlighten Olivia as much as she would have liked. Patiently, she said, "Well, the whole town's not been *here,* in the hotel where I live," she said with a good-natured smile—one that the bellman, who'd proposed to her just last month, returned readily. "Not yet. So I haven't heard a thing."

"It's The Boston Beast," the clerk confided, leaning on his desk. He nearly smudged his guest register and upset his inkwell in the process. "The Tycoon Terror. The Business Brute!"

The bellman nodded vigorously. "It's him! Plain as day! Or night, at least. He didn't even take his own private train car. He just showed up, lickety-split, in the middle of the night!"

"Hmm. The Boston Beast, eh? You've been reading those tabloid journals from the states again, haven't you?" Olivia guessed, shifting her gaze from one talkative employee to the next. She shook her head. "I'm going to have to ask the O'Malley & Sons book agent to stop bringing them with her."

"It ain't the press. It's the truth." Wide-eyed, the desk clerk turned his guest register. He pointed at the aggressive scrawl penned on the very last line. "See? There's his name!"

"His name?" Olivia stifled a grin. She raised her brows. "Would that be The Tycoon Terror or The Business Brute?"

"Just look!" The clerk waggled his finger at the scribble.

Dubiously, Olivia peered at it. "That could be anything. It looks as if an especially tetchy chicken got a hold of a pen."

The bellman guffawed. He traded glances with the clerk, then returned his attention to her. "You're funny, Miss Mouton." He hitched up his suspenders, then nervously wet his lips. "I don't s'pose you've given any more thought to my proposal?"

Uh-oh. That was Olivia's cue to skedaddle. No good could come of it when men talked about marrying her. She'd spent the past several years dodging proposals, having learned long ago that finding what she truly wanted—a man who'd value her for her genuine self—was as likely as finding gold in a guppy bowl.

"I can think of little else," she assured the bellman with a kindly touch to his forearm. She smiled. "I promise."

"I know you've got other offers." The bellman stared at her hand as though transfixed. "I know that. Everyone does. But I would surely be honored, Miss Mouton, if you would choose me."

The clerk only chortled. "Now, hold on, there. You know Miss Mouton is famously picky. She ain't gonna be choosing you."

"Well, she's got a right to be picky!" The bellman gulped. Chivalrously, he came to Olivia's defense. "She's a famous beauty. She's recognized in every single state and territory."

He gestured helpfully—and unnecessarily—at the rows of bottled patent elixir lining the shelf behind the hotel's front desk. Every last one poked at Olivia's guilty conscience. She'd traded her hopes for the future for a lithographed likeness of herself staring out from those bottles of Milky White Complexion Beautifier and Youthful Enhancement Tonic. Now she was stuck.

Her father, finally and evidently as proud as punch, had purchased a whole case for himself. He'd used it to decorate the entire hotel—and to distribute to the other businesses in town, as well. No place she went was free of that blasted bottle.

She only wished her father had been proud of *her,* not her face. She wished he'd recognized what was special about *her.*

On the other hand, maybe there *wasn't* anything special about her, Olivia reasoned. Maybe she was just as useless and as needlessly celebrated as those bottles of elixir were.

After all, she'd looked into that peddler's remedy shortly after it had debuted. Its ingredients were scientifically ineffective at best. All Milky White Complexion Beautifier and Youthful Enhancement Tonic had going for it was the unreasonable hope it could engender in otherwise rational people.

That bestselling remedy was just like her in that regard, Olivia realized as she caught another besotted look from the bellman. Somehow, she made people believe she had something they needed…when she *knew* she didn't have anything tangible to give. She knew she was a fraud. She'd been hiding her nonbeautiful, less than prim, intellectual-stimulation-craving qualities for so long that she wasn't even sure they existed anymore.

In truth, *that* was why Olivia had turned down so many marriage proposals. That was why she dallied with answering them, the way she'd done with the poor bellman. She didn't want to disappoint anyone…but she *did* want to be more than an ornamental wife to a beauty-loving husband. She wanted everyone to see her as *more* than a beauty on a bottle first…and a person last.

The trouble was, Olivia didn't know how. She didn't know where to begin, or even if she could begin. And as she glanced from the bellman to the desk clerk, registering their expectant faces and alert postures, she understood that trying to change her life now was a fool's errand. It was set already.

"I'm sure this—" she peered at the scrawl in the guest register again, could not decrypt it and decided against using the heinous nicknames the hotel employees had used "—*guest* will be no trouble at all. In fact, he's probably quite a gentleman."

With that, Olivia said her goodbyes and sailed upstairs to The Lorndorff's seldom-used top floor, mentally preparing herself for another busy, stultifying day of needlework, ladies' group meetings, afternoon teas and outings to perform good works. On the staircase landing, she sighed.

Her dutiful daily routine was almost enough to make a lady *wish* for a dark, dangerous, seven-foot-tall, gun belt–wearing, train-commandeering, masculine mystery guest to come into her life and cause a stir—and a few pulse-pounding moments, too. But since *that* fanciful line of thinking would certainly go nowhere, Olivia would simply have to go on with living her own ordinary life…no matter how straitlaced and unsatisfying it might be.

Chapter Four

Olivia had stepped onto the hotel's top-floor landing, headed for her living quarters in The Lorndorff's cozy garret, when a rough male voice roared down the hallway.

"I told you to *get out!*"

Olivia froze, staring in the direction of that unexpected sound. Ordinarily, no one stayed in either of The Lorndorff's optimistically named "luxury suites," which were located on either side of the top floor hallway. In Morrow Creek, most people couldn't afford such fancy accommodations. Her father had once muttered something about necessarily "reserving" one of those suites for his distant investors' use, but Olivia hadn't given much thought over the years to either those unknown investors or those suites. Those lavish, empty rooms were just doors she passed without noticing on her way to her own comfy rooms beneath the eaves at the far end of the hallway.

A resounding crash interrupted her musings.

Olivia looked up, saw what appeared to be a shattered vase of flowers lying in smithereens on the hall floor and hastened forward. As she did, someone backed out of one of the suites.

Annie. Olivia's best friend stumbled backward, both arms held up in a defensive posture of appeasement. Her gaze stayed fixed on someone in the suite she was exiting. Her upswept blond hair was disheveled, her uniform's apron askew, and as Annie glanced down at the broken glass, crumpled flowers and spilled water at her feet, Olivia discerned that she was crying, too.

"I said I didn't want to be disturbed!" came that male voice again, its gravely ire twice as loud now. *"Ever!"*

"I'm sorry, sir. It's just that I…" Obviously at a loss to cope with the situation, Annie hesitated. "I was told to pay special attention to your room while you're here, Mr.—"

"Stop staring at me."

The sudden hush in that unknown guest's voice was twice as chilling as his outright shouting had been. Feeling gooseflesh prickle on her arms, Olivia hurried forward to help her friend.

"I wasn't staring!" Annie protested, but a telltale redness stained her cheeks and made a lie of her words. So did the way she kept on staring, unblinking. "I only wanted to bring you—"

The suite's door slammed shut, cutting off her words.

Booted footsteps stomped across the floorboards and then fell silent, muffled by wallboards and distance and the outraged pounding of Olivia's heart as she contemplated the scene.

She had *not* been raised by her compassionate, fair-minded father to stand by while someone else behaved unkindly! Swiftly, Olivia charged forward, ready to do battle…

Only to reconsider as she caught closer sight of Annie. Her friend stared despairingly at the sodden flowers and broken vase at her feet. Her slumped shoulders and downturned mouth reminded Olivia that comforting her friend was more important than confronting a quarrelsome guest, however significant he might be to her father's business interests. She could deal with Mr. Fancypants's harrying behavior later. She would, too....

With a sigh, Annie dropped to the floor, plainly intent on cleaning up the mess their guest had made.

Oh, no. Not if Olivia arrived there first. She knelt, then began plunking glass shards into the single largest piece.

"Olivia!" At the sight of her, Annie burst into fresh tears. Looking annoyed, she dashed her palms over her eyes. "*Why* must I cry when I'm most angry?" she wailed. "I want to bash that rude beast with the remnants of this vase, not bawl over him! That man is the most horrible, the most *domineering*—"

"Don't trouble yourself. I do the same thing." Olivia gave Annie a comforting smile. She paused in her cleanup work long enough to squeeze her friend's shoulder. "We're women. We can't help that the only acceptable means of expression available to us are crying, swooning and embroidering toss pillows."

"Well, sometimes those pillows are *very* inspiring," Annie said, brightening as they cleaned. "Pithy, but rousing."

The suite's door swung abruptly open, startling them both.

A huge figure appeared in the doorway. He towered over them, wearing black clothes, black boots and a broad-brimmed black hat, somehow appearing both wild and noble at the same time. The mingled scents of whiskey and tobacco smoke emanated from him, as though he'd passed the predawn hours drinking, smoking and contemplating which vase to throw next from his room. Looking up at him, Olivia had a confused impression of costly masculine suit fabrics, uncompromising authority, and unexpected...*vulnerability?*...before he unleashed another barrage.

He hurled something else. This time a covered tray of food. It clattered to the hallway floor in a fury of silver and cutlery and cold scrambled eggs. Then he glowered down at them.

"I *heard* you." His gaze raked across them. "In *my* hotel, there will be *no* gossiping about me right under my nose!"

Olivia couldn't move. She felt...mesmerized. Helpless. Also, vexed by her own peculiar reaction. She didn't understand it.

What had he meant by *my hotel?* This wasn't *his* hotel.

During the shocked silence that fell, Annie cast a fearful glance at the man's face. A helpless chortle burst from her.

Olivia would have sworn it grew fifteen degrees warmer in the hotel hallway. The wrath emanating from their guest felt palpable. And dangerous. Making matters worse, Olivia couldn't help staring at him, too, just like Annie was doing.

Because all at once, it was beyond obvious why Annie had felt compelled to laugh at this man's terrible choice of words.

There will be no gossiping about me right under my nose!

His nose was, quite simply, huge and hooked and startlingly prominent. Olivia had never seen its like. She doubted anyone ever had. As she cast him a wary glance, she suddenly believed he'd chosen those words on purpose. He'd known full well their likely effect on Annie. As tests went, his was…casually cruel.

Realizing her mistake, Annie widened her eyes. Too late.

"I'll see you dismissed for that," he promised in the same eerily quiet voice he'd employed earlier. He didn't so much as glance in Olivia's direction. He simply slammed the door.

Left alone in the increasingly sloppy hallway, crouched awkwardly beside puddled water and scrambled eggs, Olivia and Annie frowned at each other. Annie's lower lip began trembling. Her hands shook. A tear dropped on the teacup she picked up.

"Annie." Olivia touched her arm. "My father won't think of dismissing you. He won't! He knows you need this job, and we need *you*, too! Without you, The Lorndorff won't keep running."

"No, Olivia. Even you can't fix this." Annie dried her tears on her sleeve, then kept on cleaning. "I laughed outright at a guest of the hotel! Mr. Mouton would be right to fire me."

"Impossible. I won't have it." Decisively, Olivia stood.

So did Annie. "Oh, no! I recognize that impetuous look in your eyes." She tugged on Olivia's sleeve. "Please, Olivia! Don't do anything crazy. Not on my account. I know how impulsive you can be. I know how you love a good fight, too. Remember that medicine-show man? You practically tarred and feathered him in the town square. The last thing we need—"

"Is a no-account cad making trouble for our staff," Olivia concluded resolutely. She straightened her skirts and her posture, then rapped firmly on the suite's door. "I'll handle this." She cast a sidelong glance at her friend. "Besides, that girl who lambasted that peddler all those years ago is long gone. My father told me that's when he knew I'd been spending too much time at The Lorndorff, socializing with miners and miscreants and lumbermen. He knew he'd been remiss in letting me do so. Since then… Well, I've been a perfect lady."

Annie pursed her lips doubtfully, but Olivia couldn't let her friend's skepticism affect her decision. She pounded again.

"Hello in there! Open this door at once!"

Annie widened her eyes. Her mouth formed a surprised O.

"I demand satisfaction!" Olivia announced next.

Annie gave a frantic giggle. She elbowed Olivia. "Doesn't that mean you're challenging him to a duel? Are you crazy?"

Olivia shrugged. "I can do this. I have nothing to lose."

Annie took a step back, shaking her head. "Of course you have something to lose!" she said in a harsh whisper. "Everyone loves you! Half the men in this town want to marry you!"

But strangely enough, Olivia felt that she'd never said truer words. She really didn't have much to lose. She wanted to help Annie, too. If that meant confronting a loudmouthed oaf…

She pounded harder on the door. "Listen to me and open this door! I can stay here all day, if that's what's necessary."

It would be an improvement on my scheduled quilting bee, she added to herself silently, *and the tea party that's arranged for afterward.* She felt entirely uncharitable for the thought.

The door opened. Olivia almost fell headlong into

the suite. Instead, she wound up standing toe to toe with its occupant. His eyes were bleary and blue, his jaw stubbled with an incipient beard, his expression forbidding. He glared at her. Feeling wholly intimidated—and strangely exhilarated—Olivia nonetheless refused to back down. She couldn't. She…liked this. A little. She liked the challenge of this. It *enlivened* her.

No. She had to persist because Annie was depending on her. Because Annie was…hightailing it down the hallway, her uniform's bustle swaying with her rapid footsteps, a hasty "I'll go fetch a mop and bucket!" on her lips, leaving Olivia all alone.

Alone with The Boston Beast. The Tycoon Terror. The Business Brute. *How* had he earned all those nicknames anyway?

Olivia swallowed hard. She sent her gaze up the man's black boots and trousers, over his perfectly fitted vest and shirt, across his broad shoulders to his expensive-looking suit coat and then up to his rugged, rough-hewn face. It was almost obscured by the collar of his coat and his hat brim's shadow.

Purposely, she thought, remembering his earlier words. It couldn't have been an accident that he'd called attention to his nose just when Annie had been staring at it. However perverse it was, Olivia had the sensation he'd been daring them to laugh.

What kind of man dared people to laugh at him?

What kind of man could withstand it, if he succeeded?

Having made her assessment based on the available evidence, the information she'd been privy to downstairs and a great deal of intuition, Olivia lifted her chin. "Mr. Turner, I presume?"

His assent was nothing more than a tightening of his

mouth. Olivia accepted it all the same. In for a penny, in for a pound.

"Somehow," she mused, remembering the employees' gossip at the front desk, "I thought you'd be tougher. And taller."

Olivia stepped boldly past him, swept with her skirts rustling inside his darkened suite and surveyed the scene. Her hastily calculating glimpse told her that Mr. Turner was a light traveler and an even lighter sleeper. It told her that he did, indeed, carry a gun belt and two knives. It also told her that he despised sunshine. All the suite's draperies were pulled tightly shut against the bright territorial dawn. It was…gloomy.

Although… *Were those philosophy books spilling from his valise? And was that a biography of a European industrialist on his bureau?* What kind of man traveled without much clothing—because her view informed her that he hadn't brought much more than the custom-fitted duds on his back—but with a big pile of books? Did the dictatorial Mr. Turner actually *read* when he wasn't upbraiding well-meaning people for disturbing him?

Suddenly, Olivia was dying to find out. It had been ages since she'd read a new book herself, owing to her vow to be more amenable, less headstrong and less academically minded. She still regretted that foolish vow. It was awfully difficult to keep when the book agent came to town. It would almost be worth getting to know this man, she mused absurdly, if only to have access to his book collection. But then all her thoughts fled as she sensed the hotel's orneriest new guest following her into his private suite. Her goose bumps returned anew. Her heartbeat pounded. Her palms grew damp. Her throat grew tight.

Heavens. *Now what?*

She'd simply have to improvise, Olivia decided.

His voice boomed out. "Who are you?" he demanded.

How like him, Olivia considered, not to question her correct guess at his identity. He probably assumed everyone knew—and cared—who he was. The *ever so important* Mr. Turner.

His hubris was remarkable. But so was her determination.

She turned. She could not falter now. Annie was relying on her. So, brightly, Olivia said, "*I* am your new chambermaid!"

Chapter Five

Griffin was still mentally grumbling over his unwanted visitor's earlier outrageous comment—*I thought you'd be tougher. And taller*—when she gave him a haughty look—the kind beautiful women specialized in—stepped into the center of his private suite of rooms and offered yet another ridiculous declaration.

"And you *won't* be having Miss Holloway dismissed," she went on briskly, "because *I'll* be fulfilling her duties from now on."

Griffin gave her his most coldhearted look—something that came much too easily to him now, the way money and deference and loneliness did. He hadn't known that making people respect him would also make them keep their distance from him. He did now.

"What makes you think I won't have you both dismissed?"

A careless wave. "You won't."

Her highfalutin tone suggested she was sure of it—sure of her inevitable rightness, the way Boston architects were sure that their newfangled bridges would span the river waters safely. Griffin wished he felt that certain of anything...anything except the inevitable snickering that came his way. He watched her study his suite, keeping his arms crossed, still feeling a little bit drunk on whiskey and self-pity and exhaustion.

He'd passed a largely sleepless night. He didn't want his own company, much less hers. No matter how appealing she might be. And she *was* appealing, to be sure. Dispassionately, he examined her perfect profile, her delectable figure and her graceful, feminine movements. Then he disregarded them all.

Beauty left him cold. Understandably so.

Against his will, though, her gumption stirred him.

So did her curiosity about his books. He'd noticed her interest, of course. A drunk, blindfolded bat would have noticed it. It did not fit with the frivolous-looking rest of her. Neither did her avowed intention to be his chambermaid fit with her ruffled, floral-sprigged pastel dress and delicate hands. Those soft hands had never scrubbed floors.

But those obvious contradictions could wait. In his current dark state of mind, Griffin reckoned, they could wait forever.

"*You* are not a chambermaid," he said with certainty, shaking himself into reason. "And you are *not* staying."

He took her arm, intending to herd her to the door. In his grasp, she felt like a willowy, wiggly wisp of a thing. She looked like a black-haired, blue-eyed, fine-featured China doll come to life. She smelled of roses and toast and coffee, and the fragrance of his favorite brew made Griffin's head swim.

At that moment, he heartily regretted pitching his breakfast into the hallway. But he'd needed to make his point somehow.

A man began as he meant to go on. Griffin's father

had taught him that. If he wanted to be left alone, he needed to be…

Alone. Completely alone. With no one…and no coffee.

Unexpectedly troubled by that minor facet of his new solitary existence, Griffin faltered. Just for an instant.

His new "chambermaid" noticed his moment of weakness—and undoubtedly his grumbling belly—and handily exploited both.

She wrenched free. "But I have to stay! For one thing, you *must* regret not having breakfast. I can help you with that," she exclaimed, her pert face coaxing him to agree. Likely, most people did. Even Griffin, with his longtime solitude having inured him to charm, felt pulled toward her somehow. "It's a long journey from… well, *everywhere* to here," she nattered on. "Morrow Creek is remote. From what I hear, train-car victuals don't have much to recommend them. You must be starving."

Her words called to mind…everything he wanted to forget. "No." Tensely, Griffin stared at her. "I don't need anything."

"Nonsense. Everyone needs something! Even *you,*" she cajoled. Her dimples flashed. "Take me, for instance—"

"Are all The Lorndorff's maids this chatty? Or just you?"

At his harsh interruption, she shut her mouth.

She looked wounded. Confused, too, as though most people loved hearing her ramble on nonsensically, the way she'd been doing—as though most people were immediately charmed by her and her beauty. Likely, they *were* charmed. Charmed and besotted and willing to set aside common sense for her company. Not for the first time, Griffin was reminded of the unfair privilege that the beautiful—and the consequently virtuous— enjoyed. They didn't have to watch their words. Now, at long last, neither did he.

He was a success. That helped to balance the scales.

Before he could exercise his hard-won influence, though, his "chambermaid" found her voice.

"Chatty? Only when waylaid from their work by chatty guests." She gave him an irksomely buoyant look. "Now. What would you like from the kitchen? I'll see that it's prepared to your liking. All you have to do is apologize to Miss Holloway."

Griffin blinked. He must have misheard her.

She saw his bewilderment. "You were rude to her."

He could think of nothing to say to that.

"You *threw* a vase at her. You destroyed an entire breakfast tray. You shouted and scowled and behaved quite menacingly."

He still wasn't sure how to address her complaints. Those actions had been necessary, given his situation— given his pain.

Gruffly, he defended himself. "She wouldn't leave me alone. I requested to be left alone."

"Well. I'm afraid that won't be possible here."

"It *will* be possible," he disagreed, unable to believe they were actually arguing about this. "Or I'll know the reason."

He expected compliance. Usually—and forever after—he got it. Instead, from her, Griffin merely received a smile. *Her* smile was steeped in patience, glowing with a sunset's worth of prettiness. It confused him into silence. She had to be the most sought-after woman in Morrow Creek. Why was she there, with him?

And why did she look so...*familiar* to him?

"Mr. Turner, The Lorndorff Hotel enjoys a fine reputation in the Arizona Territory and well beyond." Her peaceably clasped hands did not entreat him to listen, the way Miss Holloway's outflung palms had earlier, but rather suggested that this "chambermaid" took for granted Griffin's full attention and eventual cooperation. That was…unusual…in an employee. "Certainly you wouldn't have us endanger that reputation by ignoring one of our most important guests while he's here, would you?"

Pleasantly, she awaited his response. For a heartbeat, Griffin could not fathom who she was talking about.

Then he realized. It was him.

Hell. He hated when that happened to him. When would his success and security finally sink into his bones?

Bothered that she'd made him remember both his hungry days of skipping meals and his days of clawing for success during the same few minutes' conversation, Griffin frowned. This ended now.

Roughly, he strode to the bureau. He rummaged through his things, came up with his money clip and counted some bills.

He strode back to her with a handful of cash on offer.

"Take it. Consider your work here done," Griffin said. "I'll never say a word to damage The Lorndorff's reputation."

She frowned at the money, plainly as much at a loss for a response as he had been during her demand for an apology to the maid. Even with her brow furrowed, she somehow looked tempting.

All the more reason, he figured, to have her gone.

He knew exactly the means to managing that. Quickly, too.

"Surely this isn't the first time a man has offered you money." Griffin nodded coldly at the cash. "The difference is, this time, all you have to do to earn it is leave."

Her face jerked upward to meet his, giving him the fleeting and unfamiliar impression that she didn't care a whit about his nose or his tenement life or his poor abused heart. No one had ever looked past his nose long enough to pierce his soul—not the way she did. It was almost enough to make Griffin regret goading her. Almost, but not quite. Not when she struck back at him.

"You should be ashamed, sir! I am *not* for sale."

"Are you sure about that?" He waggled his money, belatedly realizing why she looked familiar to him. "I saw a whole passel of cheap elixir bottles downstairs that say otherwise."

Her eyes widened. Her mouth opened. "That was— It was—"

"It was proof you can be bought. There's no shame in that, as far as I'm concerned. Hell, I approve." Griffin sent his gaze over her face and figure with newfound respect, seeing beyond her fine features and evident decorum to the real, raw woman beneath. "After all, you can't pay bills with virtue, can you?"

"I *am* virtuous!" Her cheeks pinkened. "And *you* are wrong."

"Am I?"

Her annoyed gaze locked with his. "Yes."

"Hmm. That's interesting." He observed her anew, liking her courage. "I bet you wish you'd left when you had the chance."

He felt a smile sneak onto his face and was dumbfounded by it. It couldn't be that he was *enjoying* her company now that he knew she wasn't some uptight, righteous type—could it?

It seemed it could, Griffin marveled, and smiled afresh. He couldn't remember the last time he'd smiled twice in one day.

His pleasure only appeared to gall her further. "I wish I'd clobbered you with your breakfast tray. *That's* what I wish!"

He offered a *tsk, tsk* of sham politeness. "Come now. That's hardly the exemplary service The Lorndorff is known for."

An unintelligible sound of frustration came from her. Oddly enough, Griffin liked it. He liked seeing her ladylike facade crumble. He liked knowing he could affect her. He liked…*her*.

The realization made Griffin falter.

He didn't want this. He didn't want *her*.

He'd come here to be alone. He'd set out to make his supposed "chambermaid" leave, not to become smitten with her. He was not a man who failed to achieve his objectives. Not anymore.

"That sort of outburst really *does* call for dismissal," he reminded her. "You shouldn't push a man like me too far."

"Asking for an apology is not going 'too far,'" she averred. "I insist you ask for Miss Holloway's forgiveness."

Impressed by her determination, he considered it. Then he came to his senses. "No. But you're gutsy. I like that."

She gawked. "You're mad. But I should have expected that!"

Irately, her gaze whipped over his black clothes, his hat and his dark hair, as though their combined qualities entirely proved her assertion. Griffin figured they probably did, to most people. He wore black to avoid attention. He wore his hat to hide his face. He wore his hair long to distract from his hated nose. He'd done what he could, just as he'd sworn he would years ago, to make the world see a *man* when they looked at him.

He reckoned he'd done pretty well hiding the Turner curse. But this woman… She looked as if she saw every inch of badness in him. As if she saw *him* and didn't approve of what he'd become.

Well, that made them even, then, didn't it?

He'd become a man, it was true. But not a good man. Not entirely. He'd been counting on Mary to make that transformation complete. Now, though, Griffin was lost. Probably for good.

That made holing up at The Lorndorff a fine plan. The devil didn't deserve a heavenly choir. Griffin Turner didn't deserve sunshine and smiles and the friendly company of good people.

"I should have expected no better," she declared, breaking into his ruminations, "from a man who would belittle a maid, manhandle a woman *and* offer a bribe, all before breakfast!"

Her outraged tone suggested that she actually objected to his actions, not his appearance. Griffin knew that could not be the case. It never was. Especially not while she was, at that very moment, avoiding looking him straight in the face—avoiding looking at his nose. Avoiding looking at pitiable Hook Turner.

His temper flared. *This* was why he needed to be alone.

"If you're hoping to be 'manhandled,' as you say, you've come to the wrong room," he informed her coolly. "I'm not interested in empty-headed women with nothing more on their minds than posing prettily and being paid handsomely for it."

"'Empty-headed'?" She gawked at him. "You *dare* call *me*—"

"Although you did help sell thousands of bottles of that complexion concoction," Griffin went on smoothly. "I hear it's even more successful than Lydia E. Pinkham's tonic. I offer you my congratulations, miss, from one entrepreneur to another."

Sardonically, he offered her a sharp salute.

She did not appreciate the gesture. "You gravely misunderstand me, Mr. Turner. Worse, you underestimate me."

"No." He contemplated it. "I don't believe I do."

"I am more than an image on a bottle!"

"Really? What else are you?"

Rather than answer him, she paced. Then she whirled, sending her skirts swaying. "You truly are beyond the pale."

"That's not an answer to my question."

"What else am I? I'm unimpressed with you, *that's* what else I am. You're hopelessly rude. Purposely boorish—"

"I've been deemed much worse." *By my own mother, for one.* "Although not by anyone as wholesome as you." He gave a civil nod. "I'll take your attentiveness as a compliment."

"Don't. All I want from you is a bit of contrition."

"Ah. You're angling for an apology for *yourself* now, too?"

"*You* are the one who's empty-headed, Mr. Turner, if you believe I would ask for an apology for myself."

"You only crusade on behalf of your friends?"

"It's not a crusade." She gave him an uncomfortably comprehending look—one he didn't care for much.

"It's decency. Something you're not on very close terms with, evidently."

But Griffin knew that already. She couldn't hurt him by pointing out the truth, any more than she could wound him by asserting grass was green. He hauled in a breath, intending to tell her so. "I'm sorry," he surprised himself by saying.

Her eyes widened in surprise. But she didn't speak.

"That's not good enough for you?" he groused, unaccountably piqued by her unsatisfying reaction to his concession. "You want a prettier apology than that? I don't have one for you."

"Mr. Turner." Delicately, she placed her hand on his arm. He realized, to his unwelcome dismay, that he didn't know her name—and, to his further consternation, that he wanted to. "An apology isn't only for the person who receives it. It's also for the person who gives it. It's for the person who needs to see what he's done… and to try his hardest not to do it again."

Griffin frowned. Would she never quit saying things that confounded him? Something about her made him feel that she had…*something*…he needed. Something important and inexplicable.

Something he shouldn't allow himself to have.

"You shouldn't casually touch a man like me," he warned in a low voice. "Especially when you're alone with him in his private hotel suite, and he's still a little drunk."

"Drunk?" She peered at him. "That explains a great deal."

It didn't explain enough, Griffin knew as he moved beyond her reach to stand nearby. It didn't explain why he'd apologized to her…except that he'd felt a cad for not doing so. In the past decade, few people had roused a true sense of remorse in him.

That *she* had was all the more reason to avoid her.

"Don't make excuses for me," he said. "You'll regret it."

"I doubt it," she disagreed with surprising sanguinity. "Folks generally live up to people's expectations of them."

"Or down. I'll likely stay drunk for weeks to come."

"Is that your plan? Is that why you've come here?"

"No. I came here to confide all my secrets to a suitably nosy chambermaid." He gave her a deliberately bland look. "I'm lucky you're here. You're exactly what I need."

Her uncomfortable expression told him all he needed to know. She was no more a chambermaid than he was a saint.

"You're making fun of me. I see." With abundant poise, she put her palms together. "I guess I've overstayed my welcome."

She offered Griffin a wobbly, unpracticed chambermaid's curtsy. Despite his best intentions to remain unmoved by her, her awkward gesture amused him greatly. Her stubborn pride endeared her to him, too. They had that much in common—that, and a love of difficult books. He didn't want to see her leave.

He also didn't want to admit it.

It would almost have been worthwhile to agree to being pestered by maid service while he was here, Griffin reckoned, if it would mean seeing Miss Milky White every day during his stay. Having her attend to him would mean he didn't have to endure one rubbernecking dunderhead after another as various members of the hotel staff found reasons to "help" fulfill his requests.

This was not the first time he'd been the subject of prurient curiosity during a hotel visit. It wouldn't be the last. The difference was, Griffin now knew how to inure himself.

"I hope you enjoy your stay with us." Her gaze lingered tellingly—yearningly—on his books. With evident effort, she transferred her attention to the door. "Good morning to you!"

Griffin tried not to watch her leave. He did. But there was something positively entrancing about the way his "chambermaid" moved. It wasn't overtly sensual. It wasn't even especially ladylike. Her movements, it occurred to him, were appealing not because of their grace but because of their inherent liveliness. Here was a woman, he understood as he watched her stride across his suite, who was interested in everything life had to offer.

Why that should appeal so strongly to him, Griffin didn't know. He only knew that it did. And that he still *wanted* her.

"Wait," he blurted.

She turned, characteristically inquisitive…and far too decent for the likes of him. "Yes?"

"I…" *Hellfire.* All at once, he felt as bumbling as a green youth of fourteen, all thumbs and stutters. "What is your name?"

"Hmm." Her eyes sparkled. "You want to know my name?"

Was she *teasing* him? Incredibly, her tone suggested as much, yet Griffin knew that couldn't be possible. No one teased him. He'd become far too influential—far too fearsome—for that.

"Tell me your name." A beat. "Please."

This time, it was her turn to smile. "If you want to

know that—if you want me to come back—then you'll have to apologize to Miss Holloway first," she declared. "She'll let me know when you've done so to her satisfaction."

"No." Griffin could scarcely believe her audacity. She couldn't order him about. "Tell me now. I demand to know."

Her laughter rang out. "Mr. Turner, you are in the Arizona Territory! I don't know or care what you've done back in the states. Here, everyone starts fresh. Before you start expecting folks to kowtow to you, you'll have to prove yourself."

He frowned. "I'll do nothing of the kind."

A shrug. "Suit yourself. But our coffee is mighty fine. Everyone in town says so. I can promise you that you're missing out on a wonderful brew. And a tasty breakfast, too."

She opened the door to his suite. Griffin stopped her.

"Wait." He couldn't help admiring the steely strength of her posture *and* the shininess of her elaborately upswept hair. He couldn't help admiring *her*. Unfortunately, that impulse was in opposition to everything he knew he ought to want. "Do you really have nothing to lose?" he asked, reminded of her words in the hallway. If that was true, it was something else they had in common. "With your friend, Miss Holloway, I heard you say—"

"I'm afraid that's not something I intend to share with you, Mr. Turner." She cast him an indomitable over-the-shoulder look—one that, again, diligently avoided his nose. "Remember, if you begin feeling peckish, just ask for Miss Holloway at the hotel's front desk and get busy making your amends to her."

"I'd rather eat wood chips. I'd rather wear skirts!"

"I think that could be arranged. There's Mr. Copeland's lumber mill at the edge of town. He has wood chips available. As far as skirts go, well, Mrs. Crabtree—the newspaperman's wife—is a fine seamstress. I'm sure she could accommodate your request."

Her mischievous expression poked at his pride and his wish for seclusion alike. Suddenly, the notion of spending his days alone in the dark didn't hold quite as much soul-salving appeal as it once had. But if she thought he was going to beg...

"I'd rather shut down this hotel altogether," Griffin told her mulishly, "than be ordered about by a chambermaid." He didn't understand why she believed him capable of apologizing to Miss Holloway in the first place. Or why she believed him interested in doing so. The tabloid press who wrote about his ruthless business practices expected nothing of the kind from him. Unlike his "chambermaid," they showed Griffin due respect for his reputation. Unreasoningly, he wanted her to respect him, as well. "I can do it, you know."

Her smile flashed again, full of patient indulgence. "What *I* know is that *you've* had too much Old Orchard, Mr. Fancypants." Breezily, she raised her hand in a farewell gesture. "Enjoy your solitude, sir. You know how to reach me, if you need anything."

Then she curtsied again—nearly toppling over in the process—exited his suite and left Griffin on his own to brood.

Chapter Six

It took less than three and a half hours for everything in Olivia's life to change. She popped over to Miss Violet Benson's church-side home for her quilting bee—late, flushed and inattentively toting a parasol instead of her sewing supplies, having been rattled by her encounter with Mr. Turner—only to return to The Lorndorff later to find the whole place in tumult.

Outside the hotel, a pair of guests were hastily piling into a waiting wagon. A carriage stood behind it, obviously awaiting more departing guests. From the corner livery stable, taciturn Owen Cooper, the owner, strode toward the hotel while leading two saddled horses, undoubtedly delivering them to some out-of-town visitors who'd stabled their mounts with him.

Confused, Olivia picked up her pace. That was when she glimpsed the hotel's employees clustered worriedly in the lobby. Annie was there, along with the other maids. So were the desk clerk, the bellman and the dining room staff. Through the open doors leading inside, an unfamiliar, well-dressed man was visible, too. He stood on the lower steps of the hotel's oak staircase, addressing the staff from that elevated position.

Olivia ducked inside, feeling—as she always did—gratefully enveloped by The Lorndorff's cozily familiar furnishings, fine upholstered settees and sparkling crystal chandeliers.

Oddly enough, her father was nowhere in sight.

"…the future of the hotel is as yet undecided," the stranger was saying in an assured tone. "The Lorndorff may remain a hotel, much as it is today. Or it may close to guests and become Mr. Turner's private residence in Morrow Creek." He gave the hotel employees an amiable shrug. "If you don't want to work for Mr. Turner in either capacity, you may accept your final pay envelopes and be on your way. Or you may remain here, on staff, to fulfill Mr. Turner's wishes. It's your decision."

Galvanized by his words, Olivia stopped cold, surrounded by bewildered employees, gossiping guests and the workaday sounds of industry going on in the lively street outside the hotel.

Mr. Turner's wishes? As far as Olivia recalled, the cranky, hard-drinking Mr. Turner's wishes had extended to exactly three things: being left alone, making sure no one gossiped about him—especially right under his nose—and shutting down the hotel if he didn't get his way in the first two instances.

I'd rather shut down this hotel altogether than be ordered about by a chambermaid, she recollected him saying before she'd left his suite. *I can do it, you know.*

Oh, sweet heaven. Could he possibly have truly done it?

She hadn't dreamed he'd actually had the wherewithal.

The hotel *seemed* to still be functioning. But it was doing so perfunctorily, Olivia realized as she took an observant look around. It was doing so without her fa-

ther's guidance. Without her father's heart and attentiveness and care. Without the very qualities that had
made The Lorndorff legendary in the West.

This hotel was her home. Its staff was a family to her.
She loved…all of them. Now, possibly because of her—
because she'd accidentally pushed ornery Mr. Turner
into making a rash and foolhardy decision—the hotel's
operations were threatened.

Queasily, Olivia remembered her earlier, unfortu-
nate reaction to Mr. Turner's threat about closing The
Lorndorff.

You've had too much Old Orchard, Mr. Fancypants.

Her flippancy had been unwise, to be true. Still, that
didn't explain who this man was or how this was happening to the hotel. Only one of her father's wealthy
investors could have…

Oh, dear. Mr. Turner *was* one of her father's wealthy
investors, Olivia realized, and she'd offended him. *Why*
had she let her father convince her to step away from
the hotel's day-to-day business? If she'd been aware of
Mr. Turner's identity—and less incensed at his treat-
ment of Annie—she might have avoided this. She might
have placated him instead of riling him.

"You *do* realize that you must make a choice today,"
the stranger called out when the staff remained in their
places, muttering unhappily among themselves. "You
can't have it both ways. Mr. Mouton no longer runs The
Lorndorff. The sooner you come to terms with that, the
better things will be for you."

A swell of fresh dissent met his announcement. One
of the bellmen grumbled. A maid wrung her handkerchief in her hands, staring up at the stranger through
disbelieving, defiant eyes.

Olivia didn't know who this man was, but he'd have

to go through *her* before assuming control of her family's hotel.

"Excuse me!" She made her way to the front, then came to stand directly at the foot of the staircase. She stared up at him as determinedly as she could. "I am Olivia Mouton. My family owns this hotel. I don't know who you think you are, but—"

"I am Palmer Grant." He extended his hand. "Mr. Turner's associate." A smile creased his youthful face, making him appear far more likable than he deserved to, under the circumstances. "I was expecting to see you earlier in the proceedings, Miss Mouton. Given what Mr. Turner told me about you, I'd thought you'd be in the fray straightaway. He said you're a fighter."

"He doesn't know me." Baffled, Olivia rejected the very idea. As far as she'd been aware, Mr. Turner hadn't even known her name. Yet in the space of a few hours, he'd learned her name and accomplished much more, besides. Resolutely, she clutched her parasol. "But he's right about one thing—I *am* a fighter. And I'll fight to keep this hotel in my family, where it belongs."

The staff gathered around her, nodding and murmuring among themselves. They seemed to realize that Olivia knew something about this dire situation that they did not. Annie, in particular, sidled nearer. She stood staunchly beside Olivia.

"I'm afraid it's too late for fighting," Mr. Grant informed the crowd. "Mr. Turner owns a very large share of The Lorndorff Hotel. Furthermore, he owns one hundred percent of the land it's built on and the neighboring properties. The management of the hotel is his decision. It's my job to make that decision clear."

"Is he incapable of doing that himself?" Olivia asked.

"Why doesn't he come downstairs to attempt this coup on his own?"

At her questions, the crowd of staff members shifted in anticipation. But Palmer Grant merely gave a knowing grin.

"Mr. Turner is more than capable of doing...whatever he wishes, in whatever fashion he wishes, to whomever he wishes." Mr. Grant gave her an unnervingly perceptive look. "You, of all people, must realize that by now, Miss Mouton."

Olivia lifted her chin. "And my father? What about him?"

A shrug. "He disappeared into his office an hour ago."

Olivia felt her heart turn over. She cast a worried glance at Annie. Had her father given up on the hotel, just like that?

She knew he could be...retiring at times. Despite having founded The Lorndorff, Henry Mouton had never been the most aggressive of men. At heart, he was a genial host—a friend to everyone. He wasn't overly ambitious, but Olivia didn't mind that. She considered her father easygoing and loved him for it.

But surely even *he* wouldn't have surrendered the management of his hotel—his pride and joy—to Griffin Turner. Would he?

Exactly how formidable *was* Mr. Turner anyway? He hadn't earned all those nefarious nicknames for nothing. In this instance, at least, he really *was* behaving like a beast.

There was only one manner in which to handle this, Olivia decided. Courageously. And quickly. She turned to the staff.

"Everyone, I'm sorry about this confusion." Nervously, she stared out at their expectant, hopeful faces. "Clearly, there's been some sort of gross misunderstanding here. If you'll all just be patient, I promise I'll get to the bottom of this."

"It's not a misunderstanding," Mr. Grant objected easily. "The Lorndorff Hotel is under new management. From now on, Griffin Turner's word is law. The sooner you fall in line with that, the happier you'll all be." He cast an amused look at Olivia. "Or you can allow a woman whose greatest achievement is having her likeness appear on a nostrum bottle to 'lead' you."

As one, the gathered staff members turned to Olivia. She had never felt stronger—or more ready to take on a challenge and win. For her father's sake. For her friends' sake. For her home's sake. For the sake of what was the right thing to do.

The desk clerk cleared his throat. "I don't suppose Mr. Turner has asked you to marry him yet, has he? If he has, well…then we might have us a fighting chance of winning."

Everyone seemed plumb perked up by the possibility. Olivia almost hated to disabuse them. "No. He hasn't." In fact, he'd seemed unaccountably unmoved by her looks overall. "But I—"

"That's it, then. We're done for!" the bellman moaned. "If he ain't able to see how marriageable Miss Mouton is, I reckon he ain't right in the head, anyhow. There's no winnin' that."

A general murmur of assent rippled through the crowd.

Aghast, Olivia looked out at them. These were her friends and neighbors. They were practically her family. Yet even they didn't believe she could take on Mr.

Turner and win...at least not on the merits of her intelligence and ingenuity and fortitude.

Dismayed, she shifted her gaze to Mr. Grant. He had obviously read the situation as astutely as she had, because he'd already withdrawn a stack of pay envelopes from his valise.

"Do you all quit?" Mr. Grant asked, raising the envelopes. "Or will you get back to work under Mr. Turner's management?"

Breath held, Olivia waited. But it was no contest at all. One by one, all the staff members made their way dispiritedly back to their posts. They began dealing with guests, carrying baggage and refilling oil lamps...in the *new* Lorndorff Hotel.

The one that didn't feel like Olivia's home anymore.

Left alone with Palmer Grant, she watched him return the pay envelopes securely to his valise, his head tactfully bowed.

"For a man who just won," she said as she glanced at him, "you don't seem particularly happy about your triumph."

But Mr. Grant only shook his head. "This wasn't a triumph."

"Not for you, perhaps, but for Mr. Turner—"

"Not for him, either." Mr. Grant lifted his solemn face to hers, then mustered a halfhearted smile. "But if you're really as special as Griffin seems to think you are, you'll find that out for yourself soon enough." With surprising affability, he shook her hand. "Good luck, Miss Mouton. I think you'll need it."

Then Palmer Grant hefted his valise, cast one final look at the now bustling hotel and took himself off— leaving Olivia alone to figure out how she was supposed to regain her father's hotel…whether anyone believed she could accomplish it or not.

Any minute now, Griffin figured as he lay in the darkness on his hotel suite's bed, he would start to feel better.

Any minute now, the crushing weight on his chest would ease. The urge to grip a whiskey bottle would lessen. The compulsion to draw the curtains would disappear and the need to forget everything and everyone would vanish. Any minute now, a sliver of hopefulness would nudge its way into his hardened heart and carry him toward the next day and the next conquest, the way it always had in the past. The way it *had* to do today.

Under most circumstances, exercising his authority made Griffin feel better. That had been true for years. After his forced takeover of The Lorndorff Hotel yesterday, however, he felt…worse, if anything. He didn't understand it. Flexing his influence and power and wealth had always improved his outlook.

This time, inexplicably, it hadn't.

But he'd be damned if he'd back down on his decision now.

After all, what else was he supposed to do? Admit he'd made a stupid mistake, hand over the hotel to Henry Mouton—who hadn't even had the gumption to fight for it—and pull foot for someplace new? If he did that, Griffin knew, he'd lose another kind of hope: the hope that he'd see Olivia Mouton again. He wasn't ready to face that. In his darkest hour, she'd gotten to him. She'd moved him. For whatever reason, he needed her.

She made him feel…*something*. So he doggedly

stuck to his original plan. He sent out Palmer Grant for additional whiskey and cigarillos, dragged himself into bed with the lot of them and then did his utmost to forget who he was and why he was there while he waited for his supposed "chambermaid" to return.

While he waited to see if she could make him *feel* again.

Naturally enough, just when Griffin had given up hope for the fifteenth time in twenty-six hours, a gentle feminine humming came from outside his suite's door. A knock sounded. An instant later, the door swung open…and Olivia Mouton herself walked in. She looked like a dream. She smelled like roses and coffee. Still humming, she sounded like an angel.

She did not *behave* like an angel, however.

"I warned you, Mr. Turner," she said in a suspiciously cheery tone of voice, "that'd you'd underestimated me."

She deliberately opened the curtains, flooding his suite with skull-crushing daylight. She resumed her humming while she did it. Then, with that atrocious act accomplished, she turned to face him with her arms akimbo and her skirts swaying. Well, if her posture wasn't outrageously—and unjustifiably—triumphant!

Wincing from his rumpled bed, Griffin could only squint at her outline, silhouetted as it was against the stark territorial skyline outside, and wish it was midnight outside.

"You misunderstood me yesterday," she reminded him in a voice like warm butter on hotcakes. "I aim to make myself clearer from here on, so that it won't happen again."

Then she studied his room with an alarming intensity, picked up his two bottles of whiskey, scooped up his beloved cigarillos into her apron and marched away from him.

At the last instant, she grabbed his philosophy book, too.

"Whoa! Stop!" Griffin called groggily from his bed, blinking at her audacity. "You can't take that. It's mine."

She lifted her chin. "This entire hotel was mine—mine and my father's. Then you came and took it away from us. I think you should find out how *you* like losing something for a change."

This could not be happening. "I already have. I've lost—"

Mary. My chance at a future. Goodness, he wanted to say.

He couldn't. Not then. Not to her or to anyone.

"—more than you know," Griffin settled on saying. Inadequately. "I've lost more than you'll ever know."

"Yes. I'm sure it's devastating to lose a gilded statue or a fancy pile of silver cutlery or whatever it is you big-city types cherish." Her unimpressed face swam in his vision. With evident relish, she gave his favorite book a possessive tap on its leather-bound spine. "The fact remains, I'm borrowing this."

Olivia wheeled around crisply. She sashayed to the door, then paused. "I'll be back later to bring you breakfast."

"Don't bother," Griffin grumbled. "I don't want it."

"I'm bringing it anyway. I've agreed to do a job."

"I'll have you dismissed." He clutched his sheets, unable to pursue her because of his partial state of undress. "I will!"

"If you do, you'll never see me again." She gave him a thoughtful, unswerving look. "Is that really what you want?"

Griffin stared at her. Then at the ceiling. He frowned.

His silence spoke volumes. His "chambermaid" knew it.

"Hmm. I didn't think so." Gaily, she waved. "Bye for now!"

The door closed, leaving Griffin alone in blindingly bright silence. Grumpily, he leaned over. He withdrew the last of his whiskey and cigars from his hiding place beneath the bed frame. He uncapped the liquor, took a swig, then frowned at the door. He wished his consternation could pierce its painted wood and wind up affecting its true target. He wished he'd foreseen this.

It seemed Miss Olivia Mouton had discovered the concept of leverage. She'd used it to win this round between them.

If you do, you'll never see me again. Is that really what you want?

What was wrong with him? He hadn't been able to say yes.

Perhaps he *had* underestimated Olivia Mouton, Griffin realized to his amazement. Perhaps he *had* misunderstood her. But he didn't intend to make the same mistakes twice. He hadn't become The Tycoon Terror by behaving like a nitwit—a nitwit who liked coffee, roses and ladies who inexplicably smelled like both. Next time, Griffin pledged to himself, *he* would win.

In the hotel hallway, Olivia collapsed against the wall opposite Griffin Turner's private suite, feeling a well-earned hysteria burble inside her. She clutched his bottles of liquor in the crook of one arm and his leather-bound book in the other. She stared down at her apron pockets, brimful of cigarillos.

Helplessly, she felt a giggle burst from her.

"You are insane!" Annie announced. She'd been waiting in the hallway, loyally standing nearby in case Olivia felt her well-being or virtue were threatened. "Are those his things?"

"Yes." Olivia nodded. "I took them. The whiskey and cigars he doesn't need. Without them, he'll be much more amenable." Her gaze sharpened as she remembered her early days in Morrow Creek. Then, The Lorndorff had been a threadbare tent hotel frequented by rough men with rough habits. She'd learned to manage them. "Without them, I think I can convince him to see reason."

Annie shook her head. "It'll take more than a bout of teetotalism to make a man like The Boston Beast see reason."

"Don't call him that! Or those other nicknames, either."

Annie gave her a bewildered look. "Olivia, the man stole your father's hotel! I mean, I know he owned a part share—"

"We shouldn't stoop to that base level, that's all," Olivia argued. "Name-calling is beneath us. All right?"

"All right. But I still say he deserves it."

"If you treat him as though he deserves it, he'll continue to behave in ways that deserve it. Don't you see?"

Her friend frowned. "No. This sounds like some of that scientific gobbledygook you used to spout when we were younger."

There was a reason for that, Olivia knew. She'd already formulated a hypothesis about Griffin Turner. She'd already developed a theory about how she could persuade him to return management of the hotel to its rightful place: her father.

"It is," Olivia agreed as she and Annie walked together down the hallway. "Using scientific methods, I intend to conduct a systematic observation of Griffin Turner. I plan to measure and evaluate his responses to my actions, to experiment as much as is necessary with those actions, and then to test my existing hypothesis and modify it as necessary to obtain results."

"Oh. Is *that* all?" Annie laughed, grabbing the handrail as they descended the stairs. "Same old Olivia." She gave a playful wink. "And here we'd all become convinced that you preferred lithography modeling to conducting scientific experiments."

Realizing she'd said too much, Olivia stopped her friend partway down the staircase. "Please don't tell my father any of this," she begged. "I know he won't approve of my getting involved this way. But I believe this is my best chance at succeeding."

"Your best chance at succeeding?" Laughing, Annie gestured at her. "*You* are your own best chance at succeeding. You don't need a scientific plan, Olivia. You are beautiful! Use that."

But Olivia knew better. "Mr. Turner is oblivious to my looks," she argued. "No, more than that—he's openly hostile to them. He actually had the nerve to call *me* 'empty-headed.'"

"What? *You?*" Annie shook her head. "That's ridiculous."

"He said I had nothing more on my mind than posing prettily and being paid handsomely for it." *Drat those remedy bottles!*

"He deserves to be hog-tied just for that remark," her best friend observed steadfastly. "He *has* underestimated you."

"He is not the first one to do so," Olivia admitted as she continued downstairs, hugging her contraband liquor and book to her chest. "But if I have anything to say about it, he might be the last. I intend to use his arrogance to my advantage."

Annie sighed. "I still think you should bat your eyelashes or helplessly drop a handkerchief. All men love being chivalrous. They're born to rescue and protect us."

But Olivia had her doubts. "Griffin Turner isn't like all men. He's…" *Headstrong. Annoying. Confounding.* "Intriguing."

Just the thought of him left her feeling somehow excited and anticipatory and giddy. When she'd brazened her way into his room earlier, she hadn't expected to find him still abed. But she had. And she'd found him partially unclothed, too. Not that she'd purposely looked! But she hadn't been able to help glimpsing his broad, bare shoulders above the bedclothes. Reflecting on the incident now, Olivia felt 95 percent certain that Griffin Turner had been wearing nothing but underdrawers.

"He's scary, is what he is!" Annie disagreed. "He's huge and hairy. He's full of big muscles and bad temper. He has long, crazy hair like no self-respecting gentlemen should have, and he sounds so *mean*. I know it was rude of me to gawk at his nose, but honestly… you've seen it!"

"I know I have," Olivia agreed, "but it's his eyes that capture my attention more. They're so…" Hesitating, she searched for a suitably apt adjective—one that would describe the tug of emotion she felt when she looked into Griffin Turner's soulful blue eyes. If not for the anguish she'd glimpsed there, she might have believed he was beyond hope altogether. "So…"

"So utterly overshadowed by his enormous nose?"

Annie offered impishly. She gave Olivia a poke. "A person would think you've gone spoony on the big bully or something."

Had she? She *was* feeling unaccountably charitable toward him, given everything he'd done. And there was the matter of her irrepressible curiosity about him and his book-reading habits....

Nonsense. "Of course I haven't gone spoony over him!"

"Are you sure? You did look a little strange when you emerged from his suite this morning. Sort of...dreamy."

"I did?" Alarmed, Olivia glanced at her friend... only to realize that Annie was teasing her. Again. "Oh, stop it! You know all I'm doing is trying to make Mr. Turner change his mind about taking over the hotel. I have to think kindly of him. Everyone knows you get more flies with honey than vinegar."

Annie's gaze dipped to her apron's pockets—bulging with contraband cigarillos—then rose to her whiskey-and-book-filled arms. "And what do you get with pilfered goods like those?"

"Attention," Olivia returned firmly. "And, when I'm finished, a victory, too. Because as soon as I make Mr. Turner see how things really are here in Morrow Creek—as soon as I make him love the town, the hotel and the people as much as I do—he'll be as sweet as spun sugar and perfectly malleable."

"With a plan like that, he'll be unwilling to leave," Annie disagreed, raising her eyebrow. "Have you thought of that?"

Olivia brushed off her concerns. "Pishposh. He's a big-city industrialist with a money clip where his heart should be. No quantity of cleverly kindled appreciation for small-town life will make Mr. Turner give up on all his success. I'm not that influential." She gave her friend a shrewd look. "After all, he can't very well manage his other businesses from here, can he?"

"I suppose not." Annie eyed the stairwell, as though her gaze could reach upstairs to Mr. Turner's suite. "But I wouldn't put it past that slick Palmer Grant to give it a try somehow."

Chapter Seven

In Griffin's hotel suite, Palmer Grant plunked down his latest offering with all the tiresome *joie de vivre* he usually exhibited. "There! Your personal telegraph apparatus, fresh from your private train car." He aimed his head toward the curtained windows, undoubtedly indicating the mode of transport he'd used to follow Griffin straight from Boston to the Arizona Territory. "Which is parked safely on an unused length of track at the rail depot, waiting for you to come to your senses. Until then—"

"I'm not coming to my senses," Griffin argued, hugging his whiskey bottle. "I'm staying here. Indefinitely. You weren't supposed to follow me. No one was supposed to follow me."

He'd imagined, in his unhappy, drunken haze, that no one would even notice he'd gone. He should have known better.

"Not follow you?" Palmer flashed a tremendous grin, busying himself at the desk. "Of course I couldn't do that. You didn't think I'd let you run off alone, did you? We're friends!"

At that, Griffin could do no more than grumble. Despite Palmer's inexplicable joviality, they *were* friends, and had been for quite some time now. They'd worked together at the job Griffin had taken after he'd climbed the ladder at the glass factory. They'd learned. They'd conquered. And still they'd remained on good terms. Griffin couldn't explain it, but he was grateful for it. Not that he'd admit as much to Palmer.

The exasperating knuck would only gloat about it if he did.

"Now. With this, you'll be able to conduct business mostly as usual, even while you're far away from Boston." With a flourish, Palmer arranged the telegraph device more squarely on the desk. "Once the telegraph line is connected from the local station to the hotel, that is. I've already requested that."

"I didn't ask you to do any of this," Griffin pointed out from his position slung sloppily across his suite's settee. He puffed at his Mexican cigarillo. "I don't care about business anymore. I don't care about any of it. It means nothing to me."

"You will care," Palmer assured him breezily, now arranging paper and an inkwell and ledgers on the desk. "Eventually, you will. You always do." He clasped his hands together, surveying his work. His gaze roved to the pair of steamer trunks at the foot of Griffin's bed. "You're welcome for the additions to your wardrobe and personal effects, by the way. I'm happy to help."

"Thank you." Griffin squinted through his cigarillo smoke, feeling appreciative, despite himself, for those fresh clothes. "You can go back to Boston now. Give yourself a pay bonus, too."

"I already did. There are advantages to being trusted with access to your fat bank account." Palmer put out a blotting pad. "But I'm not leaving this one-saloon town without you."

"Hmm. I hope you like living in my train car, then."

"I do." Nonchalantly, Palmer studied the hotel suite. "It's more luxurious than this, actually. Why are you staying here?"

"It was available."

"So are dozens of rooms in your Beacon Hill mansion. Not to mention the other fine properties you own." A meaning-laden pause. "Such as that ramshackle town house on Tremont Street?"

As usual, Griffin ignored Palmer's hint. No one except him needed to know that that "ramshackle" town house was one of the first things Griffin had bought when he'd become successful. Originally, he'd given it to his mother. She'd moved to finer Back Bay accommodations once he'd been able to afford those.

"I like knowing I have places to live, wherever I am." *I like knowing I'll never be homeless.*

The lessons of his impoverished youth died hard. That was why Griffin had included a stipulation in his agreement with Henry Mouton that the Western hotelier always keep a suite available for him at The Lorndorff, even if he never used it.

He'd never expected to use it. Not like this.

"I like knowing I can compel you to travel across the country in pursuit of me," Griffin joked drily. "That's all."

"Fine. Be guarded, if you want to," Palmer said. "I'm used to it. You don't scare me." He eyed the telegraph machine, the ledgers and then Griffin, in turn. Briskly, he rubbed his hands together. "Now, then. What would you like to work on first?"

"More drinking."

"You've already done that. Shouldn't you diversify?"

Griffin scoffed. He ground out his cigarillo, his patience with Palmer's good-naturedness wearing thin. "If you don't like it," he said, waving toward the door, "leave me alone."

To his surprise, Palmer looked at the door, then at him and then he did exactly that. He left Griffin alone. In his darkened suite. With the accoutrements of his unsatisfying success left behind to mock him in his wake.

With the challenge of Griffin Turner in it, Olivia's life quickly took on a new rhythm. It began much earlier, for one thing, owing to the need to bring him breakfast each day as his assigned chambermaid—a position she'd certainly never expected to fill for more than a single day or two. It held much more uncertainty, for another, on account of the fact that she could never quite predict what she'd find when she opened his suite's door and stepped inside. And it required a great deal more tact and resourcefulness from her than turning down the umpteen marriage proposals she had received. Because—for one thing—Olivia could not risk showing him any weakness. She believed Griffin Turner would pounce on weakness. She believed he—with his mournful eyes and gruff rejoinders and quick, unsettlingly keen mind—would take advantage of any opening she gave him and exploit it.

Undoubtedly, that was how he'd succeeded in life so far.

At least that was what the desk clerk and the bellman and Annie kept telling her. That was what her father kept telling her, when he wasn't grumbling in the hotel corridors or moping at Jack Murphy's saloon or apologizing to Olivia for partnering with The Boston Beast in the first place. But Olivia wasn't interested in Griffin Turner's past. She was interested in affecting his future. She was interested in reaching the kind, complicated man she felt certain lingered inside him, hidden away behind dark hats and shadowy rooms and biting words.

She knew she could change his mind. It was the greatest challenge to her intellect so far. She was determined to win.

So her days fell into a routine of arriving at Griffin Turner's suite, flinging back the window curtains and beginning a day of trying to discern exactly what made him tick. If he'd been a mantelpiece clock, she'd have taken him apart to learn his mechanisms. If he'd been a book, she'd have read him from front to back and memorized all she could. If he'd been a stray dog, she'd have fed him, petted him and tamed him. But he was a man.

He was more of a man than any man she'd ever encountered.

So instead of doing all those things, Olivia settled for getting to know him. She did that while attempting, sometimes comically, to impersonate someone she decidedly wasn't: a skilled chambermaid who knew how to leave a hotel suite spotless.

Notionally, Olivia knew how to clean. Of course she did. But ever since her father had received his investment money to expand The Lorndorff—from Griffin Turner, as it turned out—he'd preferred that Olivia spend her time on more cultured pursuits. He'd preferred that she leave the cleaning to the hotel staff and devote her time to becoming more genteel.

Not being overly fond of scrubbing, Olivia had agreed.

But now, for the first time ever, she regretted taking the easy road all those years ago. Because as Olivia flounced around Mr. Turner's room each day, ineffectually dusting and sweeping and wrestling with the linens to make up the bed, she knew full well that Griffin Turner rightly suspected she was a fraud.

"You missed a spot," he pointed out not long after she'd begun tending to him, lounging—as he was fond of doing—in a sprawled, masculine heap on the settee. "See? Right there."

Olivia peered at the smudge he'd indicated—a mere dust speck on the otherwise tidy hearth rug. Easily, she dismissed it. "You'll never notice. It's always so gloomy in here anyway."

"I just did notice."

"You're probably drunk. You'll forget we discussed it."

"I'm sober." He didn't move, but his husky voice sounded fractionally more alert than was typical. That was heartening. "I'm woefully sober. You stole my whiskey, remember?"

"I didn't take your secret cache." Olivia nodded toward the bedstead, beneath which she knew he stashed liquor and cigars. "If I may offer a hint? When trying to hide your belongings from a chambermaid, it's usually best not to secrete them under the mattress. Not when she'll have to lift it to make the bed."

His mouth quirked. "Is that what you're calling it?"

"Of course!" She huffed as she went on cleaning the rug, laboriously straightening each of its tassels. "What else?"

"Making the sheets crooked. They were sideways last night."

"You can always do it yourself. I won't tell anyone."

"Yes, but then you won't come here anymore."

At his vaguely aggrieved tone, Olivia leaned on her broom. She gazed at him, with his strong-looking body carelessly slung atop the settee's upholstery, his hat pulled down to shadow his face and his elegant clothes worn as casually as homespun togs, and knew his complaining to be progress, of a sort.

The first day she'd come, Griffin had refused to leave his bed. By that afternoon, he'd stubbornly reclosed all the draperies she'd opened and uncorked his covert whiskey stash. He'd swallowed much of it. Over the next few days, he'd sulked around, put his grubby boots on her freshly dusted tables and smoked copiously. He'd refused to eat. He'd refused to bathe. He'd rejected outright her initial attempts to request that he return the hotel to her father. In fact, he'd even had the gall to suggest that her "meek" father didn't want the hotel back.

Then he'd taken to his bed. With his boots on.

In light of all that, finding him out of bed today had been almost miraculous. Learning further from the bellmen that he'd ordered a bath had been downright extraordinary. Even if he *was* lounging as lazily as a cat in his freshly changed clothes.

"Sometimes I think you'd prefer if I didn't come anymore," she said. "Sometimes I think you really *would* rather be alone."

Silence. Beneath his hat brim, his jawline hardened. It was a miracle that a few emergent beard hairs didn't pop right out.

When he spoke, though, his tone was light. "Maybe I would rather be alone," he agreed. He raised his head a fraction. "Or maybe pestering you has given me something to live for."

Oh. *Poor Mr. Turner.* Until now, he'd seemed more brooding than melancholy, Olivia couldn't help thinking. But overwhelming unhappiness could explain his apathy regarding…well, everything. Conversing. Becoming abstemious. Behaving with a modicum of manners. Experiencing daylight. His avowed down-heartedness wasn't something she could discount. Not if she wanted to reach him, to influence him and—if she was honest—to help him.

"Surely you have a great deal to live for," she argued, striving to keep her tone as light as his. She didn't want to ruin this fragile accord between them…or scare him into not confiding in her. "After all," she teased with a glance to his hiding place, "there are always whiskey and cigarillos to think of!"

"Yes." His shuttered gaze followed her as she went back to work sweeping. "There are always those. I forgot for a minute."

Something in his voice, so husky and deep, made her feel breathless. Confused by it—confused by her own burgeoning wishes to help him find something to live for, if he honestly lacked it—Olivia operated her broom with more vigor. *Sweep, sweep…*

The settee's cushions creaked. Griffin stood.

His hand clamped on her broom handle, just above her fist.

Olivia jumped in surprise. His shoulder nudged hers as he came to stand more firmly beside her, close enough to transfer his bodily warmth to hers—close enough to envelop her with the heat and assurance and absolute strength he always exuded.

How did a man come to emanate such heat? Such… intensity?

Wonderingly, Olivia glanced up. Way up, into his face. Looking at him—even in three-quarter profile as she was—still startled her. He didn't allow it often.

Usually he minded his hat's position more carefully than this. But now she could see that although Mr. Turner had not yet found the impetus to give his stubbled jaw-line a shave, he *had* decided to club his hair. It lay bundled against his neck, native fashion, tied with a strip of black leather and seeming…not quite as civil as he intended it to. As a concession to polite society, it was…

More successful as a means to emphasize his wildness.

She almost *liked* his wildness, Olivia thought crazily. It was liberating. It was fascinating. It was unlike anyone else.

So was his strength. Griffin Turner exuded fortitude as readily as he exuded a stony, combative attitude. Just then, though, his attitude seemed more distressed than aggressive.

Evidently, he'd felt her jerk away in surprise, because he shifted subtly. "I didn't mean to scare you. I'm sorry."

At his gruff apology, Olivia blinked. She stared at his hand, holding the broom very close to hers, feeling… transfixed. Feeling, she realized belatedly, very much the way she imagined the men who ogled her and tipped their hats to her and proposed to her within moments of their meeting did when she stood near.

Just then, she would have liked a proposal from him.

Instead… "You're dragging the broom," he informed her.

That was hardly romantic. "I beg your pardon?"

"You're dragging the broom." He nodded at it. "May I?"

"Certainly. Help yourself." Immeasurably curious, Olivia stepped back to offer him sole control of her broom. "I'm dying to find out what a man like you knows about brooms."

I'm dying to find out if you've ever proposed to a woman, too, she couldn't help wondering, and was shocked to find herself thinking of him in such a romantic sense. She'd never done that before, not during all the days they'd spent together. Undeniably, Griffin Turner possessed a certain raw dignity, in spite of his unusual appearance, but that didn't mean…

It didn't mean she had to think of him in *those* terms! It didn't mean she had to consider that his mouth was perfect to look at, even situated beneath his attention-hogging nose. She didn't have to reckon that, aside from that tremendous nose of his, Griffin Turner *did,* in fact, have handsome features.

Rugged, expressive, *unusual* features, to be sure, but…

Appalled, Olivia shook herself. These flights of fancy would not help her cause. Neither would letting herself get carried away. Resolutely, she returned her attention to the matter at hand: a man who was about to demonstrate sweeping techniques to her. She couldn't help giggling at the idea.

In return, he delivered her a censorious, seemingly arrogant look. He accepted the broom from her. Olivia watched in amusement, expecting him to wield it hilariously wrong, the way men typically tried to hold babies or sewing needles. If she was inexperienced with expert cleaning, menfolk in general were oblivious to it. Men, she knew, were not natural tidiers.

She couldn't wait to see him get started.

He surprised her by first leaning nearer. Up close, what Olivia could glimpse of his face was startlingly masculine and oddly compelling. Maybe she was… getting used to his appearance?

She was certainly getting used to the unique scent

of him—although *not* to the untoward impulse she felt to inhale deeply of it. Griffin Turner used a clove-oil soap, she'd learned, that was custom blended for him by a Boston apothecary. Palmer Grant had brought in a whole box of it from the East. The combination of its soapy spiciness, Griffin Turner's manly aura and the toasty notes of tobacco that clung to him was intoxicating.

He caught her stealing a lungful. She gave a sheepish face.

At least she'd learned to stop gawking at him. Olivia knew that was progress. But he seemed unaware of her improvement.

"Try not to root for my failure *quite* so obviously," he instructed with a wry expression. "Eagerness is unladylike."

Oh. He wasn't alert for her to stare at him at all. Or for her to make herself tipsy on masculine clove-oil essence. He was on the lookout for her to behave inappropriately. Just like everyone else had been for as long as she could remember.

Eagerness is unladylike. Well. That was probably true.

For an instant, Olivia felt duly chastened. Then she got over it. "I don't care if it is," she said, dizzy with a newly reawakened sense of rebellion. "Who are you going to tell? You never leave this suite or speak to anyone except me."

"I speak to Palmer Grant."

"Do you give him broom lessons?"

"You mean sweeping lessons."

Olivia waved away his specifics. "Do you?"

To her amazement, another smile tilted his mouth. It made Griffin Turner appear downright boyish. The sight of him looking that way made her wonder...had he ever been truly boyish?

Somehow, she doubted it. The thought broke her heart...and kindled a fresh desire to help him experience the youth and innocence and sense of playfulness his life may have lacked.

Doing so might awaken his kinder impulses, too. It might, aside from helping him, cause him to relinquish The Lorndorff.

"The important thing is, your 'cleaning' is sheer madness," he intruded into her thoughts to say. "I can't sit idly by and let it continue any longer. You are clumsily dragging this broom when you're meant to repeatedly push it. Like this."

To her further amazement, he demonstrated the motion. Using his strong hands and his big, burly muscles, he swept.

Olivia couldn't help being impressed. At this, Griffin Turner was remarkably adept. He made the act of sweeping seem as natural as breathing. Further, he made himself seem positively endearing while doing it. That was a trick, to be sure.

"*That,* Miss Milky White, is how you sweep a floor." He propped himself up on the broom handle—as though it was his stumpy partner in an otherwise elegant ballroom dance—appearing immeasurably pleased with his efforts. "Here. Now you try."

"Why should I, when you're doing so well?"

"Because it's *your* job. You volunteered for it."

"Volunteered? How do you know I don't need this job? How do you know I don't do this every single day?"

His gaze swept over her, cataloguing her features and her figure. "Your soft hands say you never do anything more taxing than needlework. Your stylish dress says you prefer fashion to mop buckets. Your pink cheeks say you spend time outdoors, not stuck inside a hotel. Your ineptitude at dusting, scouring, and bed making suggest you have more refined interests at heart."

He was right. She did. Except her interests lay more with intellectual pursuits than refinement. She was still reading the book she had pinched from him. She was fascinated by its chapters regarding Bentham and Rousseau. In fact, she was hoping to discuss it with him sometime soon. There was no one else she could converse with about philosophy in Morrow Creek. Regardless of those hopes, Olivia couldn't defend her housekeeping abilities. She knew they were deplorable.

"Also," he went on, "your father owns this hotel. So it's unlikely he'd enlist you for menial labor." He gave her a keen look. "In fact, I'd wager he doesn't even know you're here."

He didn't. Not precisely. So far, Olivia had managed to keep her plan inconspicuous. Henry Mouton's overall distractedness had helped with that. So had the staff's willingness to help her bluff her way into her chambermaid's duties. But she *definitely* didn't want to discuss that.

What if she did—and he requested a more competent maid?

No. If she was to make inroads with her plan to make Mr. Turner surrender The Lorndorff, she had to have access to him. She had to continue befriending him. She had stop him from any further contemplation of her past, her relationship with her father...and her reasons for behaving as a chambermaid.

As far as Mr. Turner was concerned, she was merely being friendly. And industrious. Later, she'd ask him to give over control of The Lorndorff again. Later, when he liked her.

She'd never had such a difficult time making a man like her. If only Annie was right, and all she had to do was bat her eyelashes and swoon appropriately. But since she couldn't...

She'd simply have to go on as she'd begun. While first making sure Griffin Turner didn't delve too deeply into her motivations. Searching for a suitable distraction for him, Olivia came up with, "Please don't call me Miss Milky White." This wasn't the first time he'd done so. "My name is Olivia."

"I know." He gave an amiable nod. "Yet your claim to fame is evident on those patent remedy bottles downstairs. It's—"

"It's really not very relevant to my life these days," she interrupted crisply. "I hope you'll remember that."

"How can I not, when you keep reminding me?"

"You seem to be managing capably so far."

"Mea culpa." He laid his hand over his heart. "It won't happen again." A thoughtful look. "Speaking of names—"

"I'd better get back to my work." Satisfied that she'd deterred him, Olivia grabbed the broom. Or at least she tried to. "Mr. Turner, please. I think you've proved your point. I'll try harder to sweep properly from now on. So if you'll just—"

Her next tug had little effect. He held fast to the broom.

He appeared apologetic again, too. For a man who'd seemed a latecomer to the sentiment, he was mastering it ably now.

"You're offended. That's why you're so eager to sweep."

"I'm your chambermaid. *That's* why I'm eager to sweep."

He didn't believe a word. "I'm sorry if I upset you by talking about your involvement with that complexion tonic." He seemed troubled—and perceptive in a way that no one else in town had ever managed when it came to her lithographed twin and all it represented to her. Contritely, he said, "I didn't mean to."

"Thank you. But I should still get back to work."

She gave a nod to accept his apology. And another yank to snatch the broom from him, too. It was no good. He held fast.

"Before I give this back, I want something from you."

Guardedly, Olivia peered up at him. "More cake?" she guessed. "You seemed surpassingly fond of that spice cake from Molly Copeland's bakery." She'd brought it yesterday as a deliberate ploy to soften him toward her. It had obviously worked. "If you do, I can have more delivered within the hour."

"No. Not more cake." His eyes actually sparkled at her.

Unexpectedly moved by that miniscule show of good cheer—because, after all, it meant she was making inroads at befriending him—Olivia tried again. "More cigarillos?" she asked next. "I don't approve of them, of course, but I noticed they're the same brand that the town blacksmith, Daniel McCabe smokes. I could probably fetch you more of them from the mercantile."

"No. I just decided to quit." Still holding the broom handle in tandem with her, he stepped a tiny bit closer. "Someone I know doesn't approve. I want to please her."

He meant her. Spurred on by that further proof that she was having an influential effect on him, Olivia felt her spirits soar. "Good for you," she said with a nod. "I'm proud of you."

"There's no need to get carried away. It's a minor effort."

"Still, it's an effort." Encouragingly, she smiled at him.

"So is standing here, so close to you," he said, "and not standing even closer. But I don't want to scare you again."

"I wasn't scared before," Olivia fibbed. "Just startled."

Rightly, Griffin Turner didn't appear to believe her. As though challenging her assertion, he slid his hand a few inches higher along the broom handle. Their fingers touched. At that unexpected contact, a jolt raced through her. She shivered.

He raised his eyebrow. "How about now? Are you scared now?"

"No. Not scared." *That* was an even more outrageous stretcher. With effort, she asked, "What favor did you want from me? I promise, I'm all ears." *And wobbly knees and shaky hands...*

How could a mere touch be so affecting?

"What I want," he said, making his request last a lifetime, "is for you to please call me Griffin." His smile surfaced again, seeming strangely...*rusty,* but all the more affecting for it. His hand convivially covered hers. He squeezed, boldly holding her. "Now that I've performed cleaning duties in front of you, I believe you owe me that small intimacy. Don't you?"

In that moment, all Olivia could believe was that she might topple without the support of the broom in her grasp. *Griffin Turner was holding her hand.* He was gazing at her in a decidedly hopeful fashion. He appeared open and amenable, and he was definitely, *definitely* softening toward her. She was winning.

She tried to tell herself that was all she wanted… and failed. Because he was the most enthralling man she'd met in her life, and it was impossible for her not to yearn for more from him.

"Very well." With effort, she moistened her lips—and happened to catch him watching. "Thank you very much. I will."

Griffin. It *did* seem intimate. But not half as intimate as the contact of their fingers, as the warmth spreading slowly from his body to hers, as the fact that their bodies were close enough to make their clothing overlap. Dazedly, Olivia glanced down to see her skirts pooling against his black trouser legs—to see her dress sleeve outlined in flouncy pastels against his black suit coat and woolen vest—and knew she'd overstepped.

This was a part of her experiment she hadn't counted on.

Neither had she counted on her own untoward reaction.

"Griffin." She tried to say it with a polite smile, but the pounding of her heart seemed to make it impossible to smile normally. Olivia tried a nod instead. It felt jerky. "You must call me Olivia, of course. Please. I insist you do."

But her invitation came too late. Griffin gazed into her face, saw something there that was not to his liking and yanked away his hand. She felt its loss like the coming of winter.

"Fine." His tone sounded harsh. "Olivia, it's time you left me. This place is as clean as it's likely to get for today."

"What? No!" she protested. "I haven't finished yet."

"You've finished." Closing himself off from her, Griffin wheeled his way back to his bedstead—and the single bottle of whiskey hidden beneath it. He slugged some. "I assure you."

Oh, no. She'd done something wrong. She was losing.

"I'm sorry!" Olivia cried, searching her mind for what she might have done. "Men don't usually hold my hand. I wasn't—"

His sardonic snort cut her off. "Men would give their hands to touch you. Tell me another tall one, Miss Milky White."

Hurt, Olivia clutched her broom. "I already asked you—"

"Why don't you give up this pretense?" Griffin demanded suddenly, pointing his liquor bottle at her. The amber liquid inside it sloshed. His scowl looked fearsome. "You know you're not a chambermaid. You're not truly friendly with me, either."

His suspicion wasn't unwarranted. Guiltily, Olivia bit her lip. She didn't want him to isolate himself from her. Not just because she needed his cooperation, but also because…it pained her, somehow, to see him this way. To see him suffering.

"I truly *am* intrigued by you!" she protested. "I honestly—"

"'Intrigued'?" He made it sound like a filthy insult. "People are 'intrigued' by curiosities. By *sideshow freaks.*"

"No!" *Oh, my.* How had this gone so wrong, so quickly? "I don't mean it that way." Determinedly, Olivia strode to the bed. "I *don't* see you that way. Yes, I was alarmed by you at first," she confessed, "but only because—"

"Stop." He drank more whiskey. When next he

looked at her, his eyes were haunted. "I don't want your pity. I want your absence." He gazed scornfully at her. "I want to see you leaving here and not coming back. Give me that, Olivia. Just…leave."

Woefully, Olivia clutched her broom. She wanted to fix this situation somehow. But it appeared to be too late for that.

For now, at least, her efforts were at an end.

"I'm sorry if I hurt your feelings," she said, speaking with as much poise as she could muster. "But more than that, I'm sorry you can't believe me when I tell you how I feel about you. I'm an honest woman, Griffin."

He yanked down his hat, stonily refusing to speak.

His silence only provoked her. It was as though she'd never tamped down her natural brazenness—as though she'd never strived to be ladylike by putting aside her inclination to speak freely.

Clearly, being ladylike wasn't working anyway. And she couldn't simply give up. She couldn't pretend she'd never met Griffin Turner and go back to gadding about the territory the way she had been, attending dances and wedding parties and summertime soirees. There was too much at stake here for that.

Her father had already confided in her that Griffin had every right to The Lorndorff. He'd insisted on strict terms when offering his investment. Henry Mouton had taken them. The only way out of this predicament was to appeal to Griffin's goodwill.

As if *that* existed, Olivia thought with a burst of indignation. Everything he'd done since arriving in Morrow Creek was proof it didn't. So far, she'd been wholly unable to remedy that. She took another look at him and felt her temper rise.

"No wonder you like it so gloomy in here!" she said

wildly. "It matches your disposition!" Frustrated, she glimpsed no sign that she'd affected him and felt further pushed to say more. "The problem isn't how *I* see you, Griffin. The problem is how *you* see yourself. You see shades of black and nothing else. You see darkness everywhere—" she gestured illustratively at his suite "—but only because you refuse to leave open the curtains!"

"They're open." He gestured toward them with his whiskey bottle. He took another long drink. "Nothing's changed."

"Only because you won't let it change."

"Because it *can't* change."

His mulish desolation got to her when nothing else could, dousing her ire like a bucket of water on Mc-Cabe's blacksmith's fire. Feeling unexpectedly sorry for him, Olivia stepped nearer.

"You don't really want me to leave," she cajoled. "You told me before that you didn't." *You said I gave you something to live for.* Tentatively, she touched his arm. "You said—"

Griffin reacted as though she'd struck him. With a near growl of unhappiness, he yanked himself away from her touch.

"I already told you to leave." His anguished gaze met hers briefly, then swerved away. He gave his hat a fruitless tug. There was no room for it to move any lower. "If you insist on staying, I can't be responsible for what happens between us."

His threat was not subtle. Neither was his aura of menace. Something she'd said or done had wounded him. Olivia had learned once already not to incite Griffin Turner when he was like this.

Exasperated, she took a long look at him. Then,

knowing she could make no additional progress now, she slipped from his room as quickly as she could.

She wasn't fast enough, though, to avoid hearing the bottle he threw against the door hit it hard. She wasn't fast enough to avoid hearing that whiskey bottle shatter into a thousand pieces while she fled down the hallway. And she definitely wasn't fast enough to avoid wondering...if she found the courage to come back, exactly what would happen between them next, now that they'd finally touched?

Now that they'd finally touched...and she'd enjoyed it?

Chapter Eight

When the knock at his hotel room door finally came two days after he'd made Olivia Mouton leave, Griffin knew for certain it was her. Returned to him. *Contritely returned,* he instructed his imagination to believe as he stomped to the door, ready to open it and unceremoniously toss her on her backside one more time.

Instead, Griffin was nearly smacked in the face as Palmer Grant pushed open the door and strode inside, fully fired up.

"You're costing yourself a fortune by staying here, Griffin." He shoved shut the door behind him, sealing off any possibility that a "chambermaid" might be lurking outside with a feather duster and a smile. He brandished a handful of telegraph messages. "Your business managers are losing their minds."

"They'd already done that. They partnered with me."

A sigh. "You know that's not what I mean." After tossing down the telegraph messages, Palmer flopped onto an upholstered chair. He rubbed his free hand over his face. He gave Griffin's hotel room a curious look. "Hmm. It's dark in here again."

"I like it this way." Feeling doubly morose now that

he knew Olivia had not come back to beg forgiveness, Griffin tipped back some whiskey. "I'm comfortable in the dark. It's a polite gesture. It keeps women and children from having to look at me."

It didn't have the same shielding effect on his longtime friend. Griffin didn't like the astute squint Palmer gave him.

"Aha. 'Women,' eh? This is about *her.* I wondered when it would come to this." With the amused forbearance of a saint—or a particularly addle-headed child—Palmer got up.

He went to the window. He flung open the drapes.

It was as if the pernicious ghost of Olivia Mouton had come to haunt Griffin during daylight hours…the way she did when he tried to sleep, whispering sweet things and smelling of roses.

Sometimes he wished he could sleep all the time.

"Argh." Scowling, Griffin covered his eyes with his arm. "Not you, too. You damn traitor. Leave. Now." He pointed to the door with his whiskey bottle. "Just get out."

"Fine." Palmer stood. "But I'm taking this with me."

He snatched Griffin's bottle of Old Orchard. It was a cheap brand, but it had stood by him ably. He didn't want to lose it.

Unfortunately, he was too tipsy to prevent its loss. He had to settle for glaring at Palmer as his associate tucked it securely beneath his arm in an unwitting imitation of Olivia.

"Without this," Palmer said, "maybe you'll get back to business." He glanced at the pile of telegraph messages. "Some of those need replies. You're endangering your livelihood."

Griffin didn't care. He didn't care if his money ran

out or his businesses ran aground. Success had never brought him the happiness he'd sought. Success hadn't even brought him Mary.

Granted, he hadn't seen much of Mary during the interval between his tenement beginnings and his successful life. He'd been busy working and striving and sacrificing. Still, during those hard times, he'd counted on Mary being there for him. She'd been an emblem of true success to him. Sometimes distant, sometimes busy, but always representing love and kindness and the warmhearted family Griffin had wanted and had been denied.

You thought I would actually marry you? Oh, Griffin…

Her rejection had been gentle on its surface, but no less unbearable for him to receive. Over the years, imagining his eventual proposal and Mary's delighted acceptance had gotten Griffin through some difficult times. When she'd refused him instead, she'd kicked a hole in his heart. There weren't enough fond words and Irish stew in the world to mend it.

She'd claimed that she thought of him as a brother. She'd insisted that he'd been gone for too long. She'd said that she'd found another, more devoutly Catholic man whom her parents approved of…and Griffin had realized too late that he could only have as much as the world could be forced to relinquish to him.

True love was—both then and now—*not* included.

Maybe true love was wholly illusory.

Success should have improved his life. Instead, it had brought him here, Griffin reminded himself grumpily, where Olivia Mouton lived with her smiles and her softness and her saucy way of pretending to know how to sweep. Success had made him vulnerable to her pretenses. It had made him believe—temporarily, at least—that she *liked* him…when he knew only too well she was trying to wrest control of The Lorndorff from him. He wasn't a gullible child. He didn't usually behave like one. He'd known from the start that Olivia had to have had another reason for seeing him. Why else would she have come to him every day?

Why else would she have allowed him to touch her? To *hope?*

It sure as hell wasn't because she loved cleaning. Olivia might have been eager, but her grasp of cleaning was dubious, at best. And although she looked very fetching while making a bed…

"Am I wasting my time, Griffin?" Palmer blurted. "It's been more than a week now. How long do you intend to wallow here?"

"As long as it takes. Longer. Forever, if necessary."

A commiserating look. "Would it change your mind to know you've had a letter from Mary? It came in this morning's mail."

"I don't want it." Griffin crossed his arms. "Return it."

"But you've known her since you were fourteen years old!" Palmer protested. "She deserves more than silence from you."

"Truly?" Griffin fixed him with a measuring look. "What makes you believe that? Was it her disloyalty? Her pretended devotion? Her willingness to deceive me for almost a decade?"

At Griffin's near roar of questions, Palmer shifted uncomfortably. But he held his ground. "If you want to sulk, go ahead. If you want me to keep running this damn rusticated hotel while you brood up here, I will. But *don't* speak ill of Mary."

Griffin lowered his voice. "Is that a threat?"

"It's what's necessary." Palmer lifted his chin. "For you."

"You don't know what's necessary for me." For a while, Griffin had thought Olivia was necessary for him. Obviously, he and Palmer were both terrible at this game. Realizing that, Griffin sighed. "Neither do I."

At his grudging admission, his friend went silent.

But someone else did not. When Griffin hadn't been paying attention, he realized too late, Olivia Mouton truly *had* arrived. As usual, she didn't intend to be silent in the least.

"*I* know what's necessary for you," she said from her place in the opened doorway. With conviction and sass, she strode in. "I've worked it out, and I know exactly what to do. If you're smart, you'll let me show you, before it's too late."

Too late. Her ominous tone didn't daunt Griffin. At least that was what he told himself. But when he looked at her—when he caught a whiff of her dizzying scent, saw her lively, beautiful face and felt his whole body yearn to be next to hers—he knew he was lost.

Olivia Mouton affected him. Whether he wanted that to be true or not, it was a fact as incontrovertible as the headache that came from imbibing or the ache that came from needing.

Not that he intended to reveal as much to her. Not again.

He still burned from the way she'd looked at him—from the way she'd reacted when he'd held her hand and asked her to call him *Griffin*. At first, Olivia had appeared as moved as he had been. Then, suddenly, she'd only appeared...stricken.

Undoubtedly because she'd realized she was touching The Beast. She was allowing The Beast to get closer and closer...

He'd wanted to get closer still, Griffin knew. He couldn't forget the subtle tremor that had passed through Olivia when he'd covered her hand with his. He'd felt it, too. Far less subtly. For him, it had been as though the earth had shifted...and left him groundless.

Hoping to get his feet squarely under him now, Griffin gave a stiff gesture of introduction. "Palmer, you've met Miss Olivia Mouton. Olivia, I believe you've also met my associate—"

"We're acquainted," his friend said with an inexplicably gleeful grin. He shoved the whiskey bottle at Griffin. "You might need this. Later." He tipped his hat at Olivia. "Miss Mouton, I'm sorry, but I have a prior appointment. Goodbye."

With that, Griffin's cowardly friend scampered from his suite. The door closed behind him, leaving Griffin and Olivia alone. He glanced at her...and wanted to touch her again.

Willfully, he clenched his fist instead. She could *not* make him want her just by being there. She couldn't. He refused.

And yet something in her demeanor gave him senseless hope. After all, he'd already learned not to underestimate her.

Did she know what was necessary for him? he wondered. Did she know how desperately he wanted a way out of the darkness?

As though answering his unvoiced questions, Olivia came farther into his suite. She looked composed and intelligent and utterly desirable because of it. Her beauty moved him far less than her attitude did. He could not resist her irrepressible confidence—her assuredness that he was *not* beyond hope after all. Mere prettiness could never have been as seductive.

"It's been too long since you were here." He gave a halfhearted wave at the mantelpiece. "The dust is piling up."

He'd been unwilling to admit another, less maddening chambermaid. Olivia obviously knew that already, because her smile proved that he'd done it again. He'd underestimated her.

Damn it. She didn't believe his feigned nonchalance at all.

Typically, she had the grace not to belabor the issue, but instead got straight to her reason for coming.

"I can help you, Griffin." She examined the remnants of his latest descent into the darkness—an empty whiskey bottle, shredded but unsmoked cigarillos, abandoned meals on trays that had been brought by Palmer Grant and summarily ignored. "Believe me. I can. But before I do, I want something from you."

Her echo of his earlier words wasn't lost on him. It made him remember the encounter they'd shared— and the awful way it had ended, too. But in that moment, Griffin didn't care if Olivia had jerked away in revulsion at the sight of him two days ago. He didn't care if she'd misled him into friendliness and then lost her nerve.

All he cared about, in that moment, was that she was there.

Why couldn't he stop being so vulnerable? Griffin wondered irately. He'd done it when he'd first held her hand. He was doing it again now. He'd been a fool to begin trusting her. He was about to be a fool all over again. He just couldn't help it.

"Yes?" His voice croaked out, belying the fact that—just then—he would have given her anything. "What do you want?"

"Well, *eventually,*" Olivia began confidently, "I want to discuss philosophy with you. I've finished your book, and I'm very curious to know your opinions on Bentham's theories of utilitarianism and Rousseau's thoughts on direct democracy."

He blinked…and fell a little in love with her on the spot.

Damn it. Why could he not resist her, even a smidgeon?

"I'll consider it," he hedged. "But that's eventually," he recalled her specifying a moment ago. "And first…?"

"First…" Olivia stopped near his place at the bed. She eyed its unkempt sheets as though remembering the first time she'd caught him in it. Her innocent, wide-eyed reaction to his under-the-bedclothes nudity had been memorable, to say the least. She drew in a breath. "I want to know why you can sweep so well."

At her precisely voiced question, Griffin hesitated.

Then, to his still-tipsy surprise, he told Olivia everything. He omitted not a single detail. Rats, hunger pains, abuse from his mother, abandonment by his father… They were all in his past, so he told Olivia about them. He recounted them as though they'd happened to another boy, in another life, and he didn't feel much of anything at all while he did it.

He wasn't that boy anymore. He'd locked that door.

As a man, Griffin placed Olivia on the settee. As a man, he set down his whiskey and then took his place beside her. As a man, he disclosed the bareness of his life growing up in that Boston tenement. He did so without flinching, without bawling and without lapsing into needless sentimentality. He did so unsparingly. If Olivia grew hushed and wide-eyed and eventually—confusingly—teary eyed beside him, Griffin scarcely noticed.

He was performing a recitation. It was the only way.

Matter-of-factness saved him. It saved him from feeling. It saved him from acknowledging…everything. It had been difficult—surpassingly difficult—to survive those years. Not that such delineation mattered. After all, *now* was difficult, too.

When he'd nearly finished, Griffin became aware again of the dimness of the room, the nearness of Olivia and the rasp in his voice that he still couldn't shake. He'd never revealed so much to anyone before. He had never wanted to. At some point, he saw, Olivia had taken his hand. She squeezed his fingers.

Her touch looked like a blessing. But it felt like pity.

Unreasonably distraught over that sympathetic gesture, Griffin stared down at their joined hands. He wanted to believe Olivia's touch meant more. But he knew damn well that he could not.

"So that is how I learned to sweep," he concluded. He gave her hand a final squeeze, then pulled away. "It's a shame your upbringing didn't leave you with any such useful skills."

His joke failed to meet its mark. Olivia merely gazed at him with tears in her eyes. She glanced downward, appeared to realize that he'd withdrawn his hand then shook her head.

She grabbed his hand back. She held it tight between both of hers, a fierce light brightening her eyes. "No wonder," she said with a shake of her head. "No wonder you hide away! Griffin…" Olivia broke off, probing his gaze with hers. "You're lonely."

"No. You're wrong." He shook his head. Bluster and fury and hard-drinking isolation would keep him secure. He should never have abandoned them. "Until now, I've rarely been alone. Don't you know who I am? Don't you know what I've accomplished?"

She was undeterred by his rough tone. "I told you before—all I care about is who you are *now.* You, Griffin, are lonely."

Lonely. That simple word barely began to describe the emptiness he felt. It was insufficient to mark the solitude inside him. It could not contain his deep yearning for more.

Griffin felt that yearning claw at him now, with needy fingers and a heart that wanted more. He fought back brutally.

"*You* are lonely," he accused, "with your small-town life and your 'family' of hotel workers and your apathetic father."

But Olivia refused to be dissuaded. "Another time, we'll talk about my father," she said, sliding nearer on the settee and taking his other hand. Her skirts rustled, marking her femininity and her closeness alike. "For now," she went on, still holding his hands, "I only want you to know that I'm sorry for all you went through." She inhaled deeply, keeping her gaze fixed on him. "You deserved better. You deserve better now. You deserve more than a fickle woman who'd break your heart—" for he'd told her about Mary "—and a father who'd use you for his own gains—" because Griffin's father had, indeed, taken advantage of Griffin's early ambitions for his own purposes at first "—and a mother who would be so cruel to you. You deserve better. Everyone does!"

Warily, Griffin regarded her. "Ah. This *is* pity, then," he judged. "You would treat anyone in my place this way."

"Anyone?" Olivia raised her eyebrows, then gave a lilting laugh. Meaningfully, she raised their twined hands. "No, not anyone," she specified. "But if this demonstration of my feelings is not apparent enough for you, please let me clarify."

"There's no need. I understand everything."

Another laugh. "Of course you do. All the same, allow me."

Astoundingly, Olivia released his hands. She lifted one of her hands to his jaw, then mimicked her gesture on the opposite side. With his face duly framed in her affectionate grasp, Griffin froze. *No one* touched his face. Not his mother, not his father, not the few loose women he'd known as a grown man.

Not even Mary had touched him this way, it occurred to him. Theirs had not been an overly passionate relationship. Perhaps he *had* been like a brother to her, he mused. Perhaps he'd nurtured an adolescent infatuation for too long, prompted partly by fondness for her close-knit household. Certainly, Griffin had never felt for Mary one-tenth of what he now felt for Olivia.

"Don't." Desperately, he closed his eyes, trying not to savor the light and caring touch of her palms against his face—trying not to imprison it in his memory forever after. He opened his eyes. He stared at her. "You don't want to touch me."

Griffin clung to that belief like a drowning man. He needed to. What was the alternative? To *believe* that Olivia wanted him?

Yes, he recalled her saying. *I was alarmed by you at first.*

She was the only person who'd ever admitted her initial wariness about his appearance. Now she was the only woman who'd ever touched his face willingly. That had to mean something.

Perhaps, the cynical side of him suggested, it meant that Olivia Mouton really, determinedly wanted The Lorndorff back.

But then she delivered him a mind-scramblingly playful look, stroked his jaw with her fingers and shook her head.

"You can't tell me what I want, Mr. Turner."

"Griffin," he managed, mesmerized by her nearness. "It's—"

"Griffin," Olivia repeated, her gaze warm and wonderful as she looked at him. Clearly, she was bewitched somehow. She caressed his cheeks, then brushed her thumbs over his beard stubble. "I *do* want to touch you. See? I'm doing it right now."

He couldn't help seeing. He couldn't help *feeling*. But that didn't mean…

"I'm going to go right on doing it," Olivia said in a low voice as she brought her pretty face closer to his, "because I find that your big, angular jawline provides a very convenient means to steady myself while I prepare to do *this*."

Then she took a deep breath, gazed moonily into his eyes and brought her mouth to his. Once, twice, she kissed him.

She leaned back. She lowered her hands to her lap.

Griffin stared at her, his heart pounding thunderously.

"I don't want pity," he warned with the last of his wits.

"Did that feel like pity?" Olivia posed her question with a sham sense of consternation. "Perhaps I'm not kissing you correctly. I don't have very much experience in these matters."

To his amazement, she brushed her lips against his again. Kissing Olivia, Griffin learned, was like being walloped by an angel, blessed by a temptress…driven mad by an innocent.

It was all he could do not to delve his hands in her hair, yank her still closer and bring them both down on the settee's upholstered cushions where they could continue this properly.

Sucking in a cooling lungful of air, Griffin gawked at her. "Have you lost your mind?" he blurted. "You're not supposed to want…" Wildly, he gestured between them. *"Me."*

"Mmm. You'll find that I have a long history of wanting things I'm not supposed to want. Like books. And experiments."

"And me?" Damnation. He didn't mean it as a question.

A nod. "And you." She stroked his cheek again, then shrugged. "I can't help it. I tried to stay away. I couldn't."

Distrustfully, he eyed her. "Why not?"

"I couldn't stop thinking about you holding my hand," Olivia confessed. Her gaze swung to meet his, then dropped to coolly examine her fingernails. "And… some other things."

"The hotel."

"Yes." To her credit, she didn't quibble. "Naturally. I thought about that, too. This is my home, so its future is of pressing interest to me." Olivia's wave indicated the entire hotel. "But I didn't kiss you to save my father's hotel."

Still astounded by her kiss, Griffin thought about that. If she had, it might have worked. Given the riotous effect she had on him, he might have given her anything she wanted.

Then, "I also thought about *you*. In bed," Olivia said.

Griffin bolted upright from the settee, feeling his heart race with alarm. "You should leave." He jerked his thumb toward the door, then began pacing. "You should leave right now."

Olivia eyed him with amusement. "All I want to know is, on the first day I came here, if you were *really* naked under the bedclothes. My imagination has been running wild, I'm afraid."

As she said it, Griffin stopped. Their gazes locked. He felt sure she could somehow sense him remembering that moment. It had created a sort of cock-eyed intimacy between them that could hardly have been sparked in another, more clothed, way.

"Let it," he said roughly. "The truth would scare you."

She chuckled. "I doubt that, Griffin. You're just a man. I've seen men before." Olivia's voice pursued him with maddening unreality. "Not entirely nude, of course! But this was a lawless township when I arrived here as a girl. Drunk rail workers aren't known for their delicate manners. I'm not *that* refined."

"Yes, you are. You don't know what you're saying."

"I'm saying," she said patiently, "that I'd like for you to verify my impression, please. For observation's sake. I place a great store in my observational abilities, you see, owing to my interest in the sciences, and it would be a tremendous favor to me if you would let me know—did I guess correctly?"

"Did you guess correctly about my *nakedness* on that day?" Griffin wheeled around in his suite, still pacing, hardly able to credit what he was hearing. "For the sake of *science?*"

"The scientific method, to be more precise. Yes."

He dug his nails in his palms. "I am dreaming. I must be."

"Shall I wake you up?" Her bantering tone suggested she'd already decided for herself. "With another kiss, perhaps?"

Alarmed, Griffin held out both hands to ward her off. At that, Olivia appeared undeniably disappointed. He loved that she could not—or did not try to—hide her honest reaction to him.

Heaven help him, he increasingly loved *her.* She filled his days with sunshine and chatter and helpfulness. When she looked at him... Well, she *looked* at him. She saw *him.* Not his past.

Not detestable Hook Turner, with all his inborn badness.

How could he have not scared her away already?

He'd certainly tried. He'd tried to be as formidable as possible on the day they'd met. He'd all but dared her to laugh at him—to see him as some hideous, huge-nosed, black-clothed monster. Somehow, his warnings hadn't stuck. He'd have to try harder. For Olivia's sake, he'd have to make her see the truth.

All the same, the masculine, prideful part of Griffin took exception at her notion that *she* would manage things between them, should any additional, soul-shattering kisses occur.

Despite everything, Griffin heartily hoped they occurred.

"Any more kissing will be at *my* instigation," he told her.

She wasn't the least bit dissuaded. "I liked kissing you."

Her candid admission nearly unraveled his will right there. Griffin turned around. He confronted her expectant and almost scholarly expression of interest. He groaned aloud.

"I was wearing trousers!" he confessed. "No shirt. Boots."

Olivia wrinkled her nose. "Boots in bed?"

"Now you're an expert?"

"Enough of an expert to know boots don't belong in bed."

"Neither do nosy, opinionated, book-pilfering women belong in the hotel suites of notoriously unprincipled men."

Her eyes sparkled at him. "I won't be scared away."

"You will be. When you see the truth."

"People who are afraid of the truth usually *can't* see it," Olivia told him. "They refuse to. Oftentimes quite stubbornly." In thought, she eyed him. "Take you and Mary, for instance. You were sweet on her for years. But given what you told me about your relationship, it seems to have been fairly unromantic. So—"

"Enough." Again, Griffin groaned. At the settee, he fell to his knees before Olivia. He took her face in his hands, then tilted her chin upward. He loved the way she looked, the way she sounded…even the way she opened her mouth in a surprised O.

But he *truly* loved the way she felt when he brought his mouth to hers, when he took possession of her lips and tongue and breath, when he delivered to her all the passion and confusion and trepidation he felt, ladling it all into a single heartfelt kiss. He wanted to stop her from studying him.

Instead, he stopped them both from thinking altogether.

When Griffin broke off their kiss at last, Olivia was gazing at him with stars in her eyes. He knew then that he'd done it again. He'd made a mistake. He'd misunderstood her.

Olivia didn't really see him, Griffin realized. She appeared far too dreamy for that. For both their sakes, he had to make her see. He had to make her see who he was and who he would always be. Clearly, his hat and his dark clothes and his hair had failed to do their proper jobs and sensibly deter her.

"You need to see something," he announced, standing.

"Does it involve more kissing somehow?"

She was going to kill him. "No. Please listen to me."

With unbelievable cooperativeness, she prepared to. Meticulously, Olivia straightened her voluminous flowery skirts. She clasped her hands in her lap. She smiled, then gazed up at him. Any man would have believed her an ideal feminine companion…instead of a secret firebrand who'd steal his whiskey, make him quit his cigarillos and inspire him to club his hair.

"I would settle for holding hands with you," she said.

Wordlessly, Griffin shook his head. His hands shook, too. This was going to be difficult enough without her touch to rouse him. Even a chaste handclasp would likely inspire passion now.

Now that he knew how ardently she might respond to it.

Setting aside that tantalizing truth, Griffin situated

himself in front of her. He squared his shoulders. He frowned.

"So far, I don't like this," Olivia said. "Come sit by me."

Griffin wanted nothing more. But he could not proceed while believing Olivia was purposely ignoring the truth about him.

He believed her when she said she hadn't kissed him for the sake of her father's hotel. He believed she was truthful. That left only one explanation. She'd misled herself into blindness.

So first Griffin took off his suit coat. Then he removed his woolen vest. Olivia gave him a wary look, studied his shirt and trousers then reclasped her hands. She was clearly willing to wait and see how this situation unfolded—likely for the sake of "scientific interest." "Why did you do that?"

"To show you the truth. To show you who I am."

"I've spent almost two weeks with you. I think I know—"

He cut her off by shucking his hat next. It sailed across his suite to land on his mattress and disordered bedclothes.

Not daring to confront her with the full sight of his face and his hated nose yet, Griffin kept his head down. He raised his body to its full, impressive height and strength. He reached to his nape. With a trembling hand, he released his leather tie.

He shook his head, making his long dark hair fall around his shoulders and down his broad back. He was the opposite of civilized—the opposite of desirable, especially to a prim woman like Olivia. In the same way he had days ago, he needed to dare her to shirk from him. He needed to dare her to laugh at him—to dare himself to withstand it, if she did. This was the only way to test her intentions. With a desperate mingling of hope and fear and pride warring inside him, Griffin raised his head.

At her first unimpeded view of him, Olivia gasped.

That tiny sound knifed into his heart. Feeling duly broken by it, Griffin nudged his chin a notch higher. This would not stop him. He swore it as he stood there. This was no different—*she* was no different—than anyone else. Olivia would leave in horror. He would go on. That would be the finish of it.

It would be better for both of them if this ended now.

You're lonely, he remembered her saying, and bitterly resented allowing himself to listen. He wished he hadn't. It did not help to put a name to the pain he'd become so familiar with.

Gruffly, Griffin cleared his throat. "So, you see—"

To his shame, he couldn't find the words to continue. He couldn't bring himself to drive home the truth that Olivia needed—that he was flawed, that he was damaged, that he *needed.* He needed things he had no right to ask of anyone. Like love.

A long moment passed while he struggled to say something.

For her part, Olivia sat silently. She gazed up at him, for the first time fully taking in the reality of his appearance.

Soon, Griffin couldn't bear it any longer. Sightlessly, he strode to his bedstead. He fumbled for his hat. He grabbed it.

Olivia grabbed it, too. How had she come to be there?

Wearing a determined, impassioned look, she took it from him. Numbly, Griffin let her. He felt too worn down not to.

Maybe, he thought wryly, he shouldn't have drunk so much.

"Can't you see?" he made himself ask. "*This* is why I've never married." *This badness that's inherent in me—that's linked forever to my Turner nose.* "This is why Mary refused me. Why people fear me. Everyone sees it. Surely you must—"

Olivia stopped his recitation with a sudden, lunging kiss. It was clumsy but affecting—inexperienced but wholehearted.

It was…perfect. Perfect because it was from Olivia. Griffin hardly dared to wonder what it signified. He knew what he hoped it signified. That she *cared* for him. That was audacious enough.

Afterward, she had the temerity to smile at him. Musingly, she brushed back his hair. "All I see is a man who's been alone for too long." A wider grin. "I told you—it's no use telling me what to do. I'm exceedingly contrary and *very* strong-minded."

Griffin had never, ever loved two personality traits more.

"I told you I knew what to do to help you, and I do," Olivia continued resolutely. "Put yourself in my hands, Griffin. I promise, I'm not the empty-headed, feather-dusting, terrible bed-making, lithographed gadabout you think I am. Let me prove it to you."

At that, Griffin had no recourse. He'd been broken. Now, in a heartbeat, Olivia had begun rebuilding him. She'd *seen* him. More than that, unbelievably, she seemed to have accepted him.

The realization made him feel positively buoyant.

"Can you promise another kiss?" he asked, making light of all she'd undertaken. "If you can, I just might be persuaded."

"Oh, you might, mightn't you?"

"Maybe." He nodded. "It's possible."

"You don't fool me," Olivia scoffed, rightly guessing at his willingness. "You're already persuaded." Spiritedly, she took his hand. "That means it's past time to get started."

Against all reason, Griffin could hardly wait.

Chapter Nine

From the moment Olivia appeared downstairs at the hotel on Griffin's arm on the following Saturday morning, intending to officially embark on her campaign to save him, she began to have grave misgivings about the task she'd undertaken.

Not because she didn't want to help Griffin. She did. He'd trusted her with something monumental when he'd confided in her about his terrible past. He'd trusted her to help him. Olivia fully intended to do that. She intended to cure Griffin's loneliness and bring him into the light. Whether doing so returned The Lorndorff to her family was inconsequential.

Although she did still hope to regain the hotel....

What she didn't anticipate, though, was that helping Griffin would necessarily mean bringing him into *her* world. There, despite her protestations, she really wasn't much more than a famous lithography model with a remedy bottle to her credit. In Morrow Creek, Olivia remembered belatedly, everyone saw her as nothing more than a beautiful woman with a long string of suitors and a baffling inability to choose among them.

It began with the bellman. His crestfallen expression was the first detail to catch Olivia's attention as she descended the hotel stairs and entered the lobby, escorted by Griffin.

The bellman pretended to busy himself with some luggage while she approached, but his dejected look did not wane.

"Good morning!" Olivia called. She murmured an apology to Griffin. She excused herself, then trod the few short steps that separated her from the hotel's front desk. Concernedly, she eyed the bellman. She touched his arm. "Are you all right?"

"Right as rain." Irritably, he shrugged off her hand. "*You* seem to be doin' all right for yerself, too."

His disgruntled nod indicated Griffin, who had dressed for the day in a well-fitted ensemble of shirt, trousers, expensive brocade vest, suit coat, boots and hat—all typically in black, of course. Wearing those togs and liberated from his gloomy room, he appeared twice as commanding as usual, Olivia thought. She couldn't help remembering that the man she'd developed an infatuation with was, in fact, a captain of industry. He was also an infamous citified rogue. Those realizations should not have given a good woman a thrill—but they did thrill Olivia.

"Yes. I've agreed to show Mr. Turner the town," Olivia told the bellman. "He's new to these parts after all."

The bellman sniffed. "Seems to have taken charge pretty readily, for all that." He jutted his chin. "Didja accept his proposal? I reckon you did, once he got the sense to make it."

"He didn't propose." She smiled at him. "The fact is—"

"Don't bother explainin'. I can tell when I'm licked."

The bellman issued Griffin a malicious look. He fiddled with the luggage, then swerved his attention back to Olivia. "You're better'n him, Miss Mouton. You oughta remember that. Even if you ain't gonna marry me, you can't marry someone like *him*."

Before Olivia could think of a suitable response to that, Griffin was there. His gaze flicked to the vexing array of Milky White Complexion Beautifier and Youthful Enhancement Tonic shelved above the bellman's head, then moved to Olivia.

Protectively, he took her elbow. He looked solicitously into her face. "Miss Mouton. Is everything all right here?"

"It's fine," Olivia told him. She glanced to the bellman again. She should not have waited to decline his marriage proposal. She could see now that keeping him on tenterhooks was no favor to him. Contritely, she lay her hand on his uniformed forearm. "I'm so sorry. But we'll always be friends, won't we?"

"Sure." Another sniff. "You'll need friends. Later." The bellman's deferential glance shifted meaningfully to Griffin. "Good morning to ya, Mr. Turner, sir. Do ya need anything?"

Griffin shook his head, calling her attention to his neatly clubbed hair. With his long hair—and his oversize nose—obscured by his hat, he almost blended in. At least he did until he spoke. Then his natural authority asserted itself. No one in the territory carried quite the same…*impact* as the infamous Griffin Turner did, just by being present.

"Perhaps a cigarillo?" Griffin raised his chin, nodding to indicate the slender Mexican cigars tucked into the bellman's uniform pocket. "If I'm not mistaken,

Jimmy, those are the same brand I used to be fond of. Would you mind sharing one?"

Olivia froze. When she'd gleefully distributed the contraband goods she'd liberated from Griffin's room last week to various members of the staff, she hadn't expected him to ever find out. His knowing look said he'd already guessed everything.

Bluntly, the bellman eyed him. "How'd you know my name?"

Griffin shrugged, unbothered by his blatant suspicion. "It's my job to know. Everyone here is important to me."

"It took Mr. Mouton a week solid to learn my name." The bellman cracked a confiding grin. "He's fond o' woolgatherin'."

Their conversation continued apace as, to Olivia's amazement, the bellman went on chatting. Convivially, he gave Griffin one of his own former cigarillos. Griffin thanked him. He passed the cigarillo under his nose to appreciate its cured tobacco scent, then gave Olivia a surreptitious wink. The rascal. He was flaunting his knowledge of her antics now!

Perhaps, she realized belatedly, she'd bitten off more than she could chew. Griffin Turner was more akin to tough jerky than he was to Molly Copeland's melt-in-your-mouth spice cake.

"Well, you have yourself a nice time seein' Morrow Creek," the bellman said. "I'd better git back to work at your hotel!"

Your hotel. Taken aback, Olivia gawked at him. This was one thing she hadn't anticipated—that Griffin might actually endear himself to the hotel staff even more than her father had done.

She'd better warn her father, she realized. Henry

Mouton had to try harder to regain The Lorndorff. Olivia knew he'd been hoping to find other investors— endeavoring to buy out Griffin. That was why, it turned out, her father had spent so much time at Jack Murphy's saloon. He hadn't only been drinking. He'd also been getting Mr. Murphy's advice. The saloonkeeper was a Boston man himself and surprisingly adept in the ways of business.

Murphy also, her father had assured her, poured a fine mescal. But if another willing investor didn't appear soon, or if Griffin couldn't be persuaded to make a deal with him…

Olivia was better off following her own plan, she knew. Even if no one believed she could successfully carry it out.

"Your work is certainly appreciated, Jimmy." Griffin tipped his hat. "I'm obliged for the cigarillo. Thank-you kindly."

After a few more niceties, they parted. Olivia frowned.

"You didn't tell me you could be charming!" She shook her head at Griffin's unabashed expression, marveling as he offered a genial nod to passersby. "Whatever has gotten into you?"

He only grinned. "Perhaps you've inspired me."

Olivia doubted it. "How did you know Jimmy's name?" she demanded. "You've not been downstairs since you arrived. Is it because Mr. Grant spies for you? That must be it."

"He doesn't spy," Griffin returned easily. "He is managing The Lorndorff. Nothing more." His puzzled face turned to hers. "I'm curious to know—aside from Jimmy, the bellman, how many men have proposed to you? How many of them are awaiting answers?"

"You heard us? You were eavesdropping?"

Did that mean he'd also heard the bellman claim that she was too good for Griffin?

A backward glance. "It wasn't difficult to decipher the situation. When you arrived in the lobby on my arm, Jimmy looked like a kicked puppy. When you walked toward him to say good morning, he practically wagged his tail. I inferred the rest from there." At Olivia's aghast look, Griffin gave a pragmatic shrug. "There's something about growing up hand to mouth, in danger of getting beaten, that makes a man notice the details of things." Moving on, he made a show of admiring the chandeliers, the rugs and the hotel's luxurious decor. "I'm simply curious to know how many more men are in competition for your hand."

"Are we counting *you* among them?"

His grin widened. "That would hardly be fair to them."

"We don't have time for this," Olivia announced. She gave his arm a tug, then forcibly tucked her hand in the crook of his elbow. "We have a tour of Morrow Creek to enjoy."

That sobered him. "You were serious about that?"

"Don't worry." Olivia strode onward through the lobby, all but hauling Griffin in her wake, feeling like a tugboat pulling a big, burly, recalcitrant steamer into harbor. "The sunlight won't hurt you. Even full force, it's actually quite pleasant."

He balked. "You didn't tell me your plan led outdoors. I thought we'd be starting small. Perhaps by touring the hotel." A hopeful look. "Or having toast. I think you're fond of toast."

She was. She ate toasted buttermilk bread with jam every morning, along with her daily coffee. But she couldn't guess how Griffin knew about her fondness for her very ordinary breakfast.

"I like toast, too." He veered toward the hotel's dining room, which awaited at the lobby's far end. "Let's have some."

"No!" Fixing her feet near the double doors leading from the hotel to the town's main street, Olivia stopped. She gazed at Griffin, with his obdurate expression and his admirably clean-shaven jaw, and understood that there was only one way to combat loneliness. Head-on. "Outdoors is where the world is waiting," she explained. "Morrow Creek is beyond friendly. Trust me."

Her assurances barely penetrated Griffin's unease. He tugged his hat but did not move closer to the street. There, horses and riders passed by. Townspeople conversed and conducted business. The sounds of jangling harnesses and tromping hooves held steady, mingling with the distant barking of someone's dog.

"Trust me," she urged again. "I know what I'm doing."

Griffin swallowed hard. He gave a firm nod. "Don't blame me when people stare," he said. "They will. I'm warning you."

"And what of it?" She waved. "People stare at me all the time."

"They stare at *you* in wonder, because you're beautiful."

"That doesn't mean a thing," Olivia assured him. "No one knows better than me how empty beauty really is."

He didn't notice her inadvertent confession. He was too intent on his own. "They stare at *me* in fear, because—"

"Because you do your utmost to intimidate them!" Olivia gave him another yank, grateful that he'd accidentally overlooked her admission. All she had was beauty. She couldn't malign it now. "Come with me.

Honestly, the only reason anyone shies away from you is because you make them do it."

"No." He planted his boots. "You don't understand."

"I do," she promised him. She did. She understood that Griffin drove away people on purpose, with his threatening demeanor, shouted commands and overall antagonism. Clearly, as with Jimmy, he was capable of behaving sociably. "I also understand that sometimes the only way out is through. Come."

"Come?" A frown. "I don't like it when you're bossy."

"You will learn to adore it. Don't worry."

"You were nicer upstairs," Griffin grumbled.

"That means you've agreed to come with me, doesn't it?"

He shot her a deliberately displeased look. "Did you have to give away all my cigarillos? What happened to my whiskey?"

She sighed. "The kitchen staff enjoyed it immensely."

"Humph. Did they at least know it came from me?"

"Of course not!" Olivia fixed her gaze on the street outside. "It came from me—the Robin Hood of The Lorndorff."

"I doubt so many men would have proposed to you," Griffin opined, "if they'd known you could be this contrary."

Perturbed by that, Olivia hesitated. The real her *was* contrary. "What makes you think they don't know that already?"

"Because of the way they look at you. They have dreams of wedding Miss Milky White in their eyes. And not much more."

No one had ever phrased her situation quite so succinctly. Or so accurately. Without meaning to, Griffin had defined her nearly lifelong dilemma. Not that she wanted him to know that.

"You make me sound like a prize to be won," she told him instead. She added an intentionally lighthearted look. "And if we don't leave now, we'll be late for the jam-tasting jamboree."

"Jam tasting?" Griffin shied away in horror. "Forget I ever mentioned toast. I'm *not* a man who attends country jamborees."

Olivia laughed. "Just stick with me," she said as she lifted her chin determinedly, "and try *not* to be intimidating."

"I don't think I can help it," Griffin cautioned her.

But Olivia wasn't listening. She was already stepping into the sunlight and bringing Griffin with her. She hoped, with all her heart, that this would not be the last time she did so.

For his sake. And maybe, a tiny bit, for her sake, as well.

Chapter Ten

Several hours later, Olivia found herself with sore feet, a hoarse throat and a sunny, private spot beside Morrow Creek's namesake creek. A few feet beyond her aching toes, the water burbled along its banks, glimmering in the sunlight. All around her, tall ponderosa pines and scrubby mountain oaks crowded the steep landscape, turning it green and lush. Nodding wildflowers dotted the patchy grass. The territorial mountains rose in the distance, revealing Morrow Creek for the valley town it was.

From here, though, the town might as well be miles away. At this distance from the creek bridge, even the noisy sounds of horse traffic didn't carry. The afternoon school bell and the blacksmith's hammer were swallowed up by the cloudless skies overhead, and the town's houses and buildings stood far away from this secluded spot. Nothing penetrated the trees and grass and mountainside except for birdsong and rustling leaves.

"Ah." In patented delight, Griffin reclined on a rock slab beside her. He pillowed his dark leonine head on his arms, his hat abandoned beside him. Apparently, when he'd bared himself to her, he'd lost his need to hide—

at least as long as he was out of the view of strangers. "This is good. It's worth all the dillydallying and silly conversations leading up to it."

That was *not* a polite way to refer to the many rounds of calls they'd made so far, visiting several of Olivia's friends and neighbors and experiencing the sights and sounds of Morrow Creek. But it was accurate. Together, she and Griffin had strolled the main street. They'd popped into the impressively busy offices of the *Pioneer Press*. They'd browsed Hofer's popular mercantile, said hello to a throng of children playing outside the schoolhouse where Sarah McCabe taught on schooldays, perused the lumber mill with its piles of felled timer and—of course—attended the jam-tasting jamboree. They'd encountered a number of townspeople on their way. Only a few had openly gawked at Griffin, to Olivia's satisfaction.

"I thought you'd like it here," she told him. She longed to massage her tired feet, but it would not be ladylike to remove her high-buttoned shoes. "That's why I saved it for last."

"Ah." He cracked open one eye. "You're a savorer, then."

"A savorer?"

"Someone who likes to wait for good things—who likes to delay the gratification of them for as long as possible."

"I suppose so." Pulling up her knees to her chest with her skirts flowing around her, Olivia nodded. "Isn't everyone?"

"No. Some of us know you have to grab the goodness while it's within reach, else lose it forever." Griffin levered upward on his elbow. He studied her. "Scarcity teaches that lesson."

"You're wealthy. You don't have scarcity anymore."

He disagreed. "I'll have scarcity forever." He touched his chest, indicating his heart. She doubted he was aware of it. He lay back again, letting the sunshine soak into him. Eyes closed, he said, "Just like you'll have marriage proposals forever."

Ugh. Reminded of one of the most trying elements of their day so far, Olivia squinted into the treetops. She'd never realized before exactly how much of her life was defined by the receiving—and subsequent evasion—of marriage proposals.

My son William proposed to Miss Mouton, one of the women at the jam-tasting event had confided to Griffin. *She was quite right to turn him down, though. He was scarcely eighteen.*

Or, *my brother proposed to Miss Mouton last winter,* a woman at Hofer's mercantile had said. *He's still awaiting an answer.*

Or, *I proposed to Miss Mouton myself,* a bucker had said while greeting them outside Copeland's lumber mill, *well on a year ago now.* He'd given a wink. *Any day now, she'll come round.*

Taken as a whole, glimpsed through an outsider's eyes, the entire compilation had been dismaying. Olivia could almost feel the town's fervent wishes bearing down on her even now. More than anything, her friends and neighbors wanted her to be a wife, to be perfectly proper, to be *different* than she was.

She feared she was running out of reasons to resist that.

"Eventually I'll be old." She gave a blithe wave, watching a butterfly alight on a Griffin's bent knee—watching him notice that butterfly with evident delight. "No one will want me then."

Griffin laughed. "Is that your plan? To delay your suitors until you're feeble and gray? It's novel, I'll give you that."

"What choice do I have?" Olivia shot an irate look toward the grosbeaks twittering in the nearby oak tree branches. "If I say no outright, I'll disappoint people. If I say yes—"

"You'll disappoint yourself," Griffin finished for her.

Surprised, she glanced at him. For a man who appeared to love nothing more strongly than an afternoon sunbath, Griffin was unexpectedly perceptive. "Yes. I have no wish to marry."

"How can you not," he asked, "when you're so lonely?"

For a moment, the only sounds were those birds and the peaceful ripple of Morrow Creek wending its way downstream.

Then… "What makes you think I'm lonely?" This was different from his earlier charge of loneliness. Then, he'd been reacting to her statement that *he* was lonely. Now… "Of course I'm not!"

Pondering that, Griffin kept his eyes closed. His profile jutted skyward, angular and raw. His cheekbones were as sharp as marble. His forehead was regal enough to merit a crown. His lips were full and sensual. Only his nose marred the image of him as perfectly masculine. She began to think he wouldn't speak.

Her certainty about that was woefully short-lived.

"Olivia, you've deliberately hidden yourself from everyone," Griffin said in a rumbling, self-certain tone. "With me, you were so eager to discuss Bentham and Rousseau that you committed petty larceny of my philosophy book. With Mrs. Hofer, you chatted about hats for nearly an hour. With me, you claimed a lifelong fascination with science—and proved your interest by conducting a fairly shameless 'observation' of me in my bed. Yet with Miss Adeline Wilson, you pledged your undying devotion to dressmaking patterns and intricate crewelwork. Given those vast differences, how could you be anything except lonely?"

"You don't understand. Am I not allowed to have diverse interests?" *Even if a few are false?* Olivia wasn't happy he'd brought up her borrowing of his philosophy book and her inability to quit thinking about his provocatively unclothed form…even if she *had* categorized her peeking as "scientific observation" to him. And herself. "Everyone chats socially."

"Yes," Griffin agreed. "But not everyone feels as lonely as you do when they do so. I've watched you all day. I can see it in you." He delivered her a serious look. "I feel it in you. If anyone can, it's me. Unless your own hypothesis is wrong?"

Uncomfortably, she stared at him, feeling irksomely unable to take delight in his casual use of that scientific term—even if it did prove that they had intellectual pastimes in common.

Lonely? It was true that she often felt misunderstood, Olivia mused. It was true that she had no one to explore her deepest interests with. That she felt apart from workaday goings on in town. But everyone was kind to her. Everyone *wanted* her. Annie had been right about that, at least. She was not a victim of hardship, like Griffin. She was not despondent, like him.

She might be, though, if he refused to discuss Rousseau and Bentham with her. She was counting on their mutual interest. She was counting on exploring that interest in a way she could do with no one else. But that didn't make him an expert on her.

"You've made sure they don't understand you," Griffin went on, placidly but relentlessly. "What I don't understand is why."

"What *you* don't understand is far more comprehensive than that," Olivia snapped. "I'm beginning to regret bringing you here." She brushed off her skirts, defensively preparing to get to her feet. "It seems the creek side makes you babble nonsense."

He laughed. Without so much as opening his eyes, Griffin grabbed her arm. Wordlessly, he stopped her from standing.

"I don't think it's nonsense," he said in a steady tone. "Given that you're ready to stomp off in a huff…neither do you."

Olivia wanted to take umbrage at that statement. Honestly, she did. But something about the way Griffin lazily stroked his fingers along the sensitive skin of her inner arm made her senses riot in response instead. Her breath caught. Her skin tingled. All her attempts to command her mind—instead of her traitorous body—to take charge of this situation failed utterly.

Squirming breathlessly in place, Olivia wondered how Griffin's touch could possibly be so rousing…and how she could possibly remain annoyed with him while experiencing it. Caught up in the sensation, she couldn't help remembering how it had felt to kiss him. How exciting it had been. How new, how foreign, how stimulating and passionate it had felt. Kissing Griffin had been the most stirring event she'd ever experienced.

Even now, she wanted more. More of him.

"We're the same, you and I," he said, breaking into her wicked thoughts. "We're both apart from everyone else. We're both alone. The only question now is what to do about it."

His gaze meandered to her face. She would have sworn he could read her thoughts—could know her illicit desires from the heated blush on her cheeks and the telltale hitch in her breath.

"*You* should change your ways," Olivia said immediately. "Stop being quite so…oversize. And so brooding. And so fierce."

"Ha." He caressed her wrist. "I can't help my size."

Her heart pounded. "And all the rest?"

"Hmm." His hold on her wrist tightened. He gave a gentle pull. Like magic, Olivia tumbled atop him with a breathless *oof.*

Griffin caught her, not at all brooding or fierce in that moment—and not at all bothered by their improper nearness, either. Olivia felt it intensely. She felt his chest, as hard as the river rocks beneath her hands. She felt his arms, as mighty as any tree trunks could have been, holding her close. She felt his thigh, covered now by her skirts, warmed by the sun and flexing with the strength to hold them both in place.

It occurred to her that he might have been doing the very thing he'd spoken about before—grabbing the goodness in his life before it could escape him forever. Was *she* the goodness?

Against all reason, Olivia wanted to be. For him.

"Why have you escaped the imperative to change?" he asked in a vaguely aggrieved tone. He turned his face again to the sunshine, as though it had been his plan to embrace her this way all along. "That hardly seems fair. If I have to mend my disorderly ways," Griffin told her, "then you should also. You should confess your love of philosophy, proclaim your interest in science and shout your contrariness to the rooftops."

"No." She pretended certainty when she felt nothing

of the kind. Not given all he'd said just now. "I think I should kiss you again instead. Yes, that *must* be it. It feels right."

Anything that evaded this conversation felt tangibly right. But kissing Griffin had other, more exhilarating benefits to it.

For one thing, kissing Griffin made Olivia feel *free*. Even bound as she was to Morrow Creek, its conventions and her own role among her friends and neighbors, with Griffin she felt free. Free to be just as she was. Because *he* certainly was in no position to judge her—although he was positioned to disagree.

"That's not it. Kissing is not the answer to this." He gave her a fleeting and endearingly concerned frown. "I'm serious about this. I mean what I say. You cannot be happy with—"

"With you? Oh, yes. I can." She touched his face, loving its contours and its warmth and its uniqueness. She leaned upward. She puckered up. "Here. Let me show you what I mean."

Inexpertly but fervently, she kissed him. Even better, he kissed her back. Their coming together amazed her still. It amazed her with its passion, with its tenderness… with its necessity. Olivia didn't know where she found the daring to behave this way when it came to Griffin. She'd certainly never been this sensually minded or this adventurous before *he'd* come into her life.

Now she was. Now she knew that his mouth made her forget everything. Held in his arms, she felt without thinking. She gave without reservations. She cared for him in a way that was both unequivocal and undeniable…and almost frightening in its intensity. She'd set out to comfort Griffin with this daylong out-

ing of theirs, it was true—but she'd ended up tantalizing herself with their intimacy. Now she needed more.

He, as a gentleman, would likely *not* be first to offer.
She didn't believe the stories about him—the scandal-
ous tales of The Tycoon Terror and The Business Brute.
With her, he was…gentled.

With her, at least, The Boston Beast was tamed.

Maybe that was why Olivia felt free to loosen the
leather tie at his nape. She pulled it free, then boldly
went on kissing him while she delved her hands in his
dark, tangled hair. With his mouth still pressed against
hers, Griffin gave a startled sound.

He caught her hand, held it in his then broke their
kiss.

"Don't." His heavy brows lowered. "You don't want
to—"

"I thought we'd settled this already." She smiled at
him. "You won't get anywhere trying to tell me what
to do."

Demonstrating as much, Olivia wriggled her hand
free. She caught hold of a length of his hair, then tenderly stroked it away from his face. Griffin closed his
eyes…and allowed it.

Humbled by his trust in her, Olivia gave him a loving look, not caring that he couldn't see it. He'd exposed
himself to her this way before, in his suite, she recalled.
Then, she'd been shocked at his insistence. At his ferocity. And yes, at his rawboned appearance, too. But
she'd also been captivated by him…and struck by her
own undeniable interest in touching him.

Indulging that interest now, Olivia lay on her side
near him, scandalously close to being atop him, and
went on stroking his hair. It felt surprisingly silken
against her fingers, long and wavy and exhilaratingly

different, and she knew that it was only one of the many things that appealed to her about him.

In Griffin, Olivia realized, she'd encountered a man who had dared to forge his own path in life, regardless of what anyone thought of him. Although the direction he'd taken had made him unhappy, she nonetheless admired him for his courage.

She admired him for his humor, too. How many men, she wondered, could have faced all that Griffin had faced and emerge with a sense of playfulness intact? How many men could have endured hunger and abuse and rejection, then made themselves into successful men of industry? How many men could have known outright ridicule—for he'd told her, somewhat tipsily, of his Hook Turner nickname—and then faced the world at all?

She could readily imagine him as a struggling boy. But she knew him now as a man, and she respected him for his strength.

Not that Griffin didn't need armor, of a sort, Olivia acknowledged to herself as she went on touching him. He used his big hat and his black clothes and his mighty scowl to protect himself. He used his gruff manners to create distance. He used his overlong hair to distract people from his nose, shielding himself against the thoughtlessness of strangers. Knowing that he'd gone to such lengths to be on guard—only to disarm himself for her—Olivia felt indescribably privileged to be touching him.

With his eyes closed against the sunshine, Griffin exhaled. Close against her, his body eased. "I could stay here forever."

"I could touch you forever." To prove it, she trailed her fingertips over his forehead, along his temple then down to his cheek. His jaw. His shadowy beard had already begun to reassert itself, Olivia noticed. She felt doubly thrilled to experience its prickly softness. This was nothing she'd ever encountered before. A frisson of excitement made her wriggle. "I know I shouldn't. I know it's wrong," she confessed. "But—"

"If this is wrong, just send me straight to perdition."

His unrepentant expression made her laugh. It also made her care for him twice as much. Lightly, she said, "We might both be condemned there, for being so wanton."

At that, Griffin opened his eyes. The tenderness in his gaze surprised her. Olivia had the distinct impression that no one had ever touched him with kindness before...and that he found the experience to be almost miraculous.

Poor Griffin. *Had* no one ever touched him with kindness before? If so, Olivia decided, he needed to be shown affection *much* more than usual. He needed to be caressed and hugged and kissed often. He needed to be loved, properly and well.

"This isn't wanton," Griffin disagreed. "It's beyond innocent—more than you know." His mouth quirked, as though he understood something about men and women coming together that she didn't. Undoubtedly, he did. "But I don't want anything bad to happen to you, Olivia. Especially not because of me." He caught her roving hand in his. He gave her a solemn look. "I'll leave before endangering you. I swear it. I have to be on guard for both of us. I have to protect you! If I'd thought anyone would come this way, I would never have allowed... any of *this*."

His gesture with his free hand indicated their nearly cradled bodies, their intimate position atop the worn slab of rock, their closeness that felt as right as it did thrilling.

"You're not the only one who gets a say in this," Olivia teased in low-voiced, crotchety mimicry of him. As trysts went, she decided, theirs felt…like the beginning of something wonderful. "If I recall correctly, I could have resisted."

"You could have *tried* to resist when I pulled you down with me," Griffin agreed. The rapscallion's twinkle in his eyes acknowledged the likely failure she would have met if she'd done so—and reminded her of his far greater sophistication, too. "I'm grateful you didn't. Still. I won't endanger your reputation."

"Hmm." Undeterred, Olivia pursed her mouth in an elaborate show of considering his promise. "That is chivalrous of you. But if you have your way, I'll endanger my reputation myself by proclaiming a love of science and behaving erratically."

"Behaving contrarily, as comes naturally to you." His mouth crooked anew. His hand dropped to her shoulder, holding her comfortably against his chest. "It's not the same thing."

"It is in Morrow Creek. Folks here don't understand—"

"You?" His knowing look seemed to find its way inside her—to discern all the shamefully disagreeable and too-bookish parts that she'd strived to hide beneath ladylike sewing and frivolous parties. "They might understand you, if you let them."

Ah. They were back to this, then. Olivia grinned. "Very tenacious of you. Very clever. No wonder you excel at business."

"No wonder you excel at dissembling. You didn't think you were actually getting away with distracting me, did you?"

"I seemed to be. Until now."

"The thing to remember about me," Griffin declared, "is that I never talk as much as I listen. I never give away what might be useful to hide. And I excel at solving a puzzle."

"Me, too!" Brightening, Olivia angled her neck to peer at his mountainous profile. "I'm excellent at jigsaws, tangrams—"

"In this case," he said dauntingly, "*you* are the puzzle."

Oh. "Surely you must have guessed a great deal about me."

"Not as much as I'd like to know."

"But that can't be true," Olivia argued, secretly pleased that he wanted to know her at all. "To you, I am an open book! More than anyone else in the territory, you have seen all the various aspects of me." She made a rueful face. "The good, the bad and the distressingly awful at housekeeping included."

Perhaps that was why, it occurred to her, she felt so free with him. At first, she hadn't even liked Griffin Turner. She'd had no reason to pretend to be anyone other than who she was. By the time they'd stirred up a camaraderie, it had been too late to alter the past. She was who she was…and so was he. Together.

"I have boundless curiosity about you," he told her. "I aim to satisfy it. I know I can." He cracked a cavalier grin, appearing more content than she'd ever seen him. "But first, I think I'd better soak up some more sunshine while it's here."

With a sigh of contentment, Griffin closed his eyes again. Still holding her close, he surrendered to the outdoors, to the babble of the creek, to the peacefulness of their surroundings.

Still holding her close, he surrendered to her, just as though he might never have a chance to do so again.

For a moment, Olivia felt distressed. Clearly, Griffin felt pushed to absorb all the sunshine he could now, before it slipped away. He *needed* to enjoy it now, because he felt certain it would tumble out of his reach. It was sad that Griffin still experienced such scarcity in his life. Olivia wanted to ease that needfulness in him— to assure and care for him. Maybe, if she was entirely honest, to love him. But then, liberated by his position and lulled by his easy manner, she relaxed, too.

Stealing away to cuddle beside the creek bed, she learned, had much to recommend it. Even more than she'd anticipated.

Before long, though, her curiosity got the better of her. Daringly, Olivia let her gaze slide away from Griffin's tranquil face, moving lower to the rest of him. His shoulders were broad and strong, perfectly suited for wearing finely tailored clothes—or working hard to earn those selfsame clothes. His chest was barrel shaped and muscular, ideally equipped to cushion her tumble atop him—or safeguard his troubled heart. His midsection was lean, his arms tough and adept at holding her, his legs long and limber in repose. As for the rest of him…

Audaciously, Olivia slipped her attention to the front of Griffin's trousers. With her breath held, she regarded the buttons and seams that hid the most masculine part of him.

Suddenly, the gusseting techniques she'd learned while taking sewing lessons from twice-widowed Mrs. Sunley made sense.

Beside her, Griffin drew a breath. He'd roused himself. "I'd give a hundred dollars to know what scholarly, scientific thoughts have put *that* fetching expression on your face."

Olivia started. She felt her face heat. "Nothing at all."

"Tell me another stretcher, Miss Mouton," he teased. "I don't swallow it. You seemed downright enraptured just now."

She had been. *By him.* With effort, Olivia whipped her gaze back to his face. "I was just considering all the things I don't know about…and pondering my own curiosity to discover them."

"I see." *He didn't.* "Maybe I can help you."

"You can't!" *He could.* Frantically, Olivia wiggled her way to an upright position. With her legs curled demurely beneath her skirts, she stared down at Griffin. "I don't need to know."

She wished she could know. So many things.

Including everything there was to know about him.

For the first time, Olivia was forced to acknowledge that superficial details like suits and books and hard-drinking habits could not define Griffin. Not in the way she wanted them to. They could not tell her how he looked when he drowsily awakened in the morning. How he sounded when he brought the day to a close with a murmured farewell at midnight. How he felt when he pulled his beloved close, kissed her passionately, and shared himself with her in all his unclothed grandeur. Madly, she wanted to. But she had not earned that private knowledge, Olivia reckoned. Given their situation, she likely never would.

After all, she was supposed to be considering the fate of The Lorndorff…not becoming smitten by the high-handed investor who'd assumed control of it *and* half the town's whiskey supply.

Not that she'd glimpsed him imbibing a drop for days....

She was supposed to be minding her ladylike manners, too. If she had any sense whatsoever, Griffin would be off-limits to her. Until she was duly married, *any* man would be forbidden. But truthfully, it felt far too late to heed any of those constraints. Olivia felt much too needful herself for that.

"Once you've decided to be yourself among the townspeople here," he declared, unaware of her improper thoughts, "you might find that you learn many new things." His quizzical gaze took in her newly upright posture. He accepted it in his stride, seeming to understand that—for now, at least—their tranquil idyll had come to a close. Agreeably, he sat up, too. "You'd be surprised how much time for philosophical theorizing can be freed up simply by cutting back on discussions of ladies' hats."

"I do not *only* discuss hats," Olivia retorted, suddenly feeling all too aware that the very things everyone valued her for in Morrow Creek were just amusing vagaries to him. "I'm also a member of the ladies' auxiliary league, two sewing circles, the town picnic planning committee and the women's ornithology club. It meets at my very favorite place in the world."

He raised an eyebrow. "The Lorndorff?"

"Somewhere else." Relieved to have a momentary distraction—and a puzzle for him for a change, Olivia waved away his guess. "My home is important, of course. It always will be." *Even if you steal it away.* "But I can't count it as my favorite place."

Griffin considered that. "It must be Reverend Benson's church, then. Given all your talk of perdition earlier on—"

"That was your undertaking. I only expressed concern for our good morals. You're the one who volunteered to pay for our supposedly licentious sins in such a drastic fashion."

"I did." His soulful, suddenly sizzling gaze moved to capture hers. "And if that's what's destined to happen, I think I'd like to earn my perdition more fully first."

Olivia couldn't guess what he had in mind. She was too innocent for that. But the look in his eyes suggested it would be something pleasurable. Wholly pleasurable.

"Let's move on." Feeling bewilderingly overheated, she fanned herself with his hat. "Do you have another guess?"

"About your favorite place in the world?"

She nodded. "You'll never guess. No one ever does."

Griffin gave her a long, perceptive look. "Your favorite place in the world is the Book Depot and News Emporium."

Olivia's jaw dropped. "We didn't even visit there!"

"We passed by it this afternoon." Confident in his guess, he lifted his chin. "Your arm was in mine. You practically towed me clear off my feet and into that bookshop like a mule with an empty cart and a straight path to a barn full of hay."

"Pshaw. I did nothing of the kind." *I hope.*

Worried, Olivia bit her lip. She *did* have a distressing habit of veering toward that haven of books and periodicals when she had a chance. But ordinarily she limited herself. Purposely.

"Mr. Nickerson's shop is not someplace I frequent."

It was too dangerous to her boringly decorous reputation.

"Really?" Griffin angled his head. "I'd have thought you'd be there during business hours and afterward, as well…possibly with your nose pressed longingly against the window glass."

She gave an outraged snort, pretending he wasn't right. "The picture you paint of me is hardly complimentary."

"It's entirely complimentary!" he disagreed. "I happen to enjoy books myself. Two of my businesses relate to publishing."

"They do?" Olivia perked up. "That's so—" *Exciting. Ideal.* Heavens! He probably received books and periodicals at cost! No wonder he'd had a whole valise stuffed full. "Profitable for you?" she finished lamely, not wanting to reveal anything more.

It was no use. "It's just as exciting as you believe it would be," Griffin confided. "Except for the tabloids."

He couldn't mean… "You own the same tabloids that mock you? That work to create what I hear is an outrageous 'legend'?"

"You sound skeptical of my legend. You don't believe it?"

"Of course not. I believe me. Aside from which…" She goggled. "You *really* own the same tabloids that ridicule you?"

"Some of them." He lifted his shoulder offhandedly. She'd have sworn he seemed pleased by her skepticism. That made no sense whatsoever. Why have a legend, if not to impress people with? "If it's going to occur," Griffin explained, "and I know it is," he added as an aside, "I might as well profit from it."

"That's…perverse of you."

"So is your zeal to deny your interest in the Book Depot and News Emporium." Griffin grinned. "We are alike, you and I."

"I only ever visit the Book Depot during the women's ornithology club meetings," Olivia informed him. "Grace Murphy has wrangled very favorable meeting space terms. She's quite a force of nature here. She's the town's most avowed suffragist."

"You've tried to distract me, but you haven't denied my guess outright," Griffin said. "I'm right. It *is* your favorite."

Blast. Of course he was right. "Stop looking so pleased."

"When I'm with you," Griffin said, "that's proving to be difficult." He stood, then politely extended his hand to help her to her feet. "Contentedness is a peculiar feeling." Briefly, he studied the creek. "But I believe I could get used to it."

For a heartbeat, Olivia wanted nothing more than to hold his hand…and assure him that he could. So she did. Then handed him his hat, besides. After which, it felt only correct to say…

"I don't only love books, you know." She felt uncomfortably vulnerable to have been deciphered by Griffin so easily. Fruitlessly, she fixed her skirts. "There is also—"

"Music," they said in unison.

She frowned. Then regrouped. "Inventing," she declared.

"Inventing," he echoed. At her incredulous look, Griffin merely made a funny face. "You left your sketchbook behind. I realized it was yours when I examined its pages as a means to return it to its proper owner. I thought it might be Palmer's."

"No one else even knows I possess a sketchbook!"

"I reckon that makes me special."

It did. "And you haven't returned it yet!"

"It's fascinating," he said in apparent defense of his keeping it. "Palmer isn't half as imaginative as you are."

Olivia couldn't stifle a tiny smile. "They are good ideas, aren't they?" Even though she hadn't intended to share them, she *was* proud of them. Proud of herself. "It would be instructive to have a few prototypes produced. I don't plan to, of course—"

"Why not? It could readily be arranged."

"Not by you!" She didn't want him to think she'd been fishing for financing, like her father. "I can do it on my own."

"I don't doubt that. If you want to proceed the difficult way, I won't stop you." Griffin plunked on his dark hat, then took her hand. "You see? There's no need for you to hide yourself from me, Olivia. As I said, when I'm not talking, I'm listening. I'm watching." He smiled. "I like what I've learned."

"Well." Another man would have said he liked what he saw. Griffin was unique in that. But he'd never guess her most secret diversion. Olivia felt convinced of it. "That may be true. Thank you for that. But that doesn't mean you know about my love of—"

"Baseball," Griffin said.

"Pitching," she declared at the same moment, referring to her cherished position on the emergent Morrow Creek women's league, created and organized and picketed for by Grace Murphy.

Olivia actually experienced a momentary sense of triumph—until she realized that she and Griffin were simultaneously describing the same pastime. Again. Suddenly, she understood all too well Jimmy's consternation when Griffin had addressed him by name this morning. "How did you know that?"

"Easily." Griffin squeezed her hand. "You interest me."

"You do have a spy. I swear, when I see Mr. Grant—"

Griffin only chuckled. "Don't blame him. You and I *have* conversed over the past two weeks, Olivia. I've never talked so much in all my life. Why do you think I sound so raspy?"

His apparent disgruntlement over that was uproarious. But Olivia didn't have the heart to needle him. "You were drunk. I didn't think you'd remember a word of those conversations."

"I wasn't as drunk as you believed I was."

"Evidently." She pulled a frown, remembering her own blithe chitchat during those shared moments. "So all that chatter—"

"Only endeared you to me more." He kissed her. "You're lively, Olivia. When I was in the darkness, you brought the light. Whether I wanted it or not. You were strong and sweet—"

"Like a cantankerous slice of pumpkin pie?"

"—and without you, I don't think I'd have survived."

His simple declaration touched her like nothing else. Olivia sighed. She smiled. Then she gave up all her resistance.

Griffin Turner *knew* her. As incomprehensible as it was, he did. For as long as it lasted, she might as well enjoy that.

Lord knew, this feeling would not come round again.

"I'm happy you know about my fondness for baseball, then," Olivia said, setting them both straight on the footpath to town. "Because that's what we'll be undertaking later next week."

Griffin gulped. He looked adorably fretful. "Next week?"

"Yes. After the additional visitations I've planned for us, and the upcoming handcrafts show, and the town musicale," Olivia told him briskly. She paused, feeling duly proud of her plans to bring Griffin out of his hermit's suite and into the sunshine. He would enjoy the neighborliness and conviviality she showed him. She was sure of it. She was sure it might convince him to give up The Lorndorff, as well. "I've even finagled an invitation for you from the infamous Morrow Creek Men's Club. It's secret. It's only for the gentlemen of town, so I won't be attending with you. But I have an intuition that you'll be quite—"

"Up to my ears in Levin's ale, ribald jokes and faro?"

"Most likely." Clambering nimbly up the rocks with Griffin's hand to steady her, Olivia nodded. "If that doesn't make you feel lucky to be alive, I don't know what will."

"I do." Griffin stopped at the top of the ridge. He pulled her nearer, then kissed her. Reverently, he stroked her cheek. "I know what would make us both feel lucky to be alive." For an instant, his gaze turned smoldering again. Then he blinked. "But if I ever give in to it… heaven help us both." A smile. "Let's go."

Chapter Eleven

The only person more implacable than Olivia Mouton with a mission to roust a man from his bed, steal away his whiskey and bring him into the sunshine, Griffin realized four days after his creek-side outing with Olivia, was Olivia Mouton with a mission to introduce a man wholesale to Morrow Creek—and to all its many residents in a nearly nonstop parade of faces, names and backslapping bonhomie.

By the end of the first day, Griffin's jaw ached from rare, unaccustomed smiling. By the end of the second day, his ears rang with half-remembered conversations and bellowed spontaneous greetings. By the end of the third day, his hand shot out at the least provocation, permanently in a state of readiness for a handshake. His throat felt sore from interminable chatting with the townspeople and with Olivia herself.

If he was honest, Griffin would have had to admit that he liked it. He liked knowing people who—true to Olivia's example—did not care who he was, or did not know who he was, and bluntly accepted that, in the West, it was a man's right to start over.

Griffin *wanted* to start over, he discovered as he accompanied Olivia to the millinery shop, to the livery stable and to the cooper's yard. Maybe that was what had pushed him to come to the territory, he reckoned—a desire for change that he hadn't been able to acknowledge, even to himself. He wanted to forge a simpler life. He wanted to be free of the Turner legacy. He wanted to follow the straightforward example of Morrow Creek's residents and live according to his own rules. He wanted to awaken in the morning to birdsong—MacGillivray's Warbler, Olivia informed him—instead of carriage traffic. He wanted to spend his days with honest folk—the cobbler, the railway men and the hardworking staff of The Lorndorff—instead of with scheming industrialists. He wanted to smell roses and spice cake and buttermilk toast instead of factory smoke and coal fires.

He wanted to be with Olivia.

The more time Griffin spent with her, the more he believed it to be true. Their creek-side outing had been…miraculous.

Holding Olivia in his arms had shown Griffin that there was goodness and pleasure and sweetness in the world. Feeling her touch him—feeling her stroking him without shirking or steeling herself to do so—had been revelatory. So had Olivia's insistence—so unlike Mary's—that she didn't believe a word of his vaunted, ever-formidable "legend." For the first time in his life, Griffin felt improbably at peace. He wanted to share that.

He wanted to share it with Olivia, if she'd let him.

Feeling all too mindful of his missteps with Mary, Griffin was careful to be courteous, yet interested, when in Olivia's company. He did his utmost to behave honorably, yet passionately, toward her. When he held her hand, he made it plain that he was in command of their togetherness. When he kissed her, he did so not as a platonic friend, but as a man…a man who wanted more than he could reasonably expect or should practically allow himself to take.

Still, he wanted…and day by day, his hopes grew.

To him, Griffin realized as their time together lengthened, Olivia's beauty lay more in her heart than in her appearance. Her appeal resided more in her intelligence and vigor than in her feminine figure and her innocently seductive movements. Griffin knew he ought to have cherished her for the same reasons every other man did, lest he disappoint Olivia by not raving about her obvious beauty. But he simply could not.

To him, Olivia was…more than beautiful. She was kind. She was considerate. She was funny and spirited. She was genuine.

At least she was, Griffin recognized, when they were alone together. When they were in polite society, though, *his* Olivia seemed to vanish. His spunky, determined, onetime chambermaid disappeared, replaced by an insipidly pretty automaton with perfect posture, vapid interests and a senselessly loquacious manner. In polite society, Olivia lived down to the commonplace expectations her friends and neighbors held of her. She laughed over their jibing that she was "too choosy" for a husband—when Griffin knew she simply refused to settle for a man who couldn't appreciate her. She took in stride their remarks that she was "too mercurial" or "too frivolous." She showed off her needlework to her friends with apparent zest—when Griffin had seen her abandon that sedate hobby with absurd haste every time he proposed another philosophy discussion.

Prompted by those observations and countless more, Griffin resolved to help Olivia break free from the constraining box she'd placed herself in. He knew she wasn't happy there. He could glimpse it in her eyes when she launched another round of dizzy gossip or professed her undying pride in her mending abilities. Not that she was rude, or even that her feelings were apparent to anyone except him. Griffin didn't think they were. But once he'd seen the signs of unhappiness in her, he could not ignore them. Olivia had saved him. Now he meant to save her.

Unlike him, Olivia didn't need sunshine. She needed quiet rooms and books to read and sketchbooks to sketch in. She didn't need introductions. She needed understanding and tolerance and a populace who would embrace her for who she was. She didn't even need a rescuer in the form of a beastly industrialist with more determination, money and power than good sense.

Olivia needed courage. She needed *love.*

And because Griffin could not give her courage—not the way he could, and did, give her gifts and flowers and even the surprise of an enormous book delivery sent from his publishing house to her hotel—he had to make do with giving her love.

His love. He'd never offered it in such a wholehearted way before. Not even to Mary, who'd long since meandered from his thoughts. But to Olivia, Griffin did offer his love. He had to. He was so full to bursting with affection for her that he thought he might not be able to survive without expressing it.

So on a day when Griffin would have otherwise, in his old life, been brokering a contract or examining a property or upbraiding a colleague for behaving in a less-than-cutthroat fashion, instead he was holding open the door to the Morrow Creek meetinghouse for Olivia. He was ushering her inside with a sweep of his arm and an unreserved smile, feeling as proud as a peacock with a new set of tail feathers, ready to make a fool of himself if it made her smile. He was, on a temperate and peaceful territorial evening, racking his brain for new and impressive and heartfelt ways to make Olivia *feel* brave.

Brave enough to show herself. Brave enough to love him.

When he said, "Here is a seat for you," he meant *I love you*. When he said, "I'll fetch us refreshments," he meant *I love you*. When he said, "Don't become engaged to any of the dozens of men who propose while I'm gone," he meant *I love you*.

He also meant *you're mine*...and longed for it to be true. Because Olivia did receive ludicrously frequent marriage proposals. As Miss Milky White, she'd firmly established her desirability. Griffin did sometimes fear that she'd accept another man's offer of matrimony and be done with dillydallying.

He feared that she'd come to her senses, realize she'd been gallivanting about town with The Boston Beast and scamper into the arms of the first stultifyingly dull rancher who asked.

He couldn't let that happen. But more important, he couldn't allow Olivia to go on the way she had been... denying her true nature, stifling her curiosity and berating herself for her cleverness and wit and overall uniqueness. To him, she was inimitable. She was priceless. She deserved to be completely happy. For that to happen, she needed to first be herself.

Olivia believed they were there that evening—at the town musicale—to further her notions of making Griffin more sociable and less prone to shutting himself off with closed curtains and too much whiskey. But he knew better. He knew he'd quit drinking days ago. He knew he'd mastered his tendency to brood, with her help. He also knew they were really there to begin making Olivia behave more honestly…with herself, with her friends and with her neighbors. To that end, Griffin watched her closely.

Excitedly, limned by the hall's lamplight, she nudged him. "Look! The musicians are already tuning their instruments."

"So they are." He followed her eager pointing gesture to the dais. "What kind of music do you like best?"

"Oh…" Airily, she waved. "A symphony is always nice."

"Mmm." It seemed unlikely to Griffin that a symphony was in the offing, given the musicians and their number. They fit better with the town hall's homemade decor—rafters strung with crepe streamers and walls decorated with cut paper flowers—than they did with the works of Schubert or Brahms. "What else?"

"I'm…not entirely familiar with *all* musical works," Olivia confessed. "Unlike you, we can't avail ourselves of orchestras."

"I'm sure the musicians here are talented, all the same." Griffin was delighted to notice Olivia tapping her toes. Her vivaciousness was already showing. "Will there be dancing?"

She appeared astonished. Also, *tempted.* "No! That would hardly be the done thing, would it? That's not sophisticated."

Griffin stifled a grin, knowing that Morrow Creek was not known for its "sophisticated" diversions. According to Daniel McCabe, there had recently been busty dance-hall girls added to the entertainment roster at Jack Murphy's saloon. During Griffin's indoctrination into the Morrow Creek Men's Club—for they'd insisted he join, even if temporarily—he'd further learned of the annual faro tournament the town hosted, luring in notorious gamblers from around the world, and of the gaudy, outlandish medicine shows that drew crowds when they visited.

Olivia might pretend to want sophistication, but her tapping toes suggested she wanted rowdy fun, first and last.

"Well," he said, lightly covering her hand with his as the crowd quieted, "if you feel like dancing, I'll join you."

Tellingly, her eyes brightened. Then she scoffed, "Don't be ridiculous." She patted her upswept hair. "I'll behave myself."

"Perhaps," Griffin suggested as he leaned nearer, close enough to touch her cheek with his own, "I don't want you to."

Olivia's cheeks turned pink. She opened her mouth, doubtless to object. But then the music began…and so did the fun. Griffin couldn't wait for the moment when Olivia cut loose.

If only she could gain authority over her traitorous toes, Olivia knew she could present a positive, encouraging example to Griffin of the wholesome activities a person could enjoy if they liberated themselves from their hotel suite on occasion.

Instead, while listening to the raucous fiddles and solitary banjo played by the musicale's musicians, she found herself tapping her toes. Time and again, her feet attempted to dance their way out of the town hall while her body remained staunchly, sedately, effortfully in her seat beside Griffin.

He appeared to recognize her dilemma, too. A time or two, while Olivia was battling her own unladylike propensity for jigging to the music, she caught him grinning at her.

"Remember," he said, "I *will* dance with you, if you like."

"No!" she cried in an undertone, glancing around in the hope that no one else had glimpsed her undignified behavior. Her father wasn't there, but that didn't mean she could abandon all decorum. If she misbehaved, Henry Mouton—*everyone*—would know. "There is *no* dancing at the musicale! Not even to the fiddles!"

She dearly loved the fiddles. As a girl, there'd been nothing she'd enjoyed more than listening to a bow dancing across the strings—except dancing to the resulting tunes. She'd even taken up the instrument herself once, tutored by a long since departed saloonkeeper, only to abandon it for the more appropriate practice of learning to play an upright piano.

Just then, Olivia regretted every instant of scales she'd played on a keyboard. Fiddle music was just so much more…fun.

"Look." Griffin nudged her shoulder. "*They're* dancing."

She did look, down the aisle. "They're dance-hall girls!"

"So? No one is likely to confuse you for a dancing girl."

But Olivia wasn't convinced. "I've worked very hard to become a woman my father can be proud of," she said. "As far as I know, Henry Mouton never wished he'd sired a painted lady."

Griffin shrugged. "You never know until you try."

"I know." Heavens. Now her fingers were tapping

along to the tune, too! Determinedly shoving them under her skirts—where they could keep good company with her similarly shrouded tapping toes, Olivia redirected her attention to the dais. "I won't try."

She could have sworn that Griffin appeared disappointed.

But that was simply too bad, Olivia decided. She had a reputation to uphold. She couldn't do that by giving in to every untoward desire she ever had. She couldn't do that by dancing…no matter how enjoyable and memorable it would have been.

In a sense, Olivia's fortitude was rewarded in the end. Because after the musicale was finished, when she and Griffin were jovially chatting in the town hall with her friends and neighbors, something unexpected happened. All at once, amid the glowing lamplight and the hearty laughter, Griffin went still.

Olivia noticed him glance to one corner of the hall, but she didn't think much of it at first. Partly because she was in midconversation with Annie. Partly because Griffin had been occasionally examining the town hall all night. She'd originally—and dispiritedly—thought he was becoming bored by Morrow Creek's rusticated entertainments. Then she'd looked into his solemn eyes and rapt expression and realized the truth.

He was doing it. Just like her, he was savoring. He was storing up the experience of being at the musicale with her. In that moment. While it was still happening. Before it slipped away.

Not that Griffin was rude about it. Olivia doubted anyone else noticed his gaze moving, from time to time, to the hand-lettered signs and the chattering townspeople and the humble decorations overhead. But *she* noticed. She noticed, and it made her feel sad. Why could she not help Griffin feel secure?

The notion should have made her laugh. On the face of it, a man like him did not need her help feeling secure. Griffin was successful, wealthy and admired by industry. He was, by all accounts, a man to be respected for his accomplishments. But Olivia knew him for more than The Beast he was supposed to be.

She knew him. She cared for him. She might even *love* him.

Maybe that was why Annie's next question caught Olivia off guard. Her longtime friend, having noticed Griffin's inattentiveness, seized that moment to waylay Olivia.

"So," Annie said, darting a furtive glance at Griffin, "do you think you'll be able to change his mind? How close are you?"

"How close am I?" Tardily, Olivia realized that Annie must be referring to her plan to convince Griffin to relinquish control of The Lorndorff. She waved off her friend's concern. "Honestly, I haven't given it much thought lately."

"Well, you must be making progress." Annie stepped back as Griffin absently excused himself and then strode away, further enabling their gossipy conversation. "I heard," she went on, "that Mr. Turner invited your father to manage the hotel again."

"He asked him to." Olivia had learned as much from her father. "My father refused. He doesn't want to settle for 'half measures.' He thinks he can hold out. He thinks he can convince another investor to buy out Mr. Turner and solve the problem entirely." She sighed. "I think that will simply introduce another troublesome element to an already unwieldy situation. Given a large enough stake in The Lorndorff, another investor would be equally likely to force out my father...*and* he'd be an unknown quantity, besides. I say it's too risky overall."

"Hmm?" Annie frowned. "What has gotten into you? All of a sudden, you talk like a book. A business book, to be precise."

Olivia felt abashed. "Perhaps I've been spending too much time in Mr. Turner's company." *Kissing him. And relishing a great deal of insightful conversation with him.* Not that any of those opinions had been other than her own. "I'm sorry." She sipped her punch, then smiled at Annie. "Is that a new dress?"

"It *is!*" Annie gushed, making a slight turn to display her fashionable bustle. "I've been working on it for ages. In fact, I was hoping to catch the eye of a certain gentleman tonight."

"Hmm. Mr. Grant, perhaps?" Olivia suggested, much too innocently. She'd noticed Annie noticing Griffin's associate.

"*That* citified know-it-all? No, not him!" Annie declared, much too vehemently. She stood on tiptoe, then gazed avidly across the town hall. "Why? Have you seen him here?"

Olivia suppressed a grin. "He was jigging with the dance-hall girls in the leftmost aisle a while ago. Since then—"

Annie gave her a playful swat. "He was not jigging!"

I almost was. "Well, it wouldn't be wholly untoward..."

"Yes, it would!" Annie rolled her eyes. "Dance-hall girls?"

"Well, if it wasn't a dance-hall girl who was dancing," Olivia tried. "Then maybe...?" She was desperate to learn how Annie might react to a hypothetical scenario. Say, if *she* were to indulge her yen to dance in the aisle to toe-tapping fiddle music. But she never had a chance. Because in the next moment, Annie stared. "Is that Mr. Turner?" she asked, pointing.

At the same moment, the crowd parted obligingly. In the resulting gap, Griffin strode nearer, wearing his black clothes, black boots and black hat…and carrying a young boy in his arms.

The child looked three or four years of age. With his small face streaked with tears, the tousle-haired boy clung monkeylike to Griffin's shoulders, clearly unwilling to be parted from him.

"Ladies." As though there were nothing unusual about a famously hard-hearted beast of an industrialist cradling a child in his arms, Griffin nodded politely at Olivia and Annie. "I'm sorry to leave you so abruptly. I saw this tyke crying in the corner. Nobody else seemed to have noticed the little scamp."

At Griffin's attentiveness, Olivia couldn't help remembering his nonchalant statement days ago. *There's something about growing up hand to mouth, in danger of getting beaten, that makes a man notice the details of things.* Sometimes, she guessed, those details weren't dire. But they were no less important to attend to. Especially when they involved a child.

Still, she couldn't believe he'd voluntarily cradled a lost child. Most men held children about as expertly as they did brooms. But as with sweeping, Griffin seemed to come by this skill naturally. Beside her, Annie could do no more than stare, along with the townspeople standing by. Olivia merely looked at Griffin, saw him making a funny face while murmuring silly nonsense to comfort the child and felt her heart open wide.

Something about seeing this tender, protective side

of Griffin made him irresistible. He was…downright nurturing.

"If he agreed to quit bawling," Griffin announced, peering kindly into the boy's little face, "I promised him a pony."

"Griffin!" Olivia objected. "That's far too lavish."

"Mr. Turner!" Annie echoed in a similarly censorious tone. Then her gaze turned devious. "*I* like ponies. I mean, if you're faced with an abundance of the critters and require volunteers…"

"Annie!" Olivia shook her head at her friend. "No."

But Griffin was unperturbed by their wrangling. He only jostled the boy good-naturedly in his arms, then asked, "Will the two of you help me find his mother? He says his name is Jonas."

"Will we earn a pony if we do?" Annie asked cagily.

Olivia frowned at her. "Of course we'll help you," she assured Griffin. "Let's begin with the perimeter of the room."

"Perimeter?" In frustration, Annie stopped with her hands on her hips. "Can you please speak normally? I didn't read a million books when I was small," she reminded Olivia with a nonplussed look, "so I can't keep up with all your fancy talk."

"I'm sorry." Olivia gestured helpfully. "Let's look in the aisles on the outsides of the room first. That's all I mean."

"Then why didn't you say so?" Annie gave a disgruntled head shake as they trailed Griffin and his newly devoted friend, Jonas. "You're still doing it, you know," Annie complained. "Talking like a book. Like you used to talk, years ago."

Feeling a glimmer of warning at that, Olivia shrugged.

"I guess lost children bring out my studious side,"

she hedged, unwilling to admit that it wasn't a single incident that was making her revert to her old rebellious and hoydenish ways. It was Griffin. Increasingly, she wanted the same freedom in the rest of her life as she found when she was with him. It was getting harder and harder to refrain from impropriety altogether—harder to remember why she'd ever wanted to behave herself in the first place. "Come on," Olivia said to Annie, tugging her arm. "I see Mrs. McCabe, the schoolmarm. She knows everyone's children, whether they're of school age or not."

As they picked up speed, still following Griffin and Jonas, Olivia cast that adorable duo a second, contemplative glance. Now the boy was whispering something to Griffin, elaborately cupping his ear in the dramatic fashion children had, and Griffin was laughing at the confidence they'd shared. In response, Jonas beamed. His childish chuckle sounded out.

Someday, Olivia couldn't help thinking, that could be their child being held in Griffin's arms. That could be her future, shared with a man who rescued lost children, understood philosophical theories *and* volunteered to dance scandalously in the aisles to fiddle music. In so many ways, it was ideal.

Unless…

Abruptly, Olivia stopped, peering at Griffin as Jonas's mother caught up to the pair. She watched as the woman thanked Griffin effusively, then hugged Jonas to her while conversing animatedly with Griffin. Belatedly, Olivia recognized her as one of the most decorous, well-respected, God-fearing women in Morrow Creek. Undoubtedly, she'd never experienced a moment's temptation to dance to the musicale's boisterous fiddle music.

Possibly, it occurred to Olivia, Griffin hadn't, either. Was he...*testing* her?

The idea suddenly seemed all too plausible. Certainly, Griffin appeared to enjoy the lengthy talks he and Olivia shared about egalitarianism, absolute idealism, naturalism and other philosophical theories, as well as about novels they'd read and places they'd like to visit. But those conversations occurred in private, in his hotel suite. What if Griffin, like most other men, was more concerned with what occurred in public?

What if he was concerned with having a wife who could behave herself in public?

If he was, the dreamy domestic scenario Olivia had just been imagining could not possibly come true. Marriageable women did not, as a rule, behave like dancehall girls, Olivia knew. Neither did respectable women like Jonas's mother. Once upon a time, Olivia would have been happy to omit herself from their numbers. Once upon a time, she'd been proud of her adolescent freethinking and unruly conduct. But now things were different.

The things she wanted from her life were different.

Griffin had *seemed* sincere when he'd urged Olivia to dance to the fiddle music earlier, she mused. He had recognized her love of it. He'd even seemed to share it. His toes had tapped a time or two, as well. But what if he didn't approve as wholeheartedly as he seemed to? What if he'd been pushing to learn exactly how unconventional she really was?

What if Griffin was predicating his willingness to commit further on her willingness to comport herself appropriately?

Concerned, Olivia studied him a bit longer. Then, as Annie identified Mr. Grant on the other side of the room and beelined toward her—purportedly—least favorite Boston businessman, Olivia made her decision. If Griffin was testing her, she meant to pass with flying colors. She wanted Griffin to think well of her. She wanted him to think of her as more than a counterfeit chambermaid, an amenable tour guide to Morrow Creek and a sometime conversational partner. She wanted him to think of her as a woman. A *desirable* woman. A woman whose most attractive qualities were impossible to overlook . . . as he seemed to have done so far.

If she could ensure that their togetherness would grow, simply at the price of sticking to her usual upright behavior, then that was what she'd do, Olivia vowed. She would refuse to dance. She would try harder at sewing. She would keep her most divergent opinions to herself. She would be the most respectable woman she could possibly be, and she'd prove her marriageability to Griffin in the process…no matter how much fiddle music might play or how many temptations might fall in her path in the meantime.

Chapter Twelve

A half hour early for the Morrow Creek handicrafts show, Griffin ducked into the designated venue—a two-story brick house located at the far end of the town's main street—with his mind on Olivia. He'd agreed to meet her for another of his getting-to-know-Morrow-Creek sessions, but the intent of those sessions felt largely superfluous by now. Griffin had already met and—with surprising ease—befriended most of the town's residents. He guessed that ease came hand in hand with the residents' lack of familiarity with the Turners of Boston. Here, Edward Turner's nefarious business tactics and coldhearted abandonment of his family were as irrelevant as the travails of streetcar travel and the touring playhouse schedules at the Howard Athenaeum. No one in Morrow Creek looked at Griffin's face and saw in it the curse of the Turner men. No one saw pitiable Hook Turner.

They only saw *him,* Griffin, alone. And the woman who had instigated that welcome change was waiting for him to meet her.

If not for Olivia, Griffin knew, he'd never have realized the fresh chance awaiting him in Morrow Creek. If not for her, he'd likely still be sequestered in his suite at The Lorndorff, lost in self-pity and whiskey and darkness, wondering why success, money and hard-earned respect had not made him happy.

Today, he felt happy. Walking through the show-hosting household's spacious hallways and past its finely decorated rooms, Griffin surveyed the hustle and bustle of preparations for the show and knew that his newfound happiness owed itself to Olivia. He may have failed to seduce her into letting her feet dance them both into carefree enjoyment of the musicale's fiddle music a few days ago, but today would be different, he vowed.

Today he had a surprise that even Olivia, with all her grit and tenacity and dedication, would not be able to resist.

First, though, he had volunteered to help Olivia set up the displays for the handicrafts show. Spying the set of rooms where he'd been told she would be, Griffin felt his heart race faster.

Grinning at his own sap-headed sense of romanticism, he picked up speed. His boot heels rang against the polished oak floorboards. His coat billowed behind him, lending him an imposing appearance as he strode onward. Catching a glimpse of himself in the hallway's gilt-edged mirror, Griffin hesitated.

He stopped.

For the first time in years, he took a good look at himself. He wasn't sure he liked what he saw. Not because of his nose—although that detestable feature was still fully accounted for—but because of his forbidding black clothes. Above his inky collar, dark coat, midnight vest and plain black trousers, his own rugged countenance frowned back at him, framed by the wide brim of his equally dark hat and the omnipresent tangle of his tied-back dark hair. Even his thick, dark eyebrows looked menacing.

Damnation. How was he supposed to endear himself to a lighthearted and fun-loving woman like Olivia when he most resembled a hulking, oversize, expensively dressed undertaker?

Newly mortified by the thought, Griffin turned. He peered at his profile as best he could, noting his perfectly turned-out collar, his jet cufflinks and his rough, masculine stance. He *did* appear threatening. No wonder, it occurred to him, Olivia had not wanted to cut loose and dance at the musicale.

She hadn't wanted to dance with him.

Confounded, Griffin delivered his image a scowl. Until now, he'd largely strived for invisibility. But here in Morrow Creek, with Olivia, such measures might not be necessary. Here in Morrow Creek, he might get away with a more female-friendly set of clothing. He might even dare to try not tugging his hat low.

The very idea left him chockablock with trepidation. Did he dare? For the sake of winning Olivia, did he dare to step fully into the light and risk letting everyone see him without his armor of dark clothes and face-hiding hat? Getting new suits of clothes would be easy enough, Griffin mused. Palmer could issue an order to his tailors in Boston and have custom garments delivered on the train within weeks. Maybe in medium gray...

"Griffin! There you are." Olivia approached him with a smile on her face. She held out her arms, took both his hands in hers then squeezed. "If I could, I would spend time just staring at you, too," she teased with an affectionate nod at the mirror. "You have an arresting array of features, Mr. Turner."

Griffin wanted to believe that she truly liked the way he looked. Hard experience—and his own mind—told him she could not.

All the same, he felt his whole heart give way at her touch. He couldn't help grinning. Olivia made him feel...*joyful*. Absurdly so. Doubtless he was making himself a fool, even then.

"You have an arresting way of fibbing outright. My features are nothing but problematic, and both of us know it."

"Pshaw." Eyes sparkling, Olivia levered upward. She gave his cheek a hasty, private kiss. "They are *yours,* so I love them."

Caught by that, Griffin inhaled. Did she...? *Could* she...?

He wished he did not want her approval so much.

But he did. Worse, it felt tantalizingly close.

Feeling overcome, Griffin cleared his throat. Pointedly, he glanced around the hallway. From other areas of the house came the sounds of things being moved, of conversations going on, of workers performing last-minute tasks to prepare for the handicrafts show. "What do you want me to do first?"

"Nothing. I'm essentially finished, in fact. You're simply here to keep me company. And to meet people, of course."

"That can't be true." He frowned. "There must be heavy things to maneuver. Displays to set up." Willingly, Griffin shucked his long coat, then his suit coat, leaving them both to the coatrack. He rolled up his sleeves, loving the way Olivia's eyes widened at the sight of his bare forearms. "I'll manage the difficult tasks. Just point me in the right direction."

Standing there, Olivia merely stared at him. She

seemed hypnotized by his forearms. She seemed… approving.

"As you can see," Griffin added, unable to resist performing a subtle flexing movement to win even more of her approval, "I'm strong enough for anything you'd have me do."

For a moment, all Olivia seemed to want him to "do" was pull her into his arms and hold her there, the way he'd done so many times over the past days. Then, abruptly, she blinked.

"Right. Yes. Of course!" A ladylike titter burst forth from her. "I'll just introduce you to Miss Violet Benson first. She's the daughter of my very good friend, the minister, Reverend Benson. I probably have told you how very God-fearing I am."

Confused, Griffin gazed back at her. "No. You haven't."

"Well, I am." With effort, Olivia swerved her gaze away from his forearms. She smiled. "I am also well respected and decorous. Very like Jonas's mother, whom you met the other day?"

Vaguely, Griffin recalled the woman from the musicale. "I wasn't impressed with her inattentiveness to her own child," he said bluntly. "If that's what you find admirable about her—"

"I thought you found her admirable! You conversed for a long time." Olivia's brows lowered. "You seemed engrossed."

"I was making damn sure she would pay better attention to Jonas next time." Memories of his own mother's negligence poked at him, making him scowl anew. "I was making sure she wouldn't turn her neglect to abuse and blame Jonas for getting lost."

"Who would blame a child for getting lost?"

Darkly, he gazed back at her. "My mother, for one. She had an uncanny ability to make every difficulty my fault somehow."

"Oh." Olivia's compassionate gaze met his. Her hand raised gently to his shoulder. Her touch worked like magic to soothe his troubled mood. "I'm so sorry. I didn't know. That honestly never occurred to me. I saw you talking with Jonas's mother and thought you were impressed by all her good qualities."

"I might have been. If I'd seen them."

Olivia seemed perplexed. "She's very admired in town."

"If that's so, give me a less-regarded woman any day."

At Olivia's crestfallen expression, Griffin belatedly recalled her efforts to be admired in town for her own ladylike behavior. Although that was the very behavior he was trying to staunch—because it made her so unhappy—he amended his words.

After all, he could not give her bravery by scorning her efforts—misguided and unhappiness provoking though they were.

"Not that I don't admire efforts toward respectability, as well," he said, feeling out of his depth all of a sudden. "For instance, women with children should strive to be as good as they possibly can. That will benefit their children."

Olivia appeared hopeful. "And their husbands?"

Griffin had no idea. After his calamitous proposal to Mary, he'd given up hope of matrimony for himself. At least he had for a while. But lately, he'd indulged more than his fair share of fantasies about coming home to a modest Morrow Creek house with Olivia there waiting for him, brandishing a broom with comical ineffectualness and serving him bakery-bought pies by the dozen. He'd pictured Olivia coming to him on their wedding night, looking beautiful and giddy and wonderfully naked.

He'd even wondered what sort of husband he might be.

But that didn't mean he was prepared to admit any of it.

"Naturally, their husbands would benefit, too," he told her agreeably. "Doesn't every man enjoy an amenable wife?"

"*Amenable.* Yes." Olivia's pert face took on an alarming sense of purpose. "That is a very achievable quality!"

He frowned. "You're wearing that mulish expression you get sometimes," he observed. "You know… the one that keeps you persisting when you've clearly lost a game of chess with me."

"The game is never lost until it's over with," Olivia announced with a newborn sense of vigor. She tucked her arm in his, then directed them both toward the rooms where the displays were set up. "That is one of my guiding principles."

"You don't have to 'achieve' any particular quality with me," Griffin reminded her as they passed through the doorway into the first room. Worryingly, his words seemed to pass right through her. "What would I know about what husbands prefer?" he asked reasonably. "I've never even been married."

"I know. But that might change." Blithely assured now, Olivia steered him in the direction of a plainly dressed, plain-featured, dark-haired woman. She was clearly directing the volunteers' efforts. Just before they reached her, Olivia winked up at Griffin. "If the circumstances are just right, you might find yourself wanting to propose to a *very* special someone."

Feeling increasingly wary, Griffin let himself be led.

Purposefully, Olivia stopped. "Mr. Turner, I'd like you to meet Miss Violet Benson." She cast him a meaningful look. "Miss Benson is sponsoring today's handicrafts show along with the Territorial Benevolent Association. It's going to be…"

She continued speaking, but Griffin couldn't quite listen. All his attention was suddenly directed at what Olivia had said moments ago, about him changing his mind and proposing to "a *very* special someone"—and at the wink she'd tossed him, too.

Even as he politely shook hands with demure Violet Benson and said hello, Griffin couldn't help wondering…was Olivia angling for him to propose marriage to her friend? Was that why she'd mentioned her father, Reverend Benson, in such glowing terms? Was that why she'd given him that wink? Why she'd probed his attitudes toward marriage and family life and children?

No, no, no. This was all wrong. His simple mission to help Olivia break free of her self-imposed restrictions was becoming ever more complicated. He didn't want marriage to just anyone!

He wasn't entirely sure he wanted marriage to Olivia. As much as he wanted to be with her, Griffin still had doubts. He had doubts he could win her. Doubts he deserved her. Doubts he could be a good husband, given everything in his past.

The only thing he didn't have doubts about was that he wanted Olivia in a way he'd never wanted another woman before.

Fraught with unease, Griffin nonetheless mustered

a smile for both women. He had never been a man who was unduly thrown by changing circumstances. He could handle this complication in the same way he handled everything—with dogged resilience, ruthless exactitude and an unfailing attitude of positivity.

Positivity? Struck by that, Griffin hesitated. Then he realized, to his amazement, that it was true. He *did* possess a determination to see the positive in life. If he had not, he never would have survived. He never would have succeeded. Right from the moment when he'd stood up to his mother at the age of fourteen and sworn she'd be proud of him someday, Griffin had possessed a gritty positivity. He'd known he could succeed.

Just because he sometimes succumbed to the darkness didn't mean he stopped expecting the sunrise. And just because things seemed thorny with Olivia didn't mean he intended to give up.

For her sake, Griffin told himself, he would persevere.

He glanced up to find Miss Benson in midconversation.

"...a few additional items," she was saying in polite, measured tones, "that we received just this morning."

"Additional items?" Olivia looked baffled. "I thought everything for the handicrafts show was already here. People have been talking of little else except getting their items finished and brought here to the display house."

"That's true." Miss Benson shot Griffin a tentative glance. Then, as though expecting to get no further responsiveness from him, she returned quickly to Olivia. "But these are crated items. They're labeled specifically to your attention, Olivia."

"*My* attention?" She puckered her brows. "All I'm set to display is a single cross-stitched sampler, as usual."

Miss Benson shrugged. "Perhaps someone knew that you'd volunteered to help me organize the exhibition and decided to make an anonymous contribution. Not everyone is as fearless as you've always been." A bashful smile enlivened her dowdy features. "That time you dressed down the medicine-show man is practically legendary in town. Remember? I was so awed by—"

"Oh! I'm afraid we'll have to postpone reminiscing," Olivia broke in, a skittish look on her face. She aimed a pointed glance at the room's stately grandfather clock. "It's so late!"

But Griffin was having none of it. He buttonholed Miss Benson. "Legendary? Olivia?" he urged. "What happened?"

Clearly eager to tell, Miss Benson inhaled. "Well—"

"Look!" Olivia interrupted again, pointing. "There are *three* crated items near my sampler display. Let's open them!"

Griffin joined Miss Benson in frowning at her.

"Oh. Right." The minister's daughter gave a faltering gesture. Reticence appeared to come naturally to her. "Yes, I know we should. Only I was about to tell Mr. Turner about—"

"The crates can wait," Griffin said. After all, he knew full well what was in those crates. Their construction and delivery had been his doing. He smiled at Miss Benson. "I'm keenly interested in your story, Miss Benson. Please, go on."

At his urging, she flushed mottled red. She waved away his invitation, staring down at her shoes. It occurred to Griffin, too late, that Miss Benson was a woman unaccustomed to male attention. No wonder she'd looked at him glancingly, if at all.

No wonder she'd dismissed the possibility he'd listen to her when they'd been discussing the arrival of the crates.

He understood that sort of defensiveness. He'd lived it.

Miss Violet Benson deserved a man who would recognize her unique charms and appreciate them, Griffin knew. She deserved a man who would see past her drab appearance—a man who would enchant and confound and love her completely. Unfortunately, Griffin would not be that man. His heart was already spoken for...

...by the selfsame woman who was glaring impatiently at him at that very moment. He looked at Olivia, knew both that she was demanding and that he loved her for it and grinned effusively.

Miss Benson, as observant and insightful as only the sometimes overlooked could be, spotted his grin immediately.

"Go!" She shooed them away, smiling at them. "My gossip can wait."

"Thank you." Wearing a look of pure gratitude, Olivia grabbed Griffin's hand. With him in tow, she all but careered across the room to her waiting table and its three crates—one size small, one medium and one large. "Here we are!"

"We've got to stop traveling places that way," Griffin groused with a grin. "You nearly pulled my wrist out of its socket."

Olivia tossed him a skeptical look. "Little ole me? Never."

He laughed. "'Little ole you' has the might of an elephant when provoked by a mystery—or by a need to escape some gossip." He offered her an inviting look. "So, tell me…what about the medicine-show man? This isn't the first time I've heard tell—"

—of your legendary showdown with the peddler who would eventually make your face famous, Griffin meant to say. He knew parts of the story. He wanted to hear the whole of it from her.

But Olivia had already glimpsed a waiting crowbar. She jabbed the tool toward him, compelling him to take it.

"Later," she said, rubbing her hands. "Right now, let's find out what's in these mysterious crates."

Chapter Thirteen

While Griffin lifted the lid off the first crate, Olivia stood on tiptoe to see what was in it. All she saw was a burlap-wrapped bundle. Interestedly, she stepped nearer. Wearing an oddly expectant look, Griffin moved back to allow her closer.

"Go ahead," he urged. "Take it out. Unwrap it."

It was almost as though Griffin could read the curiosity that was in her heart. Maybe it was reflected in her eyes. Olivia loved a good mystery—hence her interest in puzzles.

"Go on. You'll never know what it is otherwise," he added, plainly inviting her to give in to her natural curiosity…and its two obvious companions, impatience and unfeminine assertiveness.

Eagerly, Olivia prepared to grab that bundle. Then she recalled how solicitous Griffin had been with Violet and stopped herself cold. During one conversation, Griffin had shown a greater interest in the minister's daughter than most men in Morrow Creek did in a whole year. For a long time, Violet had been sadly overlooked by the men in town. She was one of Olivia's closest friends, so Olivia couldn't help wishing things were different for her. With Griffin, they had been.

He'd clearly been impressed with Violet's reserve.

In fact, Griffin's reaction to Violet proved that he truly was blind to beauty—or to its lack. Because as goodhearted and well liked as Violet Benson was, she was also one of the plainest women in town. It was simply the accepted wisdom that Violet was a perpetual wallflower, first to volunteer for things and last to be asked to dance. But given Griffin's attitude to Violet, Olivia knew now more than ever that she had no chance of impressing him with her most avowed asset: her looks. That made it doubly crucial that she impress him with her saintly good character. If she tried very hard to develop one. Immediately.

To that end, Olivia conjured an air of reticence. It felt a bad fit. Nonetheless, she persisted. "No. I couldn't possibly!" Graciously, she inclined her head. "Please, you look first."

Her invitation was met with a perplexed look. "It's yours."

"We don't know that," she argued. "Yes, it was delivered to me, in my care, for the handicrafts show. But that doesn't—"

"It's yours," Griffin insisted. "Trust me. I know."

With effort, Olivia clasped her hands behind her back. She shook her head. "Please, Mr. Turner. I insist you look first."

Her attempt to sound politely restrained was unimpressive, at best. How had she managed to fool her friends and neighbors into believing she was truly ladylike for all these years?

"Olivia." Griffin delivered her a too-insightful look. "What's the matter? You sound as though butter wouldn't melt in your mouth—when we both know you keep some piquant words in there." He stepped closer. "Do I have to remind you?"

Silently, Olivia held steady. She *needed* him.

She needed him to believe she was every bit as refined as Violet was. And Jonas's mother was. Even though, when reminded of her, he'd seemed unmoved. In fact, his vehemence toward Jonas's mother had caught Olivia by surprise. She'd been using that good woman as a convenient model of temperance, but now…

Griffin gazed down at her. His nearness made her yearn, very inappropriately, to be held in his arms. That feeling only grew more heated when, undoubtedly demonstrating her knack for "piquant" speech, he tossed back her own words from earlier.

"If I could," Griffin said in a low, seductive tone, "I would spend time just staring at you, too." He stopped, then gave her an exasperated look. "What is that, if not you being predictably and wonderfully honest with your thoughts?"

"It was me being inappropriate."

He gave her a direct look. "Was it untrue?"

Olivia gazed up at him. "It was true. I *do* like the way you look. When I see you now, I see…you. I like that. I like *you*."

Whatever emotion Griffin felt at that, he hid it ably.

"I like the way you look, too," he said gruffly. Then, "Look inside the crate. People are starting to arrive."

Olivia glanced up, saw the townspeople coming in and made her decision. "I'll look first if you'll promise to look next."

"I already know what's in these three crates."

That stopped her. "How could you?"

"Just…" Exasperatedly, Griffin held her by the shoulders, steered her into position in front of the smallest opened crate then commanded her to look. "I'll open the other two crates."

Obligingly, Olivia did look. She picked up the object inside, unwrapped it then gazed at it in total disbelief.

"It's a toothbrush." She peered more closely. "It's my toothbrush. The one I sketched! The one I invented!" She whipped her dubious gaze to Griffin. "You made a prototype for me?"

"Your design was very clever. I couldn't resist," Griffin said. "A reservoir handle that could contain a dentifrice agent dispensed via a screw-threaded mechanism? It's ingenious."

Olivia boggled at it. Then she lunged for the next crate.

Still clutching her innovative toothbrush in her fist, she grabbed the next item. She flipped it over. A tidy pile of sturdy stitched fabric met her gaze. At first, Olivia thought it really was some shy stranger's contribution to the handicrafts show.

Then she recognized it. "My lady's rational skirt for cycling!" With patent amazement, she held up the garment. It was fashioned in two parts. One was a bloomerstyle underlayer. The other was a skirt-style overlayer for modesty. Excitedly, Olivia pointed at it. "This will enable women everywhere to enjoy the freedom of cycling." Marveling at its construction, she shook her head. "We have a Bicycling Association in town, you know. I have to show this to Grace Murphy. She'll be so proud."

"That will make two of us." Griffin cast a hasty glance at the people filing into the handicrafts show. He gestured to a spot beside Olivia's sampler. "You'll have to come here to see the third one. It's too big to uncrate and put on the table."

That could only be one of…well, several items, Olivia knew. Giving the contents of her sketchbook a hasty mental review, she set down her cycling skirt sample. She placed her toothbrush prototype on top of it. She inhaled, shot Griffin a helplessly excited glance then looked toward the spot he'd indicated.

A device made of polished, turned wood stood there, fitted with a wheel. The wheel itself was outfitted with hanger arms, slats and shelves, forming a sort of circular bookcase.

"It's my book-holding carousel! You made a prototype of this, too?" Wonderingly, Olivia trod around it. She gave it a gentle push. The revolving mechanism spun the wheel, just as designed. The next shelf—one of six—held an open book. Tears leaped to her eyes. "It's my favorite! With this, you can read several books at once." She marveled. "*How* did you make this?"

"With a great deal of help from my new friends, the lumber mill owner, the blacksmith and the saloon-keeper," Griffin said. "Did you know Murphy has a secret past of inventing things himself? His creations caused such a furor he fled Boston."

"Mr. Copeland, Mr. McCabe and Mr. Murphy were too kind." Amazedly, Olivia transferred her attention to the lady's skirt and the toothbrush. "I'm guessing their wives may have helped with your plan, as well. I see ladies' handiwork here."

"Everyone was surprisingly helpful," Griffin told her. He gazed concernedly at her tears. "As soon as I mentioned—"

"You didn't say these things were for me, did you?" Olivia yelped, dashing away her sentimental tears. Sud-

denly she felt all too aware that her years of decorum
were for nothing if her outlandish hobby of inventing
things came to light. It was unfeminine enough to be
bookish and interested in science. It would be a hundred
times worse to be a verifiable entrepreneur, filing patents and creating inventions and working to sell them.

Even freethinking suffragist Grace Murphy—née
Crabtree—hadn't gone that far toward female equality.
And she'd been detained in Sheriff Caffey's jailhouse
a time or two for her courageous efforts on behalf of
women's rights.

"No. I didn't say they were for you." With a patient
smile, Griffin thumbed away an errant tear—one she'd
plainly missed—from her cheek. "I thought you would
say that by displaying your work here at the handicrafts
show. The book carousel should be of particular interest. Although I wish I'd brought more books—"

"I can't tell people about these. I can't!" Urgently,
Olivia gestured at the prototypes. "People will think—"

"That you're brilliant? Rightly so."

"That I'm strange! That I'm eccentric. That I'm—"

"Brave?" Griffin stepped nearer. He held her shoulders, then smiled at her. "Do it, Olivia. Show everyone
who you are."

"I can't." Resolutely, she shook her head. Didn't he
know how much depended on not doing that? This had
to be another of Griffin's tests, Olivia reasoned. He had
bags of money. Having these prototypes made would
have been inconsequential to him.

"You can," he insisted. His gaze met hers. "There
was more light in your eyes when you looked at your
inventions than there was in the entire time you were
cross-stitching your sampler."

"You don't know that," she grumbled, remember-

ing the pricked fingers and tangled embroidery floss
she'd endured. "You weren't there for the entire time I
was stitching it."

"I was there long enough to know that you might tol-
erate needlework, but you *love* inventing things. Just
admit it."

Obstinately, Olivia refused. "You don't know me."

"Then let me know you. Let everyone know you."
His impassioned gaze worked to persuade her. "Can't
you see? You must show yourself. Otherwise you'll
never really be happy."

If that was Griffin's notion of irony, Olivia didn't
care for it. What did he know about showing himself
to everyone? He did everything he could to remain in-
visible and unknowable.

"You're making fun of me." Even that was a kinder
scenario than the one wherein Griffin was testing her
suitability to be a bride. "You know I should prefer needlework, and since I don't—"

Oops. Drat it all. Feeling nearly overcome, Olivia
stopped.

She gestured in frustration toward the prototypes
Griffin had made—toward the shapes of her imagination, revealed now in ivory and bristles, in muslin
and thread…in wood and metalwork fittings. She could
scarcely believe she was seeing them.

She could scarcely believe he'd made them for her.

Even more, she could scarcely believe she was dis-
owning them. But Griffin was more important to her
than her longtime flights of fancy. Making an impression on him had to prevail. How else could she love
him? How else could she prove herself?

"*You* claim them." Olivia lifted her chin. "I've just

developed a frightful headache," she fibbed. "I'm going home."

"Olivia." Griffin appeared utterly downhearted. He grabbed her arm, even as more attendees to the handicrafts show arrived—even as conversations swirled around them and people began touring the various tabletop displays. "Please stay. *Please.* I didn't mean to upset you. I thought you'd be happy."

"I am happy. I'm thrilled by these!" Pulling her arm from his grasp, she gave a helpless wave at the models he'd fashioned of her inventions. They represented a real opportunity to move forward. With these prototypes, Olivia knew, she could file for patents. She could take steps to a new life. She could…alienate herself from her family and friends. She sighed. "They're wonderful. Truly, they are. But if you think I can claim them—"

"I know you can claim them. They're remarkable!"

"—then you don't know me at all." Even more determinedly, Olivia squared her shoulders. She glanced around the handicrafts show. "I'm sorry, Griffin. I wish I could be different."

"I don't want you to be different. I want you to be *you.*"

Olivia only shook her head. "That's very convincing," she told him with the shadow of a grin. "But I'll believe that line the day you show up hatless, wearing clothes that aren't black."

For a moment, Griffin looked almost crafty. Then…

"Fine." He smiled at her. "I didn't become the man I am by giving up, Olivia. I'm going to make you admit the truth."

The truth. Unfortunately, that statement only confirmed her suspicions. Griffin was testing her, Olivia reasoned. The most bedeviling part was, she had no idea whether she'd passed.

Given that she sometimes feared, in her own heart, that she might be nothing more than an empty beauty— that her life's highlight truly might have been appearing on that remedy bottle—Olivia reckoned she might not have passed Griffin's test at all.

But then she realized another unexpected truth. The only reason Griffin would test her was if he was considering *marrying* her! Pondering that, Olivia shot him an observant glance.

He stared back, hands on his hips, looking manful and sturdy and broad shouldered…and so adorably mulish that she wanted to fling her arms around him and hug him straight into next week. He *did* care about her. That meant she still had hope.

She had hope that Griffin might love her—might even propose to her. She also had hope that he might relinquish The Lorndorff altogether, for the sake of her happiness. Once those things had happened, she could be happy and enjoy harmony at home, too.

With a new lightness, Olivia touched Griffin's arm. Doing so made her remember what he'd looked like, partly naked, that day in his hotel suite bed. It made her recall what he'd felt like while holding her close. Boldly, she slid her hand past his cuffed shirtsleeve, down to his bare, hair-sprinkled forearm.

His skin felt shockingly hot. Excitingly firm.

He jolted at her touch, and her imagination flared anew. She'd had no idea she could affect him merely with her touch….

This fraught encounter with her invention prototypes didn't have to be a setback, Olivia told herself. It could be another beginning. Now that she knew she possessed some leverage with Griffin, she didn't have to be quite so fearful of the outcomes of their encounters. Now that she knew Griffin wanted her…

…she was free to want him back. Unreservedly.

"I just might make you admit the truth, too," Olivia said, echoing his earlier words. "Just wait and see if I don't."

Then she sashayed away, said her goodbyes to Violet Benson and the other members of the Territorial Benevolent Association and made her way back to The Lorndorff to formulate her plans.

Chapter Fourteen

Before arriving alone in Morrow Creek, stealing in under cover of darkness, Griffin had experienced baseball games. After all, the pastime of baseball was tremendously popular in Boston. Griffin was acquainted with Harry Wright. He'd followed the career of pitcher Albert Spalding. He'd reported on the sporting exploits of the Red Stockings, the Beaneaters, and the Red Caps in his own newspapers. But despite his diverse and longstanding understanding of the game of "baseball," Griffin realized very quickly that the sport was played... *differently* in Morrow Creek.

In the Arizona Territory, he'd learned, many things were.

For one thing, Griffin noticed as he strode past the modest schoolhouse and approached the designated baseball field, a distinct festival atmosphere prevailed. Townspeople streamed toward the game site with cheerful expressions. They held picnic baskets in hand, covered with gingham checked cloths, swinging them to and fro as they walked. They brought hand-stitched baseballs and rudimentary homemade bats. They laughed.

Where Griffin came from, sporting events were serious business. Gamblers wagered fortunes on them. Players staked their livelihoods and reputations on winning them. Spectators started rowdy brawls over them. But here in Morrow Creek, where rosy-cheeked children whooped their way toward the field and women sewed homemade team symbols on their husbands' shirts and men struck silly strongman poses—like barnstorming Signor Lawanda come to clobber the bases—everything was different.

It was, to Griffin's mind, miles and miles better.

Of course, that opinion probably owed more to the presence of Olivia, he knew, than to any real appreciation of sport. Because as he spied her waiting in the distance, speaking with a group of her friends and holding a bat herself, Griffin felt himself involuntarily walk faster. His heartbeat raced, too.

More than that, it felt as if his whole heart expanded.

Honestly, Griffin had expected that to quit happening by now. How much affection could one meager heart hold after all?

Maybe his heart had extra room, having been empty for so long…at least until he'd met Olivia.

"Whoa, there." Beside him, nearly at a trot now, Palmer Grant shoved out his arm. "Slow down, Turner. Do you want these ladies to believe we're eager to see them play baseball?"

"I *am* eager to see them play baseball," Griffin returned honestly. He'd learned from Olivia—and from the members of the Morrow Creek Men's Club—that in the town's established league, the men played their games first. Then the women played their games last. "As curiosities go, it's bound to be entertaining. Besides, Olivia strongly implied that it's somehow scandalous."

She'd said, in fact, that suffragist Mrs. Murphy had gone to some lengths to have the women's league approved. She'd staged a protest, then instigated a strike among the women who sewed the regulation-weight horsehair baseballs used by the men's leagues. She'd seized and then hidden all the existing baseballs so the men couldn't practice unless they came to terms. In the end, she'd been successful…with some compromises.

"You interpreted that to mean it's worth *racing* to?" His associate stared at him. "Where's your dignity, man?"

"I've never needed dignity less than I do around here." Griffin grinned, still striding onward. "It's damn refreshing."

At that, Palmer stopped altogether. Incredulously, he peered at Griffin. "I knew you were sweet on Miss Mouton. But it's worse than that. Do you actually *enjoy* this rustic town?"

Griffin stopped, too. He shrugged. "Don't you?"

"Don't I—" Palmer stuttered. He frowned. "My outlook on the matter doesn't count. We're talking about you. You *and* your increasing willingness to participate in this…looniness." As proof, he shook his head at the sturdy homespun clothes Griffin had borrowed to play baseball in. He straightened his own collar with a fussy gesture. "As soon as you come to your senses—"

"Again, that's not going to happen."

"—we'll be heading back to Boston, where the streets are paved, the restaurants serve good steaks and the women are sophisticated. Remember that?" Palmer asked. "Remember your mansion? Your *other* mansion? Your business and properties—"

"None of that matters." Griffin waved hello to Olivia.

Palmer exhaled in evident exasperation. "You ordered new suits! I took that to mean you were ready to return home."

"No. But thank you for relaying my wishes to the tailor. With a rush on the job, I think those suits will arrive soon."

"You can't stay here forever, Griffin," Palmer persisted. "Henry Mouton has more gumption than you counted on. You know he's contacting potential investors to buy out your shares of the hotel." An even more aggrieved look. "He's telegraphed Simon Blackhouse! You know...of the California Blackhouses?"

Hearing that notorious family name made Griffin frown.

"The Blackhouses? Mouton didn't say anything about them."

"Undoubtedly, he's keeping his strategy close to his vest."

"He's playing with fire, is what he's doing." Griffin knew of the Blackhouses. If anything, their line was worse than his own. They'd had a fortune for generations—and no morals to stymie that fortune's disreputable use. Extortion, cheating, threats of violence... nothing was too extreme if it satisfied the Blackhouse family's pleasure-seeking ways. "Did you warn Mouton off?"

"I tried." Palmer frowned. "He seemed to think it was a trick. After you offered to let him manage The Lorndorff again, Mouton started thinking everything we did or said was a trick."

Griffin sighed. Henry Mouton was a sore trial, to be sure.

Griffin had extended an olive branch to Mouton with

that management offer. Admittedly, it had been a half
measure. Mouton had had too much pride to accept it.
Still, Griffin had been willing. For Olivia's sake, he'd
been prepared to let her father come back as the hotel's
acting manager. He'd been rebuffed.

Now they were at an impasse. Griffin couldn't relinquish the hotel completely. If he did, what excuse would
he have for seeing Olivia? Her determined mission to
make Griffin surrender control of her father's hotel had
kept Olivia glued to Griffin's side. Until he felt sure
of her feelings for him, he could not abandon his only
means of making certain she stayed near.

"I'll come up with a strategy," Griffin promised,
setting aside the issue for now. "Don't worry. In the
meantime—"

He broke off, realizing that Palmer was no longer
listening. He was waving, with alarming enthusiasm,
at a woman who knelt near the improvised home plate
while sorting through a burlap bag of baseballs. *Annie*.
It was Olivia's friend Annie.

She glanced up, saw Palmer and waved equally vigorously.

"Hmm. You say you want 'sophisticated' women?"
Griffin couldn't help grinning. "She, my friend, is a
chambermaid."

"So was yours, at first! She was a chambermaid,
too."

"Yes. Olivia surprised me," Griffin admitted.
"Maybe Annie will surprise you, too." He gave her
another look. "Maybe she's more complicated than you
know. Women often are."

Palmer scoffed. "I doubt I'll find out. I'll be back in
Boston by then. You enjoy your baseball. I have other
plans."

Without so much as another hectoring reminder of Griffin's temporarily abandoned mansions and businesses, Palmer took off at a dash. He ducked between two bat-carrying men. He galloped past a cluster of children, then nearly collided with a grandmotherly woman who fittingly lectured him on decorum.

Palmer arrived at Annie's location. He swept off his hat.

The chambermaid looked up. She smiled broadly at him.

Despite Palmer's protestations to the contrary, there was little doubt that the two of them had sparked a romance. Whether their budding ardor would flourish was anyone's guess. But as Griffin watched his upright associate and Olivia's freewheeling friend chat together—spiritedly if contrastingly—he felt newly inspired to sort out things with Olivia.

He may not have succeeded with persuading Olivia to dance to the fiddle music at the town musicale. He may not have won her heart—or ignited her courage— with his presentation of her invention prototypes at the handicrafts show. In fact, given her topsy-turvy reactions on that day, Griffin wasn't sure if making those prototypes had been the right thing to do at all.

Still, Olivia *had,* afterward, allowed him to bring those models secretly to her cozy attic rooms at The Lorndorff. And she *had* cried happy tears upon seeing the prototypes again. And she *had* hugged Griffin thank-you with such ferocity that he'd thought his ribs might crack. So that was progress, of a sort.

In fact, it was *heartening* progress, Griffin decided as he loped toward the baseball field himself. Olivia's grateful reaction proved he was on the right course.

From here, he only had to persevere. He only had to help Olivia help herself.

The upcoming baseball game was an opportunity to do just that, Griffin realized as he neared her position and saw that—unlike her fellow members of the women's league—Olivia was not wearing a sturdy dress, outrageously hemmed to her ankles to allow free movement. She was not clad in sensible brogan shoes with low heels, suitable for a sportswoman's athletic needs. Instead, Olivia stood bundled in a lightweight coat with its collar up to her neck, doubtless broiling in the heat.

Even in the mountainous town of Morrow Creek, it wasn't cool enough to require outerwear. Not at this time of day, at least. Glimpsing Olivia's buttoned-up coat, Griffin puzzled.

Something was not quite right here.

"Miss Mouton!" He greeted her formally, since they were in public, by clasping her hand in his. He smiled, undoubtedly looking naively smitten. "It's a beautiful day for baseball."

"Yes, it is!" She smiled back at him, still holding her bat. The breeze loosened tendrils of hair from her chignon, then tossed them across her face. "I'm glad you're here, Mr. Turner."

With a moue of frustration, Olivia hooked those soft tendrils with her fingertip. She tucked them behind her ear. That impatient gesture only pulled Griffin's attention to her lovely hands, to her winsome face…to her soft, alluring lips.

Olivia glanced up at him welcomingly, and all at once, Griffin didn't care that they were in public. He didn't care that the residents of Morrow Creek had gathered all around them with boisterous goodwill, lugging bats and balls and improvised baseball bases. Given Olivia's nearness, Griffin wanted more.

He wanted to touch her hair himself. He wanted to pull her closer for a kiss. He wanted to embrace her, to explore her sweet womanly curves with his hands, to give in to all the most ungentlemanly impulses he strived so hard *not* to surrender to when they were alone together in his hotel suite.

So far, he'd done a good job of suppressing those sensual needs. Now, in the space between his hello and his handclasp, they came roaring back to him, twice as intense and a million times more demanding.

He'd never been more aware of Olivia as a bountiful and passionate woman—or himself as a strong-bodied and virile man.

The air between them felt atingle with mounting sensuality, rife with a sense of forbidden possibility. Together, he and Olivia could share so much more than they already had, Griffin knew. Together, they could be one. But a woman like Olivia deserved more from him than desire and wild imaginings and longings to kiss her. She deserved everything he had.

So, chivalrously, Griffin gave it. He gave her respect and admiration. He gave her gallantry. He smiled anew, and vowed to himself not to seduce her…however much he wanted to.

He nodded at her coat. "Have you caught a chill?"

His studied tone made her smile. "Indeed, I haven't."

"Yet you're bundled up as if you expect a blizzard," Griffin said. "Won't you find it difficult to play?"

"I don't expect to." Olivia glanced to the side, exchanged a few words with another female player then returned her attention to him. "I don't ordinarily play in the games," she informed him. "Generally, I function as the team's secretary. I maintain notes of our meetings, catalogue our equipment, set the batting order among the players…things like that."

"You don't play? Why?"

"Because it's appropriate." She shrugged, her bat still held capably in hand. "Because it's…sufficient for me."

Griffin doubted it. For a long moment, he studied her. He knew her love of activity. He understood her interest in sports.

Suddenly, he realized the truth. "This is like Nickerson's Book Depot and News Emporium," he declared. "You want to be part of the baseball league, but you don't trust yourself to play. So you surround yourself with baseball, then don't partake of it."

Olivia laughed, even as people passed by them, preparing either to play in the game or spectate. "What? Don't be silly!"

Dauntlessly, Griffin persisted. "This is not a course of action that will lead inevitably to some imagined downfall," he said. "You won't hit one baseball and transform into a hoyden. You won't pitch one inning and erase years of known propriety." He squeezed her arm encouragingly. "Play, Olivia. Do it."

A hopeful light came into her eyes. Still, disappointingly, she waved away his urgings. "You can't make me play baseball."

"Why stay on the fringes? If you want to, play!"

Cautiously, Olivia looked around. She bit her lip. "No one would understand. I've never played in a game. I practice, but—"

"*These* women would understand." Griffin gestured at the other female players. "They are playing, too! Isn't that right? Surely they wouldn't dare criticize you for joining them."

"It's different for them. They're not Miss Milky White." Agitatedly, she waved. "They have more than that to rely on!"

Olivia's distressed tone struck him in a way nothing else could have. Gently, Griffin took her free hand. He lifted it in his, kissed it then placed it atop her bat where it could join her other hand in grasping it. Automatically, Olivia assumed a batter's grip. Dreamy eyed, she adopted a batter's ready stance.

"You are not only Miss Milky White, either," Griffin said.

Her anxious gaze met his. "No. I'm...more than that."

He smiled. "Try not to sound so tentative. It's true."

Olivia's yearning expression almost broke his heart. Could she truly be that uncertain of her own innate appeal?

She could, if her sagging shoulders were any indication. Disappointingly, she lowered her bat to rest on the ground.

"If I have to buy and break every bottle of that blasted remedy to prove it to you," Griffin swore, "I will." He added a rascally grin. "You know how much I love smashing bottles."

At that, Olivia laughed. "If only you could."

"I think *you* could." From beyond the haphazard rows of spectators seated on the grass, Griffin heard his name being called. He flung up his hand to acknowledge that summons, then returned to Olivia...to his heart. "You could stop saying you're more than a face on a patent remedy and start proving it."

She frowned. "That's hardly a sensitive way to put it."

He shrugged. "My detractors would say I'm never

sensitive. You've already witnessed more Hook Turner miracles than anyone."

"Don't call yourself that. Please."

"Don't hide your light under a bushel. Please."

In vexation, Olivia shook her head. "I won't if you won't."

"If I thought that was true, I'd forget that nickname entirely." Griffin tugged down his hat, preparing to join the other members of the men's club for their baseball game. "Now, *you* think about how much fun you might have while playing."

"I'd rather think about how manly you look in your sporting attire." Olivia gave him a sassy, assessing glance—one that made him feel undeniably roused. "You seem very...fit, Mr. Turner."

"I *am* very fit, Miss Mouton. Watch and see." Grinning at her teasing, Griffin dared to squeeze her hand again. More seriously than he wanted, he asked, "Will you root for me?"

"Always," Olivia promised with her eyes shining up at him. "I am on your side, wherever that takes me."

Humbled by that, Griffin shook his head. "I don't deserve you. I don't deserve—" he spread his arms "—any of this."

"Yes, you do." In a gesture remarkably similar to the way he had arranged her in front of her first crated prototype, Olivia put her hands on his shoulders. She turned him around.

At least she tried. He was too big for her to move.

Subtly, Griffin helpfully cooperated. He turned.

"There. Now go," she instructed him. "Have fun today."

"You won't have fun," he pointed out. "Why should I?"

"Maybe you'll inspire me." Olivia gave him a feeble

shove. Then, when he didn't budge an inch, she added, "Do I have to start smashing up bats? I will, you know, if you don't go."

Her faux menacing tone was probably meant to mimic his. Knowing that, Griffin felt warmed all over. She *did* care.

"Watch me win." Proudly, he straightened. "For you."

Then, with a swagger that felt irrefutably real—and was probably wholly underserved—Griffin left Olivia to face her own fears…and went to confront a few of his own. As a man who'd never played a single game of baseball, he knew his performance on his team ought to be…*interesting,* if nothing else.

Chapter Fifteen

Seated on a patched old quilt amid the spectators, watching the men's baseball game enter its eighth inning, Olivia felt nearly toasted through. The sun beat down on her head. The spectators packed close together, increasing the ambient temperature. The fabric of her springtime coat seemed to have doubled in thickness since she'd first put it on that morning.

She'd never had a more daft idea than wearing it. Or, rather, wearing the ensemble she'd dressed in *beneath* it. But since Olivia didn't want anyone to know what she'd foolishly outfitted herself in that morning—in a fit of optimism, no doubt—she huddled in her coat, holding a small homemade pennant.

As handcrafted as it was, her miniature pennant added a certain jollity to the proceedings. Emblazoned with the symbol of Griffin's adopted team and joined with everyone else's similar pennants and banners, it demonstrated a certain sense of sportsmanship and town loyalty that she was proud of. Later, she'd switch pennants and cheer on her own female team. But now, while the men played, Olivia was strictly a spectator.

Not that she'd be much more than that later, she

thought wryly, remembering Griffin's urgings that she play in today's game. Like every other baseball game, Olivia had planned to spend this one as an onlooker. As much as she yearned to play, she couldn't risk unleashing her own vigor and competitiveness.

Women were only allowed to compete for the title of Best Jam in the county fair or Most Finely Stitched in displays of fancy needlework. To compete in other arenas only suggested an unfeminine thirst for accomplishment…not that *that* particular truism had ever stopped Grace Murphy from achieving amazing feats, Olivia mused as she spied the suffragist standing to the side, all while being married to her saloon-keeper husband.

Watching alertly as Grace gave Jack Murphy a distinctly robust cheer, Olivia couldn't help being intrigued. Her husband seemed to love everything about her. Even as Sheriff Caffey issued Grace a chastising look—bringing his helper, Deputy Winston, in on his very public censure—Jack Murphy only smiled. It was clear that he respected Grace *because* she was herself. No matter what anyone else thought of her antics.

"The players are quite virile, aren't they?" someone asked, breaking into Olivia's thoughts. "Especially my Mr. Davis."

At that, Olivia returned her attention to her own group of friends, situated on her worn quilt. Adeline Wilson sat prettily beside Olivia. She was the one who'd just spoken, and she looked as beautiful as she always did, especially while mooning over her longtime beau, Clayton Davis. The lumber-mill sawyer stepped up to bat. He aimed a lovelorn look at Adeline.

She returned it unabashedly. "Hit a home run, Clay!" She watched raptly as he did so. She clapped for him.

"Well done!" Olivia clapped, too. "My, he's very good!"

"Yes." Still watching her sweetheart run toward second base, Adeline nodded. "I only wish Clayton was half as good at tendering a marriage proposal as he is at clobbering a ball with a bat." She slanted Olivia a bemused look. "I don't know what his holdup is, but I'm running out of patience, to be sure."

"He must have a very good reason for waiting," Olivia assured her. Privately, she considered Adeline to be the most attractive woman in town—far more beautiful than Olivia herself. She couldn't fathom what would prevent any reasonable man from proposing to her. "You'll just have to be patient, I guess."

"I guess," Adeline grumbled good-naturedly. "For now…"

From beside Adeline, their mutual friend Violet Benson only gave a silent nod. While the game continued, so did their conversation. It hardly seemed fair, they agreed, that the men were allowed to play first, when the women were also keen. But that had been the compromise Grace had finagled with the league.

The menfolk simply weren't willing to allow anything more. As it was, most of the spectators drifted away after the men's game was finished. At the moment, though, the crowd was large.

It was a little *too* large for Olivia's liking—for the ill-advised plan she'd initiated for herself this morning. Facing a field full of almost everyone she knew, from her father to the *Pioneer Press*'s editor, Thomas Walsh, was unnerving at best.

To her left sat Mr. Walsh's sister, the famous cookery book author, Daisy Walsh, who was visiting Morrow Creek for a spell and had decided to accompany little

Élodie Cooper—daughter of the livery stable owner, widowed Owen Cooper—to the game. Both ladies, larger and smaller, applauded their menfolk. Near them, Miss Mellie Reardon appeared to root for the town's newspaper editor with a special enthusiasm. As a part-time typesetter at the press office, she had reason to be enthusiastic, but it seemed to Olivia that there was more than genial interest in Mellie's cheering. Watching her, Olivia couldn't help hoping she snared Mr. Walsh for her own, as she clearly wished to do.

"Ooh!" Violet elbowed Olivia in the ribs. "Here's your Mr. Turner, coming up to bat." She watched avidly as Griffin approached the plate. "He's playing with such heart, isn't he?"

At Violet's sincere remark, Olivia smiled. "That's a diplomatic way of describing it." She couldn't tear away her gaze from Griffin's masculine form, displayed to advantage by his athletic stance and slightly too form-fitting clothing. He'd borrowed those togs, but Olivia couldn't complain about the result. "I can promise you, Mr. Turner does everything in that fashion—as though he intends to win big or go down swinging."

"I admire that about him." Violet put her chin in her hand, gazing at Griffin as though she admired more than his determined attitude. She sighed. "He was very nice to me, you know."

Ah. With relief, Olivia remembered Griffin's gracious encounter with Violet on the day of the handicrafts show. Likely, that was all she meant. "Yes. He *is* quite nice."

He's especially nice when he's kissing me, she couldn't help thinking…and daydreamed through his first turn at bat.

Reassembling her attention, Olivia tried harder for

Griffin's next attempt. So far today, he'd missed more balls than he'd hit, but that hadn't unsettled him in the least.

"He's quite…unusual looking, isn't he?" ventured Daisy Walsh as she handed a rag doll to little Élodie. "His nose—"

"Is perfectly fine for his face," Violet stated bluntly.

"A big nose indicates big…appetites," Adeline added, leaning forward with a saucy eyebrow waggle. "It's manly."

Shocked by her brazenness, Olivia could only gawk as the other women in her group chimed in. One declared Griffin to be rugged. Another proclaimed him impressive. A third merely fanned herself with a bit of newsprint, watching Griffin bat.

Through it all, Daisy Walsh sat plainly mystified. She exchanged baffled glances with Élodie. They both shrugged.

"I guess you have to be a local to understand," Daisy said.

"Or a grown-up," Élodie added wisely. "Like my papa."

As Daisy's cheeks colored in response to that remark, Olivia frowned at all of them—except ten-year-old Élodie, of course. She couldn't help feeling that Griffin was *her* man to appreciate. Hers alone. Protectively, she watched him bat again.

He swung hard. He missed mightily. His ensemble of admirers gave a collective "aww" of commiseration. Irked, Olivia frowned.

"Smash it, Griffin!" she yelled through cupped hands, having had enough of poise. "You can do it! Hurray, Griffin!"

A wave of incredulity swept through the crowd,

strong enough to make Olivia's cheeks heat. But she just…didn't care.

Importantly, Griffin did care. He'd heard her. He winked at her, and then he pulled down his hat and prepared a sockdolager.

Olivia held her breath. Griffin wound up. He swung.

This time, his bat connected with the ball. In fact, it connected hard enough to splinter the bat in pieces—but not before the baseball soared into the sky toward left field.

Griffin stared. Then he ran.

Olivia leaped ecstatically to her feet.

Barely aware of her own actions, she jumped up and down, watching Griffin make a triumphant run around the bases. He was full of power and might, grinning like a conqueror, running hard. His black hat flew off. It wheeled away in the breeze.

Still Griffin kept running. With his face wholly revealed, he powered his way past third base. He was heading home.

"Go! Go! Go!" Olivia shrieked, waving her arms. "Go!"

When he cleared home base, Olivia thought she might swoon from excitement. Clapping madly, she hurtled herself toward the improvised wooden bench where the baseball players sat.

She was in Griffin's arms an instant later. Laughing with delight, she hugged him. "You did it! You were magnificent."

Still hatless, with his dark, unruly hair half-undone from its leather tie and his skin glistening with sweat, Griffin gave an offhanded shrug. "That'll show those glasshouse boys for not letting me onto their damn team." Full of pride, he cupped her face in his big, dirt-smudged hands. He grinned. "You *did* root for me. I heard you all the way on the field."

"Half the town heard me," Olivia joked, still struck by the fact that the reason Griffin hadn't ever played baseball wasn't—as she'd assumed—because he hadn't wanted to join in. It was because he wasn't allowed to join in. Her heart went out to him.

"Ahem." Nearby, one of the male players cleared his throat. "Can we proceed, Turner?" he asked facetiously. "Or do you plan on spooning with your sweetie some more first?"

Like startled cats, Olivia and Griffin leaped apart.

That didn't stop the entire bench of players from laughing.

Or dissuade the whole pile of spectators from hooting.

Well, it was too late for decorum now, Olivia decided, casting her friends and neighbors a discomfited glance. She needed to show Griffin a *little* of her true self, didn't she? Otherwise, he'd be duped into marrying someone she wasn't.

At that thought, she went still. She didn't want to fool Griffin. She only wanted to love him. If the woman she was wasn't good enough for that—with her love of science and fiddles, inventions and baseball, philosophy and books—well, if she wasn't good enough, Olivia thought with a sudden burst of rebellious courage, she might as well learn that hard truth now.

Because, true to her challenge to him at the handicrafts show, Griffin had appeared in public while hatless and wearing nonblack clothes. He *had* changed his ways. Olivia could see with her own eyes the tight-fitting tan britches and white Henley shirt he'd borrowed for the baseball game. As for his hat...

Well, it might never be recovered. The wind had it now.

Further, it occurred to her, it had been days since she'd last glimpsed Griffin drinking whiskey. It had been even longer since he'd smoked a cigarillo. For her sake, he'd left his hotel suite and gotten to know Morrow Creek. He'd trusted her.

Wasn't it time, Olivia wondered, that she trusted him?

You must show yourself, she remembered him saying while urging her to claim her inventions as her own. *Otherwise, you'll never really be happy.* Suddenly, she believed it was true.

"I'm sorry. We're finished," Olivia told the other player. She recognized him as local rancher Everett Bannon, whose meddlesome vaqueros had doubtless accompanied him to town today. They were a famously interfering lot of cowboys—unrepentantly so—but they all meant well. Olivia turned to Griffin. "You'd better get back to it," she advised him. "As soon as you men are finished playing, the ladies on my team have some fantastic athletic feats to show you. See? I'm already prepared."

Bravely, Olivia unbuttoned her coat. She removed it.

At the sight of what she'd worn beneath it—what she'd fearfully hidden all day, only to reveal now—Griffin's eyes widened. "Your lady's rational cycling skirt! You wore it."

"I thought it would be ideal for many different sporting activities," Olivia said. "It's a flawless fit, too. I sized the prototype to my own specifications. It was only convenient."

Griffin's approving gaze said he agreed. Unreservedly.

The increasingly impatient grumbling of the crowd

said otherwise. The spectators and players wanted to continue.

Olivia could cope with their impatience—and even with their potential disapproval—she realized. Because as long as she believed she was doing the right thing, she was. For her.

Not that her father's shocked face in the crowd didn't give her a moment's pause. It did. But she smiled at him…and Henry Mouton gamely smiled back. He was absentminded. But loving, too.

"Good luck!" Olivia curtsied in her shirtwaist and clever divided skirt. She slung her lightweight coat over her arm, done with it now. "I'm sorry for the interruption. Please, carry on!"

The players did, even as Olivia tromped gamely over to the ladies' practice area of the field. There, the former Crabtree sisters—Grace, Sarah and Molly—greeted her with enthusiasm.

"Your sporting costume is ingenious!" Grace marveled, clearly wanting one of her own. "I should have guessed, when Molly was cutting it and Sarah was sewing it, that its creation was your doing, Olivia. You've always been so imaginative."

"Your Mr. Turner brings out something special in you," Sarah added with a gentle smile. "I can see it, plain as day."

"I *knew* my spice cake could work magic!" Molly finished, cheerfully handing Olivia a bat to practice with. "Next thing you know, it'll be wedding bells for you two! Mark my words."

Hoping Molly was right, Olivia rested her bat on her shoulder. In thought, she turned to watch Griffin on the bench.

He wiped his brow. He saw her. He smiled broadly at her.

As one, all the women on Olivia's quilt audibly sighed.

Well, that clinched it. For better or worse, Olivia realized, her infatuation with Griffin was public knowledge.

She turned back, intending to practice her batting swing…and met the three sisters' inquisitive gazes instead.

Grace, in particular, appeared full of questions.

"So," she said directly and without preamble, "exactly why do they call Mr. Turner The Tycoon Terror?"

Chapter Sixteen

For as long as two hours after Griffin had concluded his first triumphant personal encounter with baseball, he still felt aglow with accomplishment. His senses felt sharper. His arms felt stronger. His whole body felt downright *enlivened*. His hands remembered the feel of the bat, his ears the crack of the hit he'd made, his eyes the clear skyward arc of the ball.

It was lunacy, but it was also undeniable. The small, ridiculed boy inside him felt victorious. Proud. *Accepted*.

Accepted by a rural group of miners and lumbermen and calico-clad town housewives, but accepted, all the same.

The knowledge of that was far better than whiskey.

After watching Olivia's ladies' baseball team take the field—divided amongst themselves to create their own opponent, as they were obliged to do—Griffin had cheered on his invention-making, fiddle-music-loving, philosophizing woman as best as he knew how. He'd shouted until he'd grown hoarse. He'd waved his arms, then pinched a team pennant from one of the women and waved that, too. He'd overflowed with pride when

Olivia had taken to home plate for her first turn at bat, wearing her rational sportswoman's skirt and winding up with a look of determination.

He'd leaped to his feet to applaud the wobbly ground ball that brought her to first base, then waved with joy—earning himself several amused sidelong glances in the process and one elbow in the ribs from the closest spectator, Adam Crabtree.

"Easy there, Turner," the founder of the *Pioneer Press* had said with a grin. "Anyone would think *you'd* hit that ball."

But Griffin had endured Crabtree's friendly joshing along with all the other men's ribbing. That he needed to do so at all was partly his fault after all. Not because he was too rowdy in his admiration of Olivia's baseball efforts, but because he had been largely responsible for the hefty crowd that remained to watch the second game, in direct contravention of what he came to understand was the usual Morrow Creek response of rolling up blankets and leaving during the ladies' league game.

Watching the women play had been an eye-opening experience. Griffin had never given much thought to female suffrage or athleticism or leadership. But watching Olivia's game made him realize a few things. First, that she was not the only woman who needed courage to wield a bat. The occasional catcalls from the spectators told him that. Second, that she was not alone in fearing to step from her usual role and risk public censure. The nervous giggling and red faces of the women players told him that. And third, that she was extraordinary among all her peers. Because Olivia alone played with mingled grit and fear. Unique in her, poise and doggedness battled for supremacy…and in the process, both of those qualities took their turns in the game.

In the end, Olivia's side did not win—although she did apply considerable effort to try to wrangle a victory.

Breathlessly, she shrugged to Griffin after the game. "I never said I was *talented* at baseball. Only that I enjoyed it."

"I was not considering the score," he confessed, admiring her glistening skin and aura of exertion. "I was watching you."

It was true. Throughout the game, Griffin had been unable to tear away his attention from Olivia. He loved her vigor and her fortitude. He loved her girlish swings of the bat. He loved the way she wiggled her hips while preparing to run, the way she encouraged all her teammates with generous hollers of praise and the way she tucked those wayward tendrils of hair away from her flushed face while preparing to take her turn.

He loved...*her*. Wholeheartedly and without hesitation.

After the game, everyone had celebrated with cold, fresh-pressed apple cider that had been brought to the field along with Molly Copeland's peach-filled hand pies. They'd toasted each other with cups full of cider and hands full of sweets, and in those moments, Griffin had felt that he truly belonged there.

In a way he never had in Boston, he belonged in Morrow Creek. He'd come to know its residents. He'd helped them devise solutions to business problems and strategies for succeeding. He'd shopped in their mercantile and at their milliner's, used their telegraph and postal services and admired their small-town handicrafts. He'd quit growling, quit grumbling and quit hiding himself away in the dark. Thanks to Olivia, Griffin had stopped scaring away the people around him and begun welcoming them, with all their quirks and foibles and homespun ideals.

It could almost be said that he'd found a family in Morrow Creek. But Griffin wasn't ready for anything so foolish as that.

He'd found…*peace* in Morrow Creek, he told himself that evening as he stripped off his dirt-smudged, borrowed baseball clothes. He'd found solace in the mountain views, in the crisp scent of the ponderosa pines, in the burble of the creek. That would be enough, he swore to himself as he eyed the tub full of steaming water he'd asked the hotel staff to bring up for him, then lowered himself gingerly into it. He'd found a new beginning, he determined as he soaped himself up with the spicy scent of clove-oil soap and felt the day's exertion slide away.

For now, *for him,* that would have to be enough.

But when a sharp knock came at his door, moments after Griffin had dried off from his bath and pulled on a pair of underdrawers, he knew himself to be a liar. Because at the sound of that knock, Griffin knew he wanted more. He wanted Olivia to be on the other side of that door, fetching and sweet, coming to give herself to him in the only way she hadn't yet.

Cursing himself for his own weakness, Griffin covered himself more fully with a dressing gown, then stomped barefoot to the door. Summoning some strength, he inhaled a deep breath. Promising to be pure of mind and heart if it was Olivia on the other side of his suite's door, he opened it.

She all but barreled past him through the opening, bringing a fresh, rose-scented breeze with her. Clad with astonishing informality in a chemise and a ladies' flowered silk wrap that fell to her feet, with her hair in a loose topknot, Olivia strode inside.

"I came for a broom." Speaking hastily, she scanned the suite's furnishings. "There's a bat in my room, and I'll never sleep until I shoo it out the window." With purpose, she trod to the suite's corner. "Aha! I knew I'd left a broom in here."

All Griffin could do was stare at her. Olivia was a genuine force of nature, full of tenacity and purposefulness and verve. He wasn't entirely sure he hadn't imagined her—until she stopped before him with her broom clasped in hand…and made a funny face.

"Thank you, Griffin. I'm sorry to disturb you, but this is an emergency." She shuddered. "I loathe those creatures!"

Like a soldier marching to war, Olivia wielded her broom. She headed for the door with it, doubtless intent on vanquishing the intruder who'd invaded her attic rooms.

Griffin doubted she'd even registered his state of informal dress, much less her own tantalizing lack of proper clothing.

Without her usual bustle, he couldn't help noticing, Olivia's own naturally curvaceous derriere looked especially enticing. Without the support of her corsetry, her pert breasts moved beneath her sheer chemise and silky wrap in a way that unfailingly drew his attention. He loved the way she looked, the way she smelled… the way she still radiated accomplishment and bravery and audacious zeal after her plucky efforts during the baseball game today.

He loved…*her,* Griffin thought again, and knew he should probably tell her sometime soon. But in the meantime…

He snapped himself to alertness. "I'll deal with your bat."

"What?" She paused with her nose adorably crinkled. Then she realized what he'd said. She waved. "No, thank you. It's fine. I'm a country girl, you know." Olivia gave a spirited grin. "Here in the Arizona Territory, a person can't rely too heavily on attacks of the vapors when critters come calling. If I came over all swoony every time a common vesper bat lost its way and sailed into my room at night, I'd spend most of my time wielding smelling salts. Instead of baseball bats."

Even her bare feet were cute, Griffin noticed. So was her zest. Delivering him a second spunky grin, Olivia wheeled around. This time, though, he was there to stop her. "I insist."

She made a mock rueful face. "On the other hand, far be it for me to refuse a gentleman's assistance." Olivia gave a silly curtsy—during which she seemed to notice, for the first time, Griffin's state of partial undress. Her eyes widened. Her gaze traveled up his underdrawers-and-dressing-gown-covered legs, up his casually clad chest and shoulders, then up to his face. Her voice took on a slightly less assured quality. She gripped her broom harder. "After I shoo that bat out the window, you can wrench down the sash. The window sticks something awful."

"I'll do more than that. I'll get rid of the bat."

"Not if I get there first!" Olivia sprinted down the hall.

Left dazed and surprised in the wake of her pounding footsteps, Griffin realized for the first time that it might be a little inconvenient to love a woman like Olivia. She was independent, single-minded and unafraid to speak her mind. She was unusual and impassioned. She was sweet, but spicy. After a brief and confusing spate of boringly reserved behavior, the original Olivia he'd met

in his hotel suite, all those days ago, was back…and she
was ready to wreak havoc with a broom again.

Listening to the first *thwack* of her broom against
the wall, sounding its way down the hall along with a
"Drat it!" from Olivia, Griffin grinned. He wouldn't
have had her any other way.

He also wouldn't let her go into battle alone. That
wasn't what a man did. It wasn't what he did, with his
newfound sense of goodness and honor. Straightening
his spine, Griffin listened to another *thwack* echo down
the hall. Then he rolled up his sleeves, assembled the
protectiveness and caring he'd always tried to deny…
and let his longtime sense of shame fall away.

He *wasn't* The Boston Beast anymore.

Now, he could go to Olivia's room to help her—
even with both of them dressed so informally—and not
budge a fraction in his gentlemanly resolve. He could
shut the stuck window sash for her. He could comfort
her, congratulate her and remind her again how splendid
she'd been today. He could do all that, Griffin pledged,
and not be beastly for an instant.

So, ready to show Olivia his new integrity, Griffin
left his suite. He shut his door and tramped down the
hall to her rooms. There, her door stood open, letting
him glimpse the wonderful softness and alluring femininity of Olivia's private living space, with its pastel
upholstery, lace trims and glowing lamplight. He'd been
there before, Griffin recalled, when he'd brought her the
invention prototypes. But that visit had been different.
It had been brief and almost businesslike, full of appre-
hensiveness from both of them, on account of their earlier encounter at the Morrow Creek handicrafts show.

This time, Griffin knew, his visit would be different.
For one thing, they were both wearing nightclothes.

For another, the atmosphere in The Lorndorff was snugly hushed, now that it was long past sunset and most people were asleep. Not to mention, Griffin realized as he cleared the threshold and stepped inside, Olivia had enjoyed a recent bath of her own. Her zinc-lined wooden tub still stood filled with soapy water.

Instantly, his mind conjured up a provocative image of Olivia in that tub, naked and bubbly and utterly relaxed. He could almost smell the rose-scented lather she'd used…could almost feel the slick glide of the foamy water across her smooth, pale skin. He loved her skin, so different from his…

Then Griffin heard another vigorous whack of the broom against the wall, heard Olivia exclaim loudly, and made himself quit thinking altogether. Bathing beauty or not, Olivia needed him. He could not fail her now.

Even if he *did,* all of a sudden, have several cogent misgivings about his own ability to be near her…and be the morally incorruptible man she believed him to be, both at the same time.

With her broom in hand and her hair falling in bothersome tendrils around her face, Olivia chased her bat invader to the other side of her rooms. They were composed of a sleeping area, where her bed was, and a sitting area, where her settee and reading table and lit lamp were. Spotting the bat flapping madly in the shadows there, she delivered a mighty wallop.

Argh. The varmint had the gall to flap away, unharmed.

She knew she had the wherewithal to shoo away the tiny thing. Hadn't she managed several base hits during the baseball game today? Hadn't she earned cheers from Griffin? She had.

Reminded anew of her bravery and skill, Olivia swung her broom in a wild arc. This time, she successfully frightened away the bat. It flew past her head, then zoomed straight out the window. Its mad flurry of wings almost made her shriek aloud.

Success! Unfortunately, it came at a price. Olivia ended her swing of the broom…and landed it in the bathtub. Again.

Thwack. The bristles sent water splashing everywhere.

Unlike the other occasions tonight when she'd done that, splattering herself with leftover soapy water, this time she showered Griffin. He'd arrived in her room, broad shouldered and brave, only to be doused with the remnants of her bathwater.

Olivia didn't realize it at first. She turned in a celebratory circle, holding her broom aloft in victory, then saw something big, dark and sodden standing there. *Griffin.*

"Oh! Griffin!" She dropped her broom with a clatter. "I'm so sorry." She hurried to him. Then, "I vanquished the bat!"

She couldn't help saying so. She felt reasonably proud.

"I'll close the window." Heedless of his damp dressing gown—attire that left very little to the imagination, given its free-fitting design—Griffin strode to the window. With a single strong shove, he closed the sash. He brushed his hands together. He eyed the cozy pitched underside of the eaves with an inexplicable sense of accomplishment, then nodded at the door. He must have closed it to trap the bat. A moment ago, that had been a fine idea. *Now*…

"There," he announced. "All better."

He did not quite meet her eyes, however, and Olivia thought she knew why. He was just too kind to object to being soaked.

"It's *not* all better!" Grabbing a towel, she rushed to Griffin's new position. She ignored the dappled water spots on the floorboards and rug—signs of her skirmish, along with the fallen book near her toes—then stopped in front of Griffin. "I truly am sorry," she said. "Sometimes I get carried away."

"I never get carried away." He seemed oddly proud of that. "You can count on me, Olivia, *not* to get carried away."

She felt dubious about that claim. Also, confused. Of all the qualities she prized in Griffin, levelheadedness was not among them. She indicated her towel. "Just let me dry you off."

Vigorously, Olivia pushed the towel at his chest.

Trying to dry him, she discovered quickly, felt like dabbing a mountainside with a handkerchief. Beneath her towel, Griffin's chest felt firm and unexpectedly... *interesting.*

That probably meant that she should do a more diligent job of drying him, Olivia reasoned. After all, she owed him that much. She couldn't very well invade Griffin's suite, steal his broom—even though it was the hotel's property, left behind during one of her cleaning excursions—and then simply skedaddle when the going got rough and the gentleman got waterlogged.

Not that Griffin appeared particularly gentlemanly. Not at the moment. With his unbound hair, big bare feet and informal attire, he seemed... Well, *available* to her, was what most came to mind when Olivia looked at him. She'd never been in such intimate circumstances with him before. As she went on dabbing him earnestly with the towel, she learned, too late, that this situation piqued her natural sense of curiosity.

In fact, it dangerously inflamed her natural sense of curiosity.

Olivia was dying to know more about Griffin. Suddenly, she wanted to rub him down all over. She wanted to feel his muscles bunching beneath her seeking hands, wanted to hear him whisper her name in the wonderfully husky way he had, wanted to explore all the stimulatingly masculine contours that lay beneath his dressing gown. As bedtime attire went, his citified version was practically indecent. It was maybe even—possibly—defective.

Even now, Olivia observed, Griffin's fancy dressing gown shifted back and forth with her vigorous attempts to dry him off. Unlike a normal men's cotton nightshirt, it couldn't even keep him decently covered. A flash of hair-sprinkled chest was revealed here. A glimmer of muscular torso was revealed there. A wedge of naked shoulder, a glimpse of bare, sinewy upper arm…

Belatedly, the full reality of her situation occurred to her. Save for his underdrawers, of course—which shocked her in themselves—Griffin was entirely *naked* under his dressing gown!

And *she* was practically undressing him with her towel.

Startled, Olivia leaped back a pace. Granted, she wasn't employing her bare hands alone for the scandalous job she'd undertaken. She *was* using a towel. It formed a partial modesty barrier between them. But that didn't change the facts. She, Olivia Mouton, had a man in her rooms…and she wanted him there.

Given the way Griffin had been obediently standing there, allowing her to verifiably manhandle him, he wanted to be there.

As she looked up at him, he swallowed hard. "I should go."

"Don't go!" Olivia dabbed his head. "You're still wet."

Her industriousness didn't impress him as much as she'd have liked. It didn't work to the degree that he allowed her to continue drying him. Instead, Griffin stopped her towel-holding hand. "Your bat's defeated," he said. "Your window's closed."

"So is my door," she pointed out. "No one will know if you stay awhile." Hastily, she added, "It's only sociable. After all, we've been alone together many times before. I feel so comfortable with you, Griffin," Olivia urged. "I trust you."

He seemed simultaneously pleased and pained by her admission. Why that should be, Olivia didn't know.

All she knew was that she couldn't help wondering exactly what Griffin looked like under his dressing gown and underdrawers. The glimpses she'd had only served to fire up her imagination. Was his whole chest sprinkled with fine dark hair, like the triangular bit revealed by his dressing gown? Were his legs as muscular as his forearms? Would his belly feel as firm to touch as his chest did? How tightly had he tied the sash of his dressing gown? Would it come loose with a gentle tug, or would more force be required? Exactly how much gusseting was necessary in his underdrawers… and why? Full of those questions and countless more, Olivia gazed inquisitively at him.

Griffin saw her looking…and groaned aloud.

"When you look at me that way, I can't think straight."

"I'll do the thinking for both of us." She took the

towel from him and tossed it down with a definitive motion. "Stay. Please. Everyone knows I've been to your suite. They know we've been alone together already! This time should be no different."

It *felt* different, though. It felt…vaguely tingly and warm.

Griffin shook his head. "Everyone in the hotel has been looking the other way because they want you to save their jobs. They want you to return The Lorndorff to the way it used to be."

Instead of allowing it to be turned into my private residence, Olivia imagined him adding, *the way Palmer Grant must have revealed it might be.* She was surprised to hear Griffin mention her attempts to have the hotel reverted to her family's control—to ensure her friends kept their jobs. But she wasn't the least bit interested in discussing those topics tonight.

She lowered her gaze to his chest. "I missed a spot."

Another groan. "You're going to have your way, aren't you?"

"Why should tonight be any different from usual?"

"It shouldn't." Squaring his shoulders, Griffin gave her a determined smile. "You're right. This is only sociable."

"See?" Olivia felt satisfied to have convinced him.

"Only…" His rumbling tone drew her attention. So did the way Griffin's gaze dipped to her collarbone. "You're wet, too."

Carefully, he lowered his finger to a water spot on her silk wrap. He stroked it, as though trying to make it vanish.

Instead, at his touch, that tiny spot seemed to penetrate her skin even further. Heat flared where his finger touched, then spread in a widening circle. Olivia thought she might swoon with excitement—or at least fall into his arms to be held by him. Perhaps inviting Griffin into her rooms hadn't been wise....

"You were impressive today, Olivia." His dark gaze lifted to meet hers. "I've never known anyone as special as you."

At that, her heart turned over. Impulsively, Olivia grabbed Griffin's hand. She clasped it in both of hers, cradling it to her chest. "I care for you *so* much, Griffin. I can hardly say—"

"Words fail me, too." His gaze dropped to their joined hands. Something wicked and intent flared in his expression. "You feel *so*..." Another helpless groan escaped him. Visibly tongue-tied, Griffin used his free hand to pull her nearer. "All I can do is show you." He shook his head. "I'm no poet," he confessed. "But I've never felt like this before."

"Never?" She could scarcely breathe. Her heart pounded.

Silently, Griffin shook his head. The lamplight danced across his masculine features, making them look shadowy and notoriously rugged...but no less appealing to her, all the same. Olivia loved looking at him. She loved looking at him because she loved *him*. Soon, she'd have to tell him so. But first...

"I haven't, either," she admitted. She tipped up her face and found herself almost nose to nose with Griffin. They inhaled the same air, shared the same space... even their heartbeats felt united. Olivia fancied they were meant for this, together. "I've been proposed to," she said, "but I've never felt this way. Not for anyone." Daringly, she released his hand. She stroked his face, loving the newly smooth feel of his jaw. "You shaved!"

As romantic announcements went, hers was decidedly lacking.

But Griffin only offered her a winningly roguish smile.

"I imagined I might kiss you good-night. I wanted to be ready." His smile broadened. "I probably shouldn't admit it, but I do that every night. I think of you, and I think of how rough my beard is, and I prepare for something that can't ever be."

She'd thought she was the only one who imagined the two of them together—the only one who wanted a future. A family. A life to share and adventures to have and kisses for days and days.

On the verge of confessing as much, Olivia hesitated. She didn't want to reveal too much. What if Griffin really didn't want to marry her? What if he *had* found her lacking?

But then she realized…Griffin had seen all of her. The nice and the irksome and the baseball-playing included. Contrary to her fears, Griffin believed she was *more* than Miss Milky White.

When she was in his arms, Olivia believed that, too.

"A beauty like you should have more than a beast like me," Griffin told her, gazing into her eyes now. "But if you'll have me, Olivia, I promise to try to protect you. I promise—"

Olivia lunged upward. She cut him off with a kiss.

"I promise to give you all the love you've never had," she vowed fervently. "I promise to give you… *everything*."

With unfathomable emotion, Griffin gazed at her. He swallowed, tried to speak and failed. He squeezed her close, then exhaled a shuddering breath. "You're priceless, Olivia."

"You're *mine*," she replied, knowing exactly how battered and bruised he'd been…how unfairly treated and cruelly ignored. She knew she could change that. She *wanted* to change that. For him. For her. "I swear, Griffin. I can make up for it all—"

This time, he stopped her with a kiss.

"I keep telling you." His smile flashed, brief and brilliant. "You don't have to do anything except be you."

Then he lowered his mouth to hers, brought their bathwater-dappled bodies together and gave her everything that was in his heart to give. What Griffin had to give, Olivia learned as he kissed her then, was considerable. It was love. It was him.

Surrendering to both of those immutable forces at last, Olivia leaned into Griffin's arms. She wrapped him in her embrace, then kissed him back. This was real. It was right.

For tonight, at least, it was everything she needed.

If tomorrow, everything changed…

On the cusp of going further with that thought, Olivia looked at Griffin's face. She saw the telltale signs of intense focus in his expression, knew he was doing his best to savor their time together, and decided right then to do the same herself.

Fearlessly, she touched the lapels of his dressing gown. Lovingly, she studied his expression. Impishly, she asked…

"Would you mind very much taking this off? Soon?" Her breath caught and held at her own audacity. But Olivia had never been a woman for half measures. So she provided an incentive. "You know…for the sake of satisfying my scientific curiosity?"

Chapter Seventeen

If Olivia had been any other woman, Griffin knew, he might have been able to stick to his vow to behave with honor and goodness. He might have been able to view her luscious body—clad only in a virginal white chemise and a satiny wrap—and retain some integrity. He might have been able to feel her hands eagerly probing his chest—all but undressing him with her towel and her eyes—and selflessly left her feminine, welcoming rooms behind. He might have been able to bridle the beast inside him long enough to be the man that Olivia seemed to believe he was.

Instead, it was *Olivia* who appeared before him in nightclothes that revealed her delectable shape and soft, lovely skin. It was *Olivia* who touched him with verve and enthusiasm and seductive naïveté. It was *Olivia* who begged him to stay, who told him she trusted him, who very nearly told him she loved him, with her heart in her eyes and his hand clasped in hers.

I promise to give you all the love you've never had, she'd told him breathlessly. *I promise to give you... everything.*

Until that moment, Griffin hadn't known how much

he'd needed love to feel completed. Or how much he'd believed success would bring him that love…and then, when his proposal to Mary had been rejected, how devastated he'd been that it hadn't.

But tonight, with Olivia, everything had changed.

Tonight, with Olivia, Griffin felt the stirrings of a real new beginning for him—a beginning that could lead to the life and love he had always wanted…and had always been denied.

Olivia didn't deny him. Instead, she savored him. She looked at him as though she could never get enough of his eyes, his hair and even his oversize body. Griffin couldn't help preening beneath her gaze. He'd waited a lifetime to be desired. Now, faced with true desire in Olivia's eyes, he could no more resist her than he could sprout wings and fly back to Boston.

Especially not after Olivia eyed him so pertly, grasped his dressing gown's lapels and delivered her coup de grâce.

Would you mind very much taking this off? Soon?

You know…for the sake of satisfying my scientific curiosity?

At that, Griffin looked into her beloved face and could only think of one suitable response. "One of these days, your 'scientific curiosity' is going to be the end of me."

"But not today," she said smartly. "Not tonight."

"Not tonight. Not with you." Gratefully, Griffin cupped her chin in his hand. Lightly, he tilted her face to his. "Not when I feel that without you, I would stop existing altogether."

He lowered his mouth to hers, and—like every other time he'd kissed Olivia—doing so was a revelation to him. Holding her was like capturing sweetness; pressing his lips to hers was like tasting its pleasure without any of its sinfulness. With Olivia, a kiss felt pure. It felt like saying, without clumsy words and insufficient gestures, that he loved her, needed her...wanted her.

Greedily, Griffin buried his other hand in her upswept hair, all the better to bring her closer, then kissed her more deeply. Now that he'd begun, it was as though he'd waited a lifetime to kiss Olivia this way. He couldn't get enough of her soft lips, her helpless little moans, her freehearted way of kissing him right back, with needfulness and innocent joy. Their mouths met again, more urgently this time, and Griffin felt his self-control plunge even further. He needed to stop. He couldn't stop. Not if it meant not touching Olivia, not feeling her warm, lithe body in his arms, not knowing that it was him she crowded closer to, abandoning his lapels to throw her arms around him instead, nearly stepping on his toes to bring herself nearer.

Quickly—*very* quickly—Griffin lost all memory of his plans to be good. He felt Olivia's modest round bosoms press against his chest and couldn't remember a time when he hadn't been feeling her against him that way. He dropped his hand from her chin to her waist and hauled her still closer and felt a surge of possessive caring that nearly knocked him to his knees.

He needed Olivia. He needed to be with her. He needed to see her, to touch her, to hear her murmur his name.

He needed to pleasure her. The imperative to do so made Griffin lose awareness of everything except her and him and the feel of their bodies sliding together as their next kiss went on and on. He forgot the pink and lace-filled surroundings of her rooms. Everything blurred as he drank in Olivia's breathy cries, as he

swept his tongue against hers, as he lowered his hand
to her derriere and squeezed, delighting in the womanly curves he found there. All he wanted was Olivia.
All he needed was to give himself to her—to take everything she'd offered and more.

I promise to give you...everything, Olivia had sworn.

In the long, passionate moments that followed her
declaration, Griffin took what she'd given him, with his
hands and his heart and his body. He kissed her until
they both gasped. He stroked her until her wrapped robe
was as askew as his dressing gown was, revealing the
creamy white slope of her shoulder, the ribbons that
fastened her chemise...the pink jut of her nipples, just
barely visible through her chaste garment.

Inflamed by the sight of her, Griffin touched Olivia
there, too. He cradled her breasts in his palms, buried
his face in her rose-scented hair and lost himself in the
incredible feelings racing through him. He'd never met
a woman who was more responsive than Olivia. He'd
never thought he'd find anyone who made him feel more
welcome or wanted. But somehow, Olivia did.

As he caressed her, she sighed—and pushed herself
urgently, wantonly into his hands. As he kissed her, she
moaned—and kissed him back with a fervor to match
his own, burying her fingers in his hair and holding
his head to hers. As he pulled her into his embrace, she
smiled with wicked, weak-kneed delight—and called
his name in an impossibly intimate tone, urging him
onward in a way that let him know he wasn't alone.

He wanted her. Olivia wanted him.

Together, they were...perfect. Soon, they'd be one.

Tenderly, Griffin lifted Olivia in his arms. A few
long strides brought them both to her bed, with its
snowy coverlet and lace-trimmed pillows. A single ges-

ture of surrender brought them both down on its fluffy mattress. Lowering Olivia first, Griffin followed her with his knee between her spread thighs and his inadequate clothes all but falling off him, gazing at her in wonder and gladness. He braced himself on his arm, then smiled.

"You're so beautiful." He stroked her tumbledown hair away from her face. Then, reverently, he drew his knuckle along her cheek, loving her softness. "So beautiful, and so much more than beautiful." He kissed her, knowing it was true. "If I never see another sunrise, I'll be happy having seen you in all your beauty tonight. I won't ever need anything more than this."

Shyly, Olivia smiled, too. "And you." Her eager gaze roved over his disheveled dressing gown, then dipped to the glimpse of his bare abdomen revealed above his underdrawers. She seemed to heartily approve. "You're so big and strong. So handsome."

She could say that because his flaws weren't evident so far down his body, Griffin knew. She could say that because his nose was practically miles away from his midsection, his drawers and his—apparently fascinating, if Olivia's attention were any indication—drawstring closure to those underdrawers. "I'm not handsome," he objected. "Anything else. Big, yes. Strong—"

"Yes. You are." Suddenly serious, Olivia grasped his face. "I see *all* of you, Griffin," she promised. "And I love it."

I love you, he imagined her saying, but he just couldn't bear it. Not then. Not when so many new feelings already roiled inside him. Instead, Griffin closed his eyes. He focused on the remarkable feeling of their bodies pressed so tightly together, then returned his attention to Olivia's face, flushed and sweet in the soft glow of the lamplight. Gently, he kissed her.

"Are you sure of this?" If he didn't ask now, he would surely lack the wits to do so later. "Of us, being together?"

"Am I sure?" Olivia gave a jubilant laugh. "I'm all but debauched already!" she teased. "If you don't finish the job now, I'll be deeply disappointed." With a mischievous grin, she kissed him. Then, bravely, she flung her arms to the sides, beside the piles of pillows that cradled her head. "I'm ready, Griffin," she told him. "If you want to undress me, you may."

Galvanized by her words, humbled by her trust in him, Griffin could only stare at her. He swallowed hard. Here was a woman who cared for him, who thought him handsome, who had the audacity to tease him and dare him into loving her. If ever Providence had thought to toss a perfect mate into his path, Olivia was that woman. She was kind and brave. She was…

…lifting one of her hands, languidly tracing a path down the almost unwrapped lapels of his dressing gown, biting her lip as she tentatively touched that garment's knotted sash…

"Or should I go first," she asked, "and undress you?"

With a groan, Griffin shook his head. "There'll be time for that later," he assured her, trying *not* to think of the new and indecorously snug fit of his long underdrawers. Instead, he thought of the barrier presented to him by Olivia's wrap…and all the ways he could defeat it. Beneath her wrap, he knew, Olivia waited for him, more unguarded than she'd ever been, bare and feminine and full of secrets he longed to explore.

"First, I want to do this." He kissed her again, losing himself in the heat and wetness of her mouth. "And this." He lowered his lips to her neck, inhaling the rosy scent of her skin. "And *this*." Through her clothes, he cupped her breasts again. He rubbed his thumbs slowly across her peaked nipples, heard her gasp in response and felt himself grow twice as hard. At this rate, his underdrawers' drawstring would prove insufficient to contain him, Griffin thought dizzily.

Then he quit thinking altogether...and just *felt*.

He felt Olivia, squirming and breathless and moaning beneath him as he went on stroking her. He felt himself, mindlessly grinding against her, needing a sensual release that their half-tumbled-off clothes still prevented. He felt both of them together, kissing and touching and wanting, sharing in a swift, heedless discovery that felt all the more precious for its intensity. Their coming together was...*unstoppable* now.

With Olivia, Griffin learned he could not always exercise patience. Or good judgment. Or even, sometimes, all the gentleness he wanted. His passion made him rough; his love for her made him try desperately to slow down. But it was no use.

He kissed her and needed more. He touched her and took more. He heard Olivia moan and couldn't help smiling with savage pride. *He* made Olivia feel wonderful, Griffin knew...and before this night was through, he knew he would make both of them feel that way. For tonight, at least, The Lorndorff was heaven on earth, and its attic rooms were where paradise could be found.

Wanting beyond everything to share that with Olivia, Griffin opened her wrapped robe. Kissing her, he slid its silky panels down her arms. Soon that garment was cast aside, but his tutelage of Olivia wasn't finished. Tenderly, Griffin lifted her arms. "Go ahead," he urged. "Hold me. Here. Like this."

He helped her wrap her arms around his middle, but Olivia needed no further encouragement. Eagerly, she held him close. She pressed a heartfelt kiss of her own to his neck.

"You feel...mmm...so good!" she cried. "I'm sorry if I'm holding you too tightly," she whispered, "only I'm not sure—"

"Not too tightly. *Never* too tightly." *Never let go.*

Unable to say as much, Griffin kissed Olivia instead. He kissed her and caressed her and felt her hands roving all over his still clothed back, and her enthusiasm—her *desire*—only urged him on. Groaning with enjoyment, Griffin took advantage of Olivia's new state of near undress by filling his hands with her chemise's hem. Mad with need, he lifted the fabric higher. Its lace-trimmed ruffles edged up past her knee, past her thigh...

Only another few tugs separated him from undressing her, but Griffin abandoned his quest there. The temptation to touch all the bare skin he'd revealed was too great to resist. Full of passion and affection and devotion, he swept his hand down Olivia's shin, up the curve of her calf, and then higher still.

Feeling her quake beneath him, he stroked her knee, knowing he should calm her...knowing they should take things much more slowly. But that seemed as impossible for Olivia as it was for him. To his shock, Griffin felt her mimicking his earlier movements. Her fingers tugged at his dressing gown's sash. Making an adorably determined face, she undid that problematic knot. She wrenched the panels apart. She took her time looking at his naked chest, his tensed midsection, his underdrawers...

Then she smiled. Moments later, his dressing gown

struck the floor beside her bed in a bundled up, triumphant heap.

"Now we can *really* be close," Olivia breathed, and Griffin had the sense, looking into her eyes, that she loved that idea.

He did, too. Lowering himself atop her, careful not to crush her with his weight, Griffin kissed her. He *loved* that Olivia was forward with him. He loved that she wasn't afraid to show herself or to see him, that both of them were vulnerable and needful and full of inhibitions that fell away at the flicker of the lamplight. Looking at Olivia, beautiful and giving against the pillows and disarrayed coverlet, Griffin had to have her. He had to love her, to kiss her…to deftly unfasten the ribbons at her chemise and pluck away the laces, one by one, until the gap he'd created let him pull down that diaphanous cotton to reveal first one perfect breast, then the next.

Awed by her, made generous by her, Griffin pleasured her everywhere. He caressed her breasts and made Olivia sigh. He kissed her nipples and made her moan. He tongued her there and made her cry out…even made her clutch his head to her chest, where his wild, long dark hair spilled across her pale skin, turning him into nothing more than a conquering creature of passion and strength…and her into nothing less than a sweet, salvation-providing maiden—one who would fill his dreams forever.

Except *this* maiden was real. *This* maiden touched him boldly. She explored his chest and his shoulders and his midsection. She gazed at him with wonder and curiosity. She dared to kiss his neck. She pulled his hair, if that was what was required to make him kiss her where she most longed for him to. With him, Olivia was free and uniquely herself, needing and giving and taking in equal measure—and near equal nakedness.

Thrilled that her boldness met his own, Griffin matched her with every caress, every kiss, every new place to explore that which had once been forbidden but was now his to take. Moments flew past, barely noticed as he returned to Olivia's knee, then slid his hand higher. Her thighs felt silken and strong; her breath panted across his bare shoulder as he touched her.

"Oh!" In a low voice, Olivia cried out. "Is that…?"

Whatever she meant to say next was lost in a breathless moan. Griffin had found her most feminine secrets. Even as she tossed her head against the pillows, he went on touching her, wholly unable to hold back a moan of his own. Knowing Olivia this way, so intimately, was… *exquisite.* Knowing that she liked the way he touched her would live inside him forever. Striving to be gentle, determined to please her, Griffin caressed her.

Olivia arched herself higher in response, helplessly trying to get closer to him. Instinctively, she flexed her thighs. Her whole body trembled, already on the verge of something she'd doubtless never experienced and would not understand…but at the same moment as Griffin began to whisper comfortingly to her, he felt Olivia's hand swerve to the front of his underdrawers.

At her touch, his entire being went rigid. Gritting his teeth, Griffin released a groan of pleasure that would have scared him—had Olivia not made a passionately similar sound at the same moment. Acting on instinct and need, again mimicking him in a way that he vigorously approved of, Olivia stroked him.

She panted his name, and Griffin was lost. He lifted his face to hers. He saw Olivia's wide-eyed, marveling look as she went on stroking his manhood, and knew that he would disgrace them both if he let her continue. Her touch was simply too potent. Her eagerness was too arousing. Her love was too much.

Panting now, too, Griffin covered her hand with his. "Wait," he breathed. "Just…*feel*."

Making himself go slowly, just for now, he went on caressing Olivia with his free hand. Her slick femininity unfurled beneath his touch, hot and pouting and desirous, and it was all Griffin could do not to lose control of himself as he felt Olivia tensing beneath him…as he felt her surrender completely.

"Oh! Griffin!" Her gaze flew to his. "I feel…"

Before she could say, Olivia came undone. Bucking wildly beneath his hand, she reached a height of pleasure he'd never imagined she would…and then, when her gleaming body finally quit shuddering, she stared at him in surprise. She breathed heavily, gave a giddy giggle then stroked his face.

"I don't know what just happened," she said in a dazed tone, "but I just couldn't help myself. I'm sorry if I—"

Passionately, Griffin kissed her. "There's nothing to be sorry for." Gently, he stroked her face, too. "If that hadn't happened, I'd be ashamed to call myself a man."

"Oh. I see." With her heart pounding, Olivia regarded him through dreamy eyes. Then, "Can that happen for you, too?"

Nearly overcome at the thought, Griffin only nodded.

But Olivia seemed to have found a new sense of liveliness. Wearing a brazen look, she examined him…all the way down to his underdrawers. She seemed startled to find her hand still atop his clothing—still atop the long, unyielding length of him.

"Oh! I quite forgot myself," Olivia said. Then,

wearing a look of pure discovery, she began stroking him again. First tentatively. Then interestedly. Then joyously…and *vigorously.*

Her reaction was so uniquely her that Griffin found himself newly amazed. Filled with an indescribable sense of joy that a woman like Olivia had come to love him, he somehow found the strength to close his eyes, cover her hand with his, then stop her diligent, insanity-inducing ministrations a second time.

"I," he said in a husky voice, "have a better idea."

"Thank you, but I'm enjoying this one," she protested.

Griffin wasn't having it. An instant later, he took control. He kissed Olivia into a fresh round of wriggling, moaning insensibility. He caressed her passionately atop her feather-filled mattress. Then he stood beside the bed, smiled at her and dropped his underdrawers. Bared to the midnight air, ready to make Olivia his at last, Griffin inhaled deeply.

Olivia leaned up on her elbow to look at him. Then…

"You're *very* thrilling to look at," she mused. Her gaze roved over his shoulders and arms, past his chest and middle, straight down to…his feet. Then, shyly, it roamed higher.

Griffin felt himself react to her intensely interested scrutiny in a predictable way. His member throbbed. Then, *right then,* he needed Olivia to reach for him, to touch him…

And she did. As though divining what he wanted— or sharing the impetus of that desire—Olivia reached out. But Griffin knew he couldn't help reacting if she caressed him again. Eager and passion filled, he rejoined her on the bed. He brought himself down over her.

He gazed into Olivia's face and let the full weight

of what they were about to share sink into him. After this, Griffin knew, they would always be part of each other. Forever.

With the same synchronicity they'd shared earlier, they came together. Olivia eagerly parted her thighs, urging him to settle between them. Griffin pulled her nearer and kissed her deeply, letting her know how remarkable this was between them.

"I want you, Griffin," Olivia said then…and there was nothing he could have done, from that moment on, to stop himself from loving her fully. He simply needed her far too much.

With a single unerring stroke, he entered her. As readily as he'd ever dreamed it would, her body welcomed him. Hot and wet and shuddering, Olivia grabbed his back with both hands. She urged him on, tossing her head against the pillows again, and as Griffin reared up to look at her, as he went on plunging himself inside her, he knew that this was a night he would never forget.

Maybe, a small and unasked-for part of him knew, it was a night he would never forgive himself for, as well.

But Griffin couldn't think about regrets or mistakes or the honor and goodness that had slipped from his fingers like water past the banks of Morrow Creek in the moment he'd begun making love to Olivia. Because she was in his arms. She was moaning in passion beneath him. She was clutching his backside in a way that shocked him and drove him on, and Griffin simply couldn't hold on any longer. Thrusting again, Griffin felt himself losing control completely…and he could do nothing except give in.

Again and again, ecstasy shook him. Aware of nothing except the need to have more of it, Griffin lost himself in Olivia's arms. He'd never known such ferocious pleasure. He'd never experienced such a complete unraveling of what he knew to be true and real and right. In that moment, love was true.

Olivia was real. Being with her was right.

A heartbeat later, some of that started to change.

But Griffin felt too caught up in the aftermath of the storm they'd both shared to think about…much of anything at all. So he only set aside the unexpected, unwanted, unforgivable feelings that swamped him in that moment. Instead, he focused on Olivia. He pulled her close. He kissed her anew. He remembered the sound of her intimate cries as he'd brought her pleasure, and he tied up those memories with a sailor's knot too tight to be broken. Because, far too late, Griffin knew that this time, he'd made a mistake much too grave to ever be forgiven for it.

Especially—most of all—by Olivia herself.

Chapter Eighteen

Awakening as the late-morning sunshine poked its way into her rooms through the closed but uncurtained window that Griffin had masterfully shut the night before, Olivia slowly became aware of the scent of clove-oil soap clinging to her rumpled sheets. Groggily, she sniffed it. Then, she smiled.

Griffin. That was Griffin's unmistakable scent. Along with the aromas of stubbornness and passion—because, when Olivia was around him, she felt certain those qualities possessed enough tangibility to be inhaled—clove-oil soap was uniquely *him*.

Drawing in another big lungful, Olivia stretched lazily. Eyes closed, she wiggled her toes beneath her coverlet. She made fists with her hands and stuck out her arms. *Ah*. Then, struck by a sudden and unfamiliar sense of vague soreness, she went still.

Oh. Yes. Griffin had loved her last night.

She still had the slightly swollen mouth, giddier than giddy feelings and unaccustomed feminine aches to prove it.

Feeling butterflies anew over her recollection of it, Olivia sighed. After everything they'd shared, she and

Griffin had cuddled. They'd talked. They'd washed themselves, laughing over the icy leftover bathwater they'd used for the sake of discretion among the hotel staff. Then they'd cuddled again, and then—after a tiny bit more elated canoodling—they'd slept.

It turned out, Olivia had learned, that being held in a man's arms had a remarkably soporific effect. Especially if that man was a woman's beloved. Because she had no sooner scooted herself into Griffin's arms, felt him kiss her cheek and heard him rumble a low-voiced *good-night* than she was fast asleep.

She'd dreamed of wedding bells and spiced wedding cake.

She'd awakened with thoughts of proposals on her mind.

That was only natural, Olivia told herself as she languidly prepared to begin her first morning as Griffin's official paramour—and he, hers. Griffin loved her. She loved him. The intimacies they'd shared last night were ample evidence of that.

She still couldn't believe she'd felt that way! She hadn't even known such sensations existed. Recalling it now nearly made Olivia blush—but that hadn't stopped her. With Griffin, she'd been downright shameless. She'd ogled him. She'd groped him. She'd wantonly let herself be thrown on her own pine-framed bed and ravished until she'd begged for more. Given all that, if Griffin *didn't* propose to her... Well, Olivia couldn't imagine it.

Of course Griffin would propose to her. A decent man did not make love to an innocent woman and then not suggest marriage! Olivia knew that. She had married friends. Most of them had indulged in certain... intimacies with their husbands before tying the knot.

People got carried away, like Olivia and Griffin had done. Or they just couldn't wait. Some women arrived at their own weddings with twice-let-out dresses concealing their newly fruitful figures. Most people in town understood that. As long as the gentleman in question behaved honorably and the lady in question remained decorous, things worked out fine.

On the other hand…

Olivia had also known fallen women, some of whom had come to Morrow Creek to make a fresh start. Some claimed to be widows. Some kept to themselves and let the gossips decide what their pasts might have involved. Either way, it wasn't entirely unusual in the Arizona Territory to encounter an unmarried woman with a pregnant belly or even with a baby in tow.

Not that Olivia wanted to be one of them! Shivering at the very thought, she stretched again, then inhaled another lungful of Griffin's signature spicy scent. It was fortunate she liked it, she thought in a burst of cheerfulness, because it was probably all over her…exactly the way Griffin himself had been. She doubted a single square inch of her had escaped his loving attentions. From her ears to her toes, from her fingertips to her… Well, to the rest of her, Olivia felt tingly and loved.

She felt as though she'd shared something momentous.

Now she was ready for the next step. Because after everything that had happened over the past few weeks, Olivia felt more indomitable than ever. She'd taken on the challenge of Griffin. She'd successfully impersonated a chambermaid. She'd introduced Griffin to Morrow Creek, attended a whirlwind of activities with him and found the courage to step into her own lady's rational cycling skirt and play a game of baseball.

From here, she reasoned, there would be no stopping her.

Smiling at that, Olivia finally popped open her eyes. At the same time, she swept her arm to the side, intending to tease Griffin. He possessed a few sensitive, surprising spots that were most fun to tickle. If she played her cards right...

She would find herself alone in bed?

Confused to find the opposite side of the bed unoccupied, Olivia frowned. She sat up in the selfsame shaft of sunshine that had awakened her, then looked around. From her bed, she could easily glimpse her entire set of rooms. Her settee and lamp were still in place. Her revolving bookcase and prototype toothbrush were right where they belonged. Her bathtub stood where she'd left it, holding much less water, now even colder.

Draped across it was her abandoned floral wrap. Nearby, her chemise had been flung inelegantly across an armchair. Olivia couldn't remember how it had gotten there. She was too busy noticing that although her discarded clothing was still strewn about, Griffin's underdrawers and dressing gown were not.

Hmm. Rubbing the sleep from her eyes, Olivia looked again. The view didn't change. Apparently, sometime during the night, Griffin had left her rooms and quietly returned to his own.

Well. Undoubtedly that was because he wanted to help her retain her modesty and her reputation, Olivia told herself.

After all, if a member of the hotel staff came upstairs to retrieve her zinc-lined wooden tub, empty it of its water and move it downstairs—as they should have done last night—it would be better for everyone if Olivia and Griffin weren't in bed together. That was only sensible, wasn't it?

Assuring herself it was—despite the sense of prickly unease that filled her at Griffin's absence—Olivia slipped out of bed.

After hastily washing her face and brushing her hair, she pulled on her wrap again. Trying to ignore her increasing sense of disquiet, she opened her door. She padded down the hall to Griffin's suite. Her hotelier's keys admitted her. Most likely, Olivia assured herself as she opened the door, Griffin would be dozing in his own bed, rightly exhausted from pleasuring her.

Or…perhaps he would *not* be in bed at all?

With rising concern, Olivia trod farther into the room. Immediately, she saw that things had changed overnight.

Griffin's trunks and possessions were gone from the foot of the bed. His suit coat no longer occupied the dressing rack near the bureau. His long overcoat wasn't on its hook; his toiletries weren't beside the washbasin and pitcher. His books and valise were packed and gone. Even the imprint of his body was missing from his bed, which had been made up and smoothed as though by a professional chambermaid's hands.

Hmm. Evidently, Griffin's skills with housekeeping weren't limited to sweeping, Olivia realized. He was apparently an adept bed maker, as well. Undoubtedly, he hadn't wanted to malign her pathetic abilities by displaying his own. Until now.

Until the day he left.

Fraught with disbelief, Olivia stared at Griffin's bed.

More than anything, seeing it uncharacteristically made up confirmed all her worst fears. He'd left The

Lorndorff. He'd left *her*. And he'd done so secretly, in the worst way possible.

Probably, he hadn't been able to face her, Olivia reasoned. Last night, Griffin had *seen* her. He'd *known* her in the most intimate and complete way possible…and, just as she'd feared, he'd ultimately found her empty. In a way no one else ever had, Griffin had gotten to know her absolutely—for her appearance and for her nascent inner qualities—and he'd rejected her.

Griffin, like everyone else, had decided Olivia really was nothing more than a face on a patent remedy bottle. His only fault was lacking the strength of character to tell her so in person—to behave as forthrightly as everyone else in Morrow Creek had and be honest with her about her own limited appeal.

Not that she should have expected more from The Boston Beast, Olivia tried to tell herself. He was notoriously bad. He was known to be cruel, known to be harsh and unforgiving…

But Olivia didn't believe that. She knew this was her fault. She had tried to be fully herself with Griffin—philosophy books, inventions and baseball playing included. He'd obviously not appreciated those aspects of her. Unlike everyone else in town, Griffin knew her… and he didn't want her. If he had, he'd have been there, greeting her with a kiss and a smile, pulling on his hat and preparing to accompany her on another outing.

But he wasn't. He was gone. And she'd been a fool.

Feeling increasingly stunned, Olivia walked closer to the bed. She touched its coverlet, hoping against hope that its smooth appearance was a trick of the light. If she could glimpse a slight crease, if she could detect Griffin's presence…

But it was no use. *He'd gone.* There was no changing that.

In a sense, his leaving had been inevitable. Griffin had never promised to stay. In fact, he had always been evasive about his plans in Morrow Creek. Whenever Olivia had pressed him about it, she'd been met with outright caginess. She'd figured his equivocation owed itself to his scheme to take over the hotel and his reluctance to discuss The Lorndorff with her.

Now she realized Griffin had been evasive not because of the hotel, but because of her. He'd been too kind to reject her attentions immediately. But eventually, as time wore on…

As time wore on, he'd had to reject her. The alternative was to commit to her. Griffin clearly hadn't wanted to do that.

With a sharp sense of despair, Olivia remembered yesterday's baseball game. *That* must have been the limit for Griffin. He'd goaded her into playing and, when confronted with her true rebellious and unladylike nature, had found her unsuitable for him. Just as she'd guessed, he had been testing her. She'd failed. Just as she should have known she would.

Truthfully, it hadn't been fair for Griffin to use his greater sophistication and considerable intellect against her—all while tempting her with fiddle music and dancing, inventions and their prototypes, athletics and women's baseball playing. But he had. And she'd fallen for it entirely. Gullibly and trustingly, Olivia had allowed herself to be led.

She had allowed herself to *love.*

Now what was she supposed to do?

Woodenly, Olivia sank onto Griffin's abandoned bed. She felt its soft mattress give way beneath her weight, felt its plush coverlet bunch up around her fingers and knew there was nothing she could do. She'd taken a chance on love. Foolishly, she'd taken a chance on loving a man whom the whole world should have warned her against. Of course, she should have known better.

Of course, she should have resisted him.

But remembering Griffin just then—recalling his smile and his gruff voice and his disarmingly attentive ways—Olivia knew she could not have resisted him. She'd been too smitten, too awestruck…too skirts over chignon for a man who had appeared to *want* her, just as she was. A man who had appeared to need her, to care for her, to know and appreciate her innermost being.

She was intelligent, Olivia reminded herself ruthlessly. She could not have been utterly wrong about Griffin. Could she?

Looking back on their time together, Olivia considered the evidence. In this, as in most things, perhaps scientific thought could save her. She couldn't risk becoming caught up in grief and sentiment—not if there was a way around it. After all…

You're so beautiful, she remembered Griffin saying last night. *So beautiful, and so much more than beautiful.* Those weren't the words of a man who had judged her and then found her wanting. Those were words of love.

I keep telling you, he'd said before that. *You don't have to do anything except be you.* Those were words of acceptance.

A beauty like you should have more than a beast like me, Griffin had said. *But if you'll have me, Olivia, I promise to try to protect you.*

Those…well, those were words of self-disdain, mingled with words of strength and loyalty and protectiveness.

Reminded of something similar Griffin had once told her, Olivia squinted. She knew he'd expressed a comparable sentiment—one that, at the time, she'd not given much further thought to.

Then she recollected it.

I'll leave before endangering you, he'd sworn to her that lazy afternoon when they'd been lolling in the sunshine beside Morrow Creek after paying their social calls. *I swear it.*

It seemed, all at once, that Griffin had done exactly that.

It seemed that Griffin had sacrificed himself—sacrificed them both—for her. His view of himself as irreparably flawed had prevailed in the end. His wrongheaded sense of honor had made him leave…had made him try to protect her from himself.

What a foolish, *foolish* man he was, Olivia realized.

She didn't need anyone to protect her! If Griffin had truly been paying attention, he'd have known that all she needed was someone to *love* her. The rest was just sketchbooks and sparrow sightings, quilting bees and quiet times…getting herself through her days as best she could, just like everyone else she knew.

Unlike everyone else she knew, though, Olivia realized, she wasn't afraid of uncertainty. She was excited by it. She hadn't been daunted by wrangling with The Tycoon Terror. If anything, she'd been drawn to Griffin even more strongly because of the danger inherent in him—because of the courage he'd made her reveal and the facets of herself she'd uncovered in the process.

Because of him, Olivia realized, she'd learned her limits. She'd learned they were only as wide as she measured them to be. No one else could peg out that yardstick for her. Just like no one else could think her thoughts or dream her dreams, no one else could tell her how far she could go or whom she could want.

Including Griffin Turner.

You're priceless, Olivia, he'd said to her last night. Then, she'd believed him. Now…she *still* believed him. A man like Griffin didn't say pretty words for no reason. In fact, given the evidence of their time together, he was likelier to grumble and complain and hide away when troubled. Perhaps he was even doing so right now—hiding away in a place she couldn't find him.

Well. Griffin Turner had drastically underestimated her, if he thought Olivia Mouton could hear something like "you're priceless" and then just tuck it away in her memory like a colored autumn leaf in a scrapbook. She was better than that! She was braver than that.

Now, more than ever, she was stronger than that.

Griffin probably hadn't set out to test her with his leaving. Inadvertently, he'd done exactly that. He'd aroused Olivia's instincts for observation and analysis, and he'd riled her sense of feminine outrage, too. She *deserved* a proposal of marriage from him. All the facts—and her heart—pointed to that.

Besides, she *loved* Griffin. She did. If she didn't make sure Griffin smiled sometimes, laughed often and resisted the occasional urge to hide away in a dark hotel suite, who would?

She'd made some promises, too, last night—promises to love Griffin and stay beside him, to help him and try to make up for the terrible mistreatments of his past. She'd meant those promises.

Now Olivia meant to keep them. After all, it wasn't

every day a woman heard, *I've never known anyone as special as you.*

It wasn't every day she met a man who would say those sweet words, and then show her with kisses and smiles and every kind of loving attention that he truly meant them.

Unless her hypothesis was wrong—and hers weren't usually wrong, because Olivia knew to think them through—Griffin was even now on his way out of Morrow Creek. He was sacrificing the friends he'd made and the progress he'd made, and he was giving up her love, too. There'd probably never been a more foolhardy notion than his idea that he had to leave to protect her.

He had to stay to love her. And to *be* loved by her!

Standing again, Olivia straightened her spine. She lifted her chin, then directed her gaze out of the hotel suite's window. In the distance, the Morrow Creek railway station stood with a train on its tracks even now, preparing to pull out. It was possible that Griffin was on that train. It was possible, given how late in the morning she'd slept, that he'd already left.

Either way, Olivia meant to track him down.

Because you didn't fall in love with someone who'd been hurt and abandoned and abused in the past…only to hurt and abandon and abuse them yourself by letting them go. With dignity and decisiveness, she intended to go to Griffin. With determination aplenty, she intended to show him that some people were steadfast, that some people could be counted on and trusted…and that *she* was at the head of that line.

When it came to him, that line might be endless. If he stayed. Because this was the only place, Olivia realized as she pulled tight her wrap and headed for the door, that Griffin had truly dared to be himself—without his dark hat, without his black clothes, without his intimidating demeanor. If he wanted to be happy, he *had* to stay here. He'd said so himself.

You must show yourself, Griffin had told her.
Otherwise, you'll never really be happy.

She'd already done that, Olivia knew. But she'd almost let her happiness slip through her hands, too. At the first bump in the road—when faced with Griffin's departure—she'd been ready to surrender being herself and go back to being Miss Milky White.

But no longer. From here on, Olivia vowed, she would pursue the life she wanted with all the verve and vigor she could muster. And she would start by pursuing the man she wanted.

After all, if Griffin had never pursued her, she might never have uncovered herself. She might never have known how courageous she could be. Or how inventive. Or how loving.

Griffin would be easy to spot, Olivia reasoned as she left his suite and returned to her own rooms. Griffin would be the man whom women were staring at, men were sizing up admiringly and children were trustingly approaching…the way little Jonas had done at the musicale. Griffin would be the man who stood apart from all the rest—not because he was alone anymore, but because when Olivia looked his way, he was all she could see.

If she hurried, she knew, she might be able to catch Griffin today, within the hour. The only question now was…

Exactly what did a fashionable lady wear to properly impress the man she meant to spend the rest of her life with?

Chapter Nineteen

Griffin had never had so much trouble leaving a damn rusticated creek-side town in his entire life.

Starting at daybreak, he'd approached the Morrow Creek train station. Clad in his most menacing black attire—to match his dark mood—he'd stomped to the window and requested a ticket. The clerk, a certain Miss Hartford, had claimed she was "plumb sold out for today." What was more, Griffin had been *sure* there was a note of triumph in Miss Hartford's voice, too.

"Sold out in all directions?" Griffin had asked, glowering.

A shrug. "Yes, sir. Sold out. It's the oddest thing."

"You can't be sold out. Don't you know who I am?"

A squint. Another shrug. "Are you a prospector? I'd like to help you out. Surely, I would. But if the train's full—"

"Never mind. I'll take a coach."

Biting back his annoyance, Griffin had stalked toward the stagecoach office next. All the way there, he'd been confronted with the now-familiar sights and sounds of Morrow Creek. The butcher, O'Neill, opening his shop. The mercantile owner, Mr. Hofer, sweeping the raised plank boardwalk in front of his store. The blacksmith, McCabe, stoking his fires. The various female typesetters of the *Pioneer Press,* animatedly discussing the latest meeting of the ladies' auxiliary league while they walked across town to the newspaper office. Every last one of those people had smiled and said hello to Griffin.

He hadn't had much patience for any of them.

Especially not once he'd reached the stagecoach office, asked for an eastbound ticket and was told they were "sold out."

Stymied, Griffin had frowned. "But I need to leave town," he'd insisted.

"You'll need to wait, I reckon," the female clerk had said, echoing Miss Hartford's victorious tone at the railway station.

"Never mind. I'll hire a horse."

But once Griffin had reached the livery stable, Owen Cooper had been away—and his laconic stableman, Gus, had been less than no help at all. He'd actually proved an impediment to leaving.

"Nope. Not a single horse available," Gus had confirmed, fiddling with the grimy bandanna around his neck. "Nor a donkey, neither. It's the strangest thing." Amiably, he'd spat some tobacco, leaned on his hay rake and added, "I'd sure love to jaw with ya a bit 'bout yore biznesses in the states, though. Ya see, the thing is— and nobody knows this 'cept you—I got me a surefire notion for a different kind o' hiring company."

Gus had commenced chatting, talking at the approximate speed of a turtle who'd spied a tasty clump of leaves, spending a full half hour or more trying to obtain Griffin's opinion of his various and prospective business ideas. By the time Griffin had managed to extricate himself from the stableman's sudden garrulous spell, he'd been downright worn-out.

Or maybe that was grief, doing him in. Because even as Griffin relentlessly strode through Morrow Creek, trying to find a way to leave it, one thought kept dogging his steps. One image kept running through his mind. One sound kept chasing after him.

I'm all but debauched already, came the sound of Olivia's sweet feminine voice, again and again, circling his thoughts. *If you don't finish the job now, I'll be deeply disappointed.*

Griffin could still envision her, flushed and breathless and smiling as she'd invited him to undress her—as she'd flung her arms onto her sweet, pure bed and all but begged him to love her.

She shouldn't have done that.

She *wouldn't* have done that. Except for him.

Because late last night—far *too* late last night—Griffin had realized the truth of things. All this time, while he'd been convincing himself that Olivia was changing him for the better, he'd been changing her for the worse. He'd taken a gentle, innocent woman and turned her into an unrepentant wanton. He'd turned Olivia Mouton into the kind of woman who would willingly bed The Boston Beast…and then smile over having done so.

No right-thinking woman wanted The Business Brute. No matter how hard Griffin had tried to convince himself he wasn't that man anymore, last night was the proof that he was.

He hadn't changed, the way he'd told himself he had. He hadn't learned goodness and honor. Instead, he'd ruined Olivia.

It would be better for them both if he left. Olivia

deserved more than him. She deserved more than he could ever be.

But Olivia was too kind, Griffin knew, to turn him away. She was too gentle to protect herself the way she ought to. That was why Griffin knew he had to do it… if only he could find a way out of the blasted prison of this town.

Only one option remained for him. Griffin didn't want to take it. But after spending more time than he wanted trying to secure a train ticket, passage on the stagecoach or even a horse to ride, he was desperate enough to try his last recourse.

He arrived at his private train car, parked on a length of track alongside the Morrow Creek depot, and opened the door.

Sunshine flooded inside, falling on the train car's luxe furnishings, velvet-upholstered furniture and paneled walls. Griffin's desk stood beside the window where he'd abandoned it, piled with paperwork, a lamp and a writing set. His cabinets waited with drawers full of papers and ledgers. His personal correspondence overflowed its designated corner of the desk.

Heaving a sigh, Griffin slung his baggage into the train car's interior, then stepped inside. His old life seemed to surround him as he did, bringing with it all the unsatisfying smells of ink and coal and industriousness. Miles to the east, Boston awaited, ready for him to return to deal brokering and socializing—ready for him to return to compensating for his inborn fault with money and success and striving.

Ironically, Griffin realized, he knew now that his damnable nose—once so torturous to him—had never been the source of his troubles at all, despite what it represented to him.

He had let his appearance matter. He had let it dictate his actions and his attitude. He had let it punish and torment him.

Olivia had cured him of that. She'd made him see that he was more than his detested Turner nose—that he was more than his money and success, too. In the process, though, she'd also made him see that he was less than he'd hoped. In some ways, Griffin knew, he was even worse than he'd feared. He had to be worse, to have taken advantage of Olivia. He had to be worse, to have turned her into someone less like herself...and more like him.

His old life had never felt more superficial. He'd never yearned less to return to it, with all its empty splendor. But faced with the choice of continuing to corrupt Olivia or leaving Morrow Creek, Griffin knew he faced no choice at all.

Olivia came first, now and always.

For her, he would have walked across fire.

Or awakened Palmer Grant when he had overimbibed.

Because *that* was the particular dragon that Griffin roused when he stepped farther into his train car—nearing the area where the conductor's information was kept so he could get the train on the rails toward Boston—and found himself staring down the barrel of a lethal-looking pistol...held by Palmer.

Irritably, Griffin nudged away the firearm.

His associate only gawked. Blearily. "Griffin?"

"Go back to bed. You're hallucinating me."

"I am?" A blink. The gun wobbled. "Are you sure?"

"Certain." Griffin frowned. "Where's the blasted conductor? How long does it take to get this monstrosity on the tracks?"

Palmer set aside his weapon. "What monstrosity?"

"The train car." With his patience at an end, Griffin deepened his frown. He didn't usually have to manage these kinds of details. Typically, these were the sort of specifics Palmer handled. All Griffin knew was that maneuvering his private train car onto the tracks and in motion would take longer than boarding another train, catching a stagecoach or hiring a horse would have. That was why he hadn't come here first. "You'll be happy to know that we're going home. Today. Now."

"Oh." Palmer frowned, too. "Wait. *I'm* not going home."

"Yes, you are. You've been itching to get back to Boston. Now you're getting your wish." Griffin cast a puzzled glance at Palmer's clothes, which he'd plainly slept in. "And a bonus."

A cash incentive would sweeten the deal. And expedite it.

Except it didn't. His associate only shook his head.

"I'm not leaving. I proposed to Annie last night—"

Griffin groaned. He did not want to hear this.

"—and she accepted!" Semidrunkenly, Palmer beamed. "We were up late celebrating. I met her family. They're farmers."

"You're not marrying into a family of farmers. I won't believe it." Griffin strode toward the compartment's nearest built-in cabinet. He wrenched it open, then riffled through the papers, looking for the information he needed. "Help me find the train schedule. Or help me circumvent it. I don't care which. Everyone in this town seems to be conspiring to make me stay, and I won't have it." He swore. "Where the hell is the—"

"They *are* conspiring to make you stay," Palmer said.

Griffin scoffed. "See? I knew you hated it here.

You're not even above concocting crazy stories about the townspeople."

"I don't hate it here. Not anymore. Not since Annie." His friend gave a besotted grin. "Also, it's not a crazy story. They *are* conspiring to make you stay. At least some of them are. Unless you've proposed to Miss Mouton. Because if you have—"

"What does Olivia have to do with this?" Griffin demanded. *Except for bringing me back to life…then making my heart feel as though it's splintering.* He clenched his fists. He couldn't have Olivia anymore. For her sake, he had to get used to that. "Of *course* I didn't propose to Miss Mouton. *I* haven't lost my mind."

"Are you suggesting I have? I take exception to that."

Griffin ignored Palmer's pugnaciously raised fists. "Get to the point. Please. Who is conspiring to make me stay?"

If he could get to the bottom of this quickly, Griffin reasoned, maybe he could still catch a regular train— and avoid steeping himself in Palmer's lovesickness for an entire journey. His friend's happiness only made him feel sadder and more alone.

"It started with Jimmy. The bellman at The Lorndorff."

Griffin remembered him. But… "*What* started with Jimmy?"

"The bets." Expansively, Palmer gestured to the train car's settee, indicating that Griffin should take a seat. "On you."

Feeling suddenly overwrought, Griffin did sit. "Explain."

His terse tone did not intimidate Palmer. His associate merely gave him a satisfied nod, executed an unsteady swivel, then began pacing. "Everyone in town knows that Miss Mouton is the most sought-after bride. When you and she started spending so much time together...well, that's when the betting pool began."

Darkly, Griffin regarded him. "I don't like this so far."

"You'll like it even less when you hear the rest," Palmer promised him. He pressed together his palms, appearing to sober up a little as he continued pacing. "You see, most of the men in town have proposed to Miss Mouton. At one time or another—"

"I'm aware of that part," Griffin cut in. He did not feel eager to contemplate which man might win her when he'd gone.

"—they've all suggested marriage to Miss Mouton," Palmer went on, undeterred, "and they've all been very kindly refused. When Jimmy understood his own offer of marriage to have been rebuffed by Miss Mouton, he decided to make the most of it."

Griffin remembered when that had most likely happened—on the day when he'd first toured Morrow Creek with Olivia.

"He 'made the most of it' by instigating a betting pool?"

A nod. "And by stacking the odds in his favor, given the inside information he had," Palmer confirmed. Reluctantly, he added, "I'd told him a time or two that I was eager for you to return to Boston. Jimmy knew you had urgent business there—"

"I don't like the sound of this, either."

"—and he became convinced that you'd leave Morrow Creek *before* you'd enacted a successful engagement." Palmer gave Griffin a direct look. "So he bet against you. Gleefully, in fact. Essentially, I believe his words were, 'Turner'll run off lickety-split after Miss

Mouton shoots 'im down, too.'" Palmer grinned. "You can imagine for yourself the smug tone."

"But we were friends!" Griffin protested. "I liked him."

"Jimmy liked you, too," his associate told him. "But he also likes money—and with your chowderheaded takeover of The Lorndorff in the works, Jimmy was afraid for his job. He wasn't sure what would happen. He didn't think Miss Mouton could persuade you to give up your plans and surrender the hotel—"

"I already have!" Griffin broke in, indignant on her behalf. He couldn't believe her own friends had so little faith in her ability. "I left a note for Henry Mouton. I signed over the deed to The Lorndorff. It's his from now on, free and clear."

Palmer raised his eyebrows. "Well. Jimmy didn't know that."

"He didn't know a lot of things," Griffin grumbled. "If I *had* proposed to Miss Mouton—" *She would have accepted,* he thought, remembering the loving way Olivia had looked at him…and he was instantly thrown back into his current predicament.

He had to get out of town. Now.

Otherwise, he might weaken and go back to her.

"If you *had* proposed…?" Palmer aped him cheerfully. "Then?"

Griffin stood. "I hope you laid in a heap of cash on the side that wanted me to leave before I proposed," he said, "because I'm clearing out of here today, one way or the other."

"Hmm." Idly, Palmer stared out the window. "How does leaving in an undertaker's wagon suit you?" he asked.

Griffin made a face. "You're still soused. You're not

even making sense anymore. This whole imbroglio is probably—"

"No." His associate pointed out the window. *"Look."*

Griffin did look. He saw that Morrow Creek residents had begun assembling near the railway depot. They were drifting en masse toward his train car. "Mmm. They don't look very happy."

"They're *not* very happy. I think they're an angry mob."

Griffin scoffed. But then he took another look. The peculiar tableau before him divided into two fairly distinct sides. One was composed of male Morrow Creek residents. The other was composed—largely, at least—of female Morrow Creek residents. "Is that the suffragist, Mrs. Murphy?" he asked.

Palmer confirmed that he thought it was. "At the lead."

"But why are they here?" Griffin aimed a baffled look at his friend. "Are they here to make sure I've gone? Or to make me stay? I thought the men were betting I was leaving town."

"They have been. But all the women have been betting you'd stay." Palmer looked at their accumulated numbers with something akin to admiration. "I'll wager they're a sight better than the men at coordinating a joint effort to keep you here—at least long enough for you to propose to Miss Mouton, that is."

That explained a great deal about Griffin's difficulty leaving town this morning. Miss Hartford, the railway depot clerk, had likely bet on his staying and proposing. The clerk at the stagecoach office had been a woman, too, he recalled. Only…

"The stableman, Gus, isn't a woman," Griffin said, feeling weirdly pleased to have jabbed a hole in Palmer's cockamamie theory. "Why would *he* want me to stay in town and propose?"

"He's fond of Miss Daisy Walsh, who's staying with the Coopers above the livery stable." Palmer gave him a disbelieving look. "Owen Cooper won the bride raffle a while ago, and—well, the upshot is, Daisy Walsh wagered for you to stay." He shook his head. "Don't you listen to *any* of the town gossip at all?"

"I've been busy." Distractedly, Griffin peered through the train-car window. He ran his hand through his long hair, feeling uncomfortably exposed. He wished he still had his hat. He'd lost it forever—along with his heart, to Olivia—on the day of the baseball game. "None of those people appear ready to accept defeat," he told Palmer, absurdly. "I have to do something."

Palmer agreed with a nod. "Annie told me all about the women's point of view. Evidently, no one's more adept than Mrs. Murphy at inspiring the womenfolk on behalf of a good cause."

Griffin knew that already, given the well-known fable of her contraband baseballs. "My...courtship...of Miss Mouton is *not* 'a good cause'!" He could scarcely believe this was happening. He had woefully underestimated both the depth of his feelings for Olivia and his urgency to protect her from himself. He eyed the still-assembling mob. "Someone brought a picnic lunch!"

"And a banjo," Palmer added, brightening. "Listen."

Griffin groaned, fully at his wit's end. Banjo music was playing outside now. Perversely, he would have preferred raucous fiddles. "What kind of town is this anyway?"

"A close-knit one, I reckon."

"You 'reckon'?" Griffin exhaled. "Damnation. You're

a lost cause, too." He gestured outside. "Go ahead. Pick a side."

"I might. I could probably make a pretty penny." Blithely, Palmer squinted out the window. He pursed his mouth in thought. "Whatever you do, at least half the town will be happy."

"No. This is madness!"

His friend shrugged. "I guess that's love for you."

His sappy tone did not make Griffin feel better.

Neither did what he said next.

"It could be worse," Palmer mused aloud. "Miss Mouton could be out there herself, waving greenbacks and taking bets."

Appalled, Griffin swerved his gaze out the window, suddenly fearful he'd see exactly that. He wasn't sure he could withstand it. To know that their time together had been a joke to her...

"It wasn't like that between us!" he yelled. "It was—"

"Yes?" Palmer asked in a silky tone. "Go on...."

Frustrated, Griffin stared him down. "It was special," he ground out through clenched teeth. "You wouldn't understand."

"Oh, I understand," Palmer disagreed calmly. "I understand that you appear to have thanked Miss Mouton for your 'special' relationship by giving her father a hotel."

Griffin frowned. That remark made his generous resolution of the situation sound so...dastardly. In reality, it had been practical. So, mulishly, Griffin refused to comment. Palmer's gross misunderstanding of the situation didn't warrant it.

"It seems to me," Palmer plowed on relentlessly anyway, "that *that* strategy is something your curmudgeonly former self would have considered sufficient."

He raised his eyebrows. "It's *not*, however, a response befitting the man you are today."

Griffin arrowed him a deadly recalcitrant glance. Olivia had, technically, gotten what she wanted, he knew. She'd won the game she'd set out to play with him by impersonating a chambermaid—by trying to make him relinquish The Lorndorff.

"Bribing someone with a hotel to assuage your guilty conscience is *not* an action that's in keeping with the man you are today," Palmer repeated laboriously, unaffected by Griffin's ire, "after being with Miss Mouton for all these weeks."

Bribing? Guilty conscience? Infuriated, Griffin paced.

No one else would have dared speak to him this way. If he knew what was good for him, Palmer Grant wouldn't have, either.

"I know where I've been these past weeks," Griffin bit out, unwilling to discuss any of this. "And with whom. And I know where I am now—which is facing an angry mob!"

"Well, it will only be half an angry mob, eventually," Palmer pointed out. "Once you make your decision, that is. And evidently, you don't know where you've been these past weeks. Or you haven't been paying attention during them." He gave Griffin an exasperated look. "Can you truly not see the changes in yourself?" He raised his arms in vexation. "By now, you should have threatened to wallop me at least three times. You should have fired me once, maligned the reputations of my grandfathers twice and then stormed off to drink some whiskey."

"I might yet," Griffin growled. "Wait and see."

But his associate only laughed. "You are *different,*

Griffin! You are different because of Olivia." At his casual use of her first name, Palmer softened his tone further. "Don't let her slip away from you. You will regret it forever if you do."

Obstinately, *aggrievedly,* Griffin contemplated that.

"You might have said the same thing of Mary," he said.

At that, silence fell in the train car. At least it did, as much as was possible between the increasing shouting coming from outside and the banjo music wafting on the breeze.

"I left Mary behind," Griffin went on roughly. "I left all hope of marriage and happiness behind with her! You didn't—"

All at once, the truth struck him. Confused, Griffin frowned. "You didn't say a thing," he told Palmer. "Why not?"

His friend gave him a wry look. "Mary was not Olivia."

He didn't need to say anything more. The truth was too evident. It was too raw, too real…and suddenly, too hopeless.

"I've ruined this!" Griffin said. "I can't fix it now."

Palmer gave an annoyingly equable look. "Well, you can't fix it by staying here, that's for certain."

"I can't fix it by leaving, either." Distraught, Griffin paced faster. He wanted to smash something. To drink to forget. To blame this on Palmer…on anyone. But he didn't. He truly *was* changed by Olivia. "Those women outside will blockade me."

"Maybe," Palmer agreed, appearing on the verge of chortling. "But I meant you can't fix this situation by staying here, in your train car. You have to go to her. Now."

Griffin stopped. "Maybe Olivia wouldn't have accepted if I'd proposed to her," he confessed. Maybe part of him had been afraid of that happening all along. "She's refused everyone else." Sardonically, he cracked a smile. "Leave it to me to fall for the one woman who's the hardest to woo. Maybe in the world."

"You always did enjoy a challenge."

Argh. What Griffin enjoyed was Olivia—seeing her smile, hearing her debate Descartes's theories with him, feeling her touch. Somehow, he had to set things right. But first…

"Did you bring any spare hats?" he asked.

Palmer appeared perplexed. "You only ever wear the one."

"Then you didn't. Just say so, will you?"

"I didn't bring any spare hats."

But he needed a hat to confront this issue, Griffin knew. He needed protection to go to Olivia—to beg her forgiveness and ask her to be his. He might even need a hat to sneak past the waiting crowd. A few of them appeared none too pleased with him.

He wouldn't be surprised if they broke out pitchforks. He couldn't believe Palmer was willingly marrying one of them.

"Don't tell me you're worried about your…" Palmer broke off, gesturing toward Griffin's hideous nose. "*Now.* Are you?"

A little. "For all I know, those townspeople haven't come to settle their bets at all," Griffin protested. "For all I know, they've come to try to chase away The Boston Beast."

Palmer's guffaw didn't help matters. Then… "No," his associate assured him in an even tone. "They haven't."

Doubly vexed, Griffin shot another speculative glance at the gathered crowd. Each side milled around in talkative clumps. They appeared to be electing representatives now. Most likely, he reasoned, the people of Morrow Creek were preparing to have their irksome wagers settled, for once and for all.

From one side, Grace Murphy stepped forward.

From the other, Olivia Mouton did.

Boggling at her, Griffin felt his heart turn over. His belly performed a somersault, too. He couldn't tell if Olivia loved him, if she hated him…if she'd merely come to collect on the *non*proposal side of the town's bet. All he knew was that Olivia looked wise and determined and unstoppably desirable.

All he knew was that, for better or worse, he was going to her. "Cross your fingers," Griffin said, then he headed outside.

Chapter Twenty

Olivia couldn't believe so many of her friends and neighbors had come to the railway station to witness her possible defeat. Likely, a few of them—the men whose marriage proposals she'd turned down over the years, for instance—were deliberately rooting for a setback for her. Doubtless, they wanted beautiful Olivia Mouton to be refused the only proposal she'd—ironically—ever truly desired. They wanted to see her humbled. They wanted to see her stripped of an advantage that Olivia knew today more than ever was wholly ineffectual.

At least it was when it really counted.

Beauty faded. Remedy bottles grew dusty. They smashed or stopped selling or simply quit convincing enough folks of their efficacy. Someday soon, Olivia knew, that medicine-show man's Milky White Complexion Beautifier and Youthful Enhancement Tonic would fade from memory. A new elixir would replace it.

Her only hope, now as ever—even when she hadn't realized it—was to rely on the parts of her that couldn't be lithographed or sketched or photographed, Olivia knew. Her only hope was to be herself, *fully* herself…

and to take her chances that when things truly mattered, she would be enough. For anything.

Considering that as she stepped forward to the front of the collected crowd, Olivia wished mightily that her wise thoughts came packaged with additional bravery. She also wished that her wise thoughts had the capacity to stop a lady from rethinking her choice of attire and hairstyle for the afternoon. Even now, Olivia gave her upswept hair a tentative pat. She fluffed her skirts, checked her high-buttoned bodice then exhaled deeply.

Nervously, she aimed a hesitant glance at Annie. From her friend, she'd learned of the goofy betting scheme that Jimmy the bellman had hatched. From her friend, she'd learned of the plans the members of the ladies' auxiliary league had made to waylay Griffin, should he ever try to leave town. Now Annie nodded.

She also gave an audacious "go ahead!" signal, making the women's side of the betting pool surge forward in anticipation.

Hoping she wouldn't disappoint their hopes for a proposal, Olivia gathered her courage. She took another step forward.

At the same time, the door to Griffin's private train car opened. Griffin himself appeared in the doorway. He looked tall and broad shouldered and undeniably grim, and Olivia had the distinct sensation that her heart skipped a beat at the sight of him. He looked so...forbidding, she thought. Also, so alone.

Maybe, it occurred to her, he perversely liked it that way?

The gentlemen's side of the betting pool appeared to agree with that supposition. As one, they murmured and moved forward.

Keeping ahead of them, Olivia raised her chin. It

wouldn't do to falter now. She'd come here to get her man. That was exactly what she intended to do. No matter how foolish she had to make herself look to do so. Just then, she didn't care a whit.

Also just then, Griffin descended the train-car steps. His visage did not become any softer. Absurdly, Olivia was reminded of the very first descriptions of Griffin she'd heard from Jimmy and the hotel desk clerk, the day after Griffin had arrived.

I heard he's the terror of Boston, they'd said, *with eyes like the devil and a fancy dark coat that drags along on the ground when he stomps by. About seven feet tall, with a fully loaded gun belt and knives strapped to both legs. Dressed all in black. Couldn't scarcely see his face, 'specially with all that hair.*

All those descriptors were still apt. Realizing it, Olivia quailed. Griffin might not have precisely reached seven feet, but it felt as though he did—and all his ability to intimidate was fully evident today. If she managed to successfully stage a public showdown with him, Olivia realized, her old quarrelsome encounter with the medicine-show man would crumble to pieces.

In its place, a new legend would rise—one where Olivia Mouton actually had the gumption to demand a proposal from a man whose approach made fully grown railway men and cowboys blanch.

Behind her, Olivia's supposed backers on the *non*-proposal side of the betting pool stopped in their tracks. Not a man among them wanted to antagonize Griffin. She was on her own.

Bravely, Olivia took another step. She squared her shoulders. She watched as Griffin strode toward the crowd.

He might have emerged, it occurred to her, simply

to settle their wagers. For all she knew, Griffin had laid bets himself.

Olivia didn't want to think which side he might have gambled on. If he was really as bad as he'd claimed, he'd have had no compunction about profiting from such a situation—about letting her believe he'd been wooing her for real…when all along he'd actually been scheming to win a devious series of bets.

On the other hand, the fact that Griffin had given The Lorndorff outright to her father was strong evidence of Griffin's sincerity. Olivia had learned of *that* surprise from her father. Although everyone in town had seemed duly impressed with her "victory" over the out-of-town industrialist who'd shaken up Morrow Creek with his mysterious arrival, Olivia had been unable to take much pleasure in her supposed triumph.

She'd been too busy trying to formulate what to say when this situation arose—as, inevitably, given her own unstoppable sense of determination, she'd thought it would.

She'd had a whale of a speech prepared, too, Olivia reflected. It had been full of vivid metaphors and passionate analogies and irrefutable logical arguments. It had been touched by emotion and leavened by whimsy. It had been magnificent.

Unfortunately, as soon as Griffin got close enough for her to glimpse the heartbreak in his eyes and the regret in his face, Olivia felt her entire carefully crafted speech melt from her mind. Her eloquence vanished, replaced by simple need.

She needed Griffin. That was the beginning and the end.

With the last shred of her intellect, Olivia transferred her gaze from Griffin's face to his head. His long dark hair lifted in the territorial breeze, making him seem wilder than ever. He hadn't replaced his hat, but she liked him this way.

"I'd like a proposal," she blurted. Her voice broke on the words, so she tried again. Knowing that her demand was likely being carried by the wind toward the onlookers behind her, Olivia added extra starchiness. "I *deserve* a proposal. I—"

Before she could say more, Griffin stunned her by dropping to his knees. His fine black trousers hit the dirt. His long black coat puddled there, too. Not caring, he grabbed her hands.

His grasp was every ounce as urgent as his expression was.

"*Please* forgive me, Olivia," Griffin said. "I'm sorry."

His hoarse, needful tone shocked her. "Get up!" She gave a jerky upward gesture, stifling an impulse to see if people were laughing. "Your suit! Your coat! They'll be ruined." She glanced backward. "Half the town is here, Griffin. People will talk."

"Let them talk. I don't care." With unabashed sincerity, Griffin looked up at her. Ludicrously, he kneed his way closer. "All I care about is you," he said. "I *need* you, Olivia. I need you like darkness needs dawn. Like whiskey needs a glass. Like flowers need creek water. I can't stand it without you."

"So…I'm bright and encircling and prone to flooding?" she couldn't help asking, unable to fathom his plan. If it was to make her look a fool, it was succeeding. Her knees wobbled. Her heart pounded. In Griffin's grasp, her hands trembled. Olivia doubted she could hold out much longer. "Is that it? Griffin, you've scarcely been without me for a single morning, so—"

"It felt like a lifetime," he swore. "I didn't know—I

couldn't see—" He broke off, groaning in dismay. "You have to believe me, Olivia. I've been without love for so long—"

At that, her heart broke a little bit.

"—that I guess I didn't trust it when it found me." He gave her hand a passionate squeeze. "I didn't trust it when you found me. I didn't think it could be true—that you would want me for yourself. For your own." He gave a pleading gesture from her to himself. "Look at us. You're fine and sweet and brave, and I'm—"

"You're wonderful!" Helplessly, Olivia dropped to her knees, too, right along with him. Not caring about the onlookers who gasped at her movement or the dirt that smudged her skirts, she ardently stroked his cheek. "You're kind, Griffin, and you're brilliant and generous, too, and I can't bear to think what would have become of me if you hadn't come to town."

A glimmer of hope brightened his eyes. "You'd have spent a lot more time embroidering things?"

Horrified by the notion, Olivia shuddered. "Maybe!" she agreed. She couldn't help smiling at the raspy mischief in his voice. "Or maybe I would have just spent my days not knowing who I really was…not knowing who I *really* wanted."

"Well…" He quirked a grin—one that reminded her of his teasing ways. "You have quite an assembly here to choose from."

"It's *you!*" Exasperated, Olivia choked back a sentimental sob. "It's you, Griffin. It's only you." Once more, she caressed him. Once more, she drank in the sight of him. She'd only been mostly sure that she'd catch up with him in time after all. "Without you, all my days lose their thrill. All my nights—"

Hastily, he cut her off before anyone could hear her

discuss all the very private, very sensual things they'd shared.

"Without you, I have no reason to be," Griffin said simply. "Without you, I wouldn't know what it means to be loved at all."

At that, tears leaped to her eyes. "You *are* loved, Griffin! Haven't I said so?"

Wordlessly, he shook his head. Her heart broke anew.

"I love you!" Olivia shouted, not caring who heard. "I love you so much, Griffin, that I can't believe the breadth and shape and size of it. My love for you—"

"Is bigger than a bread box and more crooked than a shoehorn?" Griffin joked. "Well—"

"—is big enough to hold you and me together forever," Olivia finished resolutely. "It's big enough to hold the moon and the stars and everything in between. I don't know how I got along without you, but if I have my way—"

"You'll never have to try," Griffin said, pulling her close to him. On their knees together in the dirt, they gazed at one another. Very softly, he kissed her. "I swear, Olivia, if you let me, I'll do everything it takes to give you the love you deserve. I'll fight every battle. I'll give you all I have and more." His face took on a shining countenance, as though Griffin had just remembered something especially excellent. "I have mansions and money!" he assured her. "I have social connections. I have a box at the opera house and prize-winning horses. I—"

With a kiss of her own, Olivia stopped him. She breathed in deeply, loving the sight of him. The feel of him. The *nearness* of him. She shook her head. "I don't care about any of those things. I don't care where we live or who we see. I only want *you*. I want you forever,

Griffin. I'm sorry I didn't say so before." Olivia sighed. "We might have avoided all this."

"Maybe." Griffin cast a dubious glance at the crowd. They'd kept a respectful distance, but Olivia knew there was still a chance they'd run riot. There was a lot of money at stake in those wagers. "But somehow," Griffin went on, "this feels exactly right to me. Because *you're* with me. And I'm with you."

He held her hands, then drew in a deep breath. "I don't know if I can say it right. I've never tried before." His dark-eyed gaze swept over her, solemn and meaningful. "But I love you, Olivia. I do. I love you in ways I'd never imagined. When I'm with you, I feel as though I could do anything. I feel as though my heart is too big for my chest and my arms are too short to hold you for as long as I'd like to."

"Well," Olivia inserted pertly, "that could be remedied with enough practice, I'd say. So just keep trying."

Griffin appeared to love that idea. Tenderly, he kissed her again. He nudged his knees a little closer to hers. He inhaled, then rested his forehead against hers, gazing into her eyes.

"When I look in your eyes," he said, "I can see the man I want to be. I can see the man I hope to be. And I know I almost wrecked that today, Olivia—" Griffin's voice broke, then strengthened "—but I swear, if it takes my whole life, I promise I'll love you the way no one else ever could." Lovingly, he stroked her cheek. "I promise I'll be there for you. No matter what it takes. I can do it! I'm strong and I'm smart—"

"He is both of those things," Palmer Grant interjected from the side, cradling a jubilant-looking Annie next to him. "I can vouch for the grumpy, bossy, hard-drinking son of a—"

"—and I'm equipped with more pigheaded stubbornness than any single man ought to have been endowed with," Griffin continued with self-evident intractability. "So you can count on me. I promise, you can. Just give me another chance. Please."

At that, Olivia gave him a cockeyed look. "What do you think *this* is?" she asked reasonably. "Do you think I fall down and plant myself in the dirt at the railway station for just any man?"

"I hope not," Griffin avowed. "Because if you do, I just got a damn sight less special, didn't I?"

"Never," Olivia pledged, smiling as she kissed him. "You'll be special to me always. No matter what."

For a long, blissful moment, they only gazed into each other's eyes, forehead to forehead, breathing the same fresh Morrow Creek air, not wanting to move—not wanting to change.

They were both, Olivia realized belatedly, savoring the moment.

Then the crowd began to stir. Someone stepped forward.

"None of this mush," Jimmy the bellman observed loudly, "sounds like a proposal of marriage to me. How 'bout you boys?"

"No!" As one, the assembled men roared out. "No!"

"Hold on!" Grace Murphy yelled back, speaking for the collected ladies. She motioned for the men's catcalls to quit. Her husband, the saloonkeeper, helped with that endeavor. Then, with that accomplished, Grace looked at Olivia and Griffin. "Please continue," she suggested with a courteous gesture. "Here in Morrow Creek, most of us have faith in true love."

Her sisters, Molly and Sarah, stepped up to agree.

"Nah! It ain't happenin'!" one of the menfolk said.

Someone chuckled. "She ain't sayin' yes, if it does!"

"Pshaw," added a woman. "She practically proposed to him!"

At that, Olivia looked at Griffin. He looked at her.

They both smiled. They both drew in deep, happy breaths.

"*Please* marry me," they said in unison.

A confused, collective groan came from the crowd.

"What in Sam Hill does that mean?" Gus the stable-man shouted from the back. "Did anybody hear a yes or a no?"

Amid all the turmoil, Griffin smiled at Olivia.

Olivia smiled back. *"Yes,"* they said together. "I will."

A stunned silence fell over the crowd. The banjo quit playing. Even the town's children, who'd wandered there with their parents, stopped frolicking near the station platform.

"Tarnation!" someone cried. "Does that mean we *all* lose?"

"On the contrary," Mrs. Murphy demurred. "I believe you'll find that means the ladies win their bets. And so, after a fashion, at least, do Miss Mouton and Mr. Turner."

"We men *lost* our wagerin' money?" Jimmy asked, looking astonished. "But…we were gonna add it to the kitty for the big faro tournament. It was gonna draw in heaps of high rollers!"

"Mmm. I don't think so," the town's most-known suffragist told him. "Not anymore, at least. But I *do* believe it will be a fine addition to the Temperance League's coffers."

"Temperance League?" the men groaned. "Ain't that

a kick in the pants?" A pause. Then… "Sure you ain't gonna reconsider, Miss Mouton? It still ain't too late!"

Olivia laughed, shaking her head.

And with that, the people of Morrow Creek were off, doing several of their most favorite things at once—gambling, arguing, coming together, laughing…and most of all, cooking up a brand-new addition to the town's burgeoning supply of folklore.

This tale, Olivia heard as Griffin gallantly helped her to her feet and then kissed her, seemed to involve a misunderstood beauty, an enigmatic beast and a whole passel of suspiciously "essential" town matchmakers who'd paved the way for their love and happiness. But even if the folklorists didn't *quite* get all the details perfectly and accurately right, Olivia didn't care.

Because against all the odds and beyond all her hopes, she'd found the one man who could see into her heart and love what he glimpsed there. She'd found the one man who could soak up every bit of the love she had to give him—and it was a *lot* of love, she assured Griffin as they sneaked their way past the increasingly frolicsome crowd and headed back to The Lorndorff together—and then give it right back to her.

Only somehow, Olivia realized, Griffin had managed to double the love she'd given him. He'd managed to make it as big and as strong as befit a seven-foot-tall giant who could turn around trains with his will alone… and emerge from the darkness to find a girl with a light, just waiting there for him.

From now till forever, Olivia meant to be that light for Griffin. She meant to love him and care for him and trust him.

At the bottom of The Lorndorff's stairs, Griffin

turned to her. He smiled, patently hers in that moment and happy for it.

He held out his hand. "Are you ready for this?" he asked.

"I'm ready for *everything*," Olivia promised him.

Then she took his hand, assembled all the inborn curiosity that had separated her from everyone else for so long…and used it to send her straight into her future with Griffin.

"Have I ever told you," Olivia remarked as she and Griffin reached the top of the hotel stairs after leaving the railway station, "about the time I discovered the universe?"

Still holding her hand, Griffin smiled. "I don't think so. I guess I should have known there was more?"

"Of course there's more!" She laughed. "With me, there always is."

"I wouldn't have it any other way," he assured her.

"Good." Olivia nodded. "So…?"

"So…?"

"So aren't you going to ask me?"

"Oh. Of course." Griffin delivered her his most inquisitive look, determined not to disappoint her. He felt far too grateful for the second chance he'd been given. "Tell me," he said obligingly. "What about the time you discovered the universe?"

Joyfully, Olivia squeezed his hand. "It happened when you kissed me," she told him. "It was right there in your eyes."

"Aha." Nodding, Griffin recollected that moment. "I think that was a dust mote," he teased. "Just a bit of fluff."

"It was not!" she protested. "We were at the creek!"

"I remember." For a moment, Griffin did just that. Then he smiled at her. Rakishly. "If you're fond of what my eyes can do," he said, "wait until you learn more about the rest of me."

Olivia looked as though she could hardly wait. Except...

"*After* we're married, you mean?" she asked.

"Yes," Griffin agreed staunchly. "*After* we're married."

For an uncertain, rueful moment, they looked at each other.

Then, "Let's head to Reverend Benson's right now!"

Their unified exclamation made them both laugh.

"We've got to stop doing that," Olivia said, looking giddy and full of daring. "It's going to begin annoying people."

But Griffin only shrugged. "I don't think we can stop. It's not as though we're doing it on purpose."

"That's true. Maybe it'll stop on its own. Eventually."

They contemplated that for a moment.

Then, "Probably not," they said in unison.

Laughing, they headed back downstairs again, hand in hand.

In the lobby below, Griffin stopped. He looked around the bustling hotel, soaking in the furnishings and the chandeliers.

"You know," he mused, "I think I've found a home here."

Olivia smiled mischievously. "Really? At The Lorndorff?"

"No." At her overtly cheeky tone, Griffin smiled. He deserved that, he guessed, for joking about dust motes. Very discreetly, he touched her dress's lace-trimmed bodice, making his meaning more than plain. "Right here. In your heart."

Olivia melted. "And here I had such a humdrum answer."

"You had the perfect answer," Griffin disagreed cheerfully. "Between the two of us, we have every territory covered. That right there, Miss Mouton, is the true meaning of partnership."

"That's true." With a newly assessing glance, Olivia looked him over. Lovingly. "You know," she said, "I think we're going to have a very interesting and thrilling life together."

"I know we are," Griffin promised. "I guarantee it."

Then he took Olivia's hand, and they both got started. On today, on tomorrow…and on every single fun-loving, philosophy-filled, sunshine-sparkled day that would come after that.

* * * * *

REQUEST YOUR FREE BOOKS!

 HARLEQUIN® HISTORICAL:
Where love is timeless

2 FREE NOVELS PLUS 2 **FREE GIFTS!**

YES! Please send me 2 FREE Harlequin® Historical novels and my 2 FREE gifts (gifts are worth about $10). After receiving them, if I don't wish to receive any more books, I can return the shipping statement marked "cancel." If I don't cancel, I will receive 6 brand-new novels every month and be billed just $5.44 per book in the U.S. or $5.74 per book in Canada. That's a savings of at least 16% off the cover price! It's quite a bargain! Shipping and handling is just 50¢ per book in the U.S. and 75¢ per book in Canada.* I understand that accepting the 2 free books and gifts places me under no obligation to buy anything. I can always return a shipment and cancel at any time. Even if I never buy another book, the two free books and gifts are mine to keep forever.

246/349 HDN F4ZY

Name _____ (PLEASE PRINT) _____

Address _____ Apt. # _____

City _____ State/Prov. _____ Zip/Postal Code _____

Signature (if under 18, a parent or guardian must sign)

Mail to the **Harlequin® Reader Service:**
IN U.S.A.: P.O. Box 1867, Buffalo, NY 14240-1867
IN CANADA: P.O. Box 609, Fort Erie, Ontario L2A 5X3
Want to try two free books from another line?
Call 1-800-873-8635 or visit www.ReaderService.com.

* Terms and prices subject to change without notice. Prices do not include applicable taxes. Sales tax applicable in N.Y. Canadian residents will be charged applicable taxes. Offer not valid in Quebec. This offer is limited to one order per household. Not valid for current subscribers to Harlequin Historical books. All orders subject to credit approval. Credit or debit balances in a customer's account(s) may be offset by any other outstanding balance owed by or to the customer. Please allow 4 to 6 weeks for delivery. Offer available while quantities last.

Your Privacy—The Harlequin® Reader Service is committed to protecting your privacy. Our Privacy Policy is available online at www.ReaderService.com or upon request from the Harlequin Reader Service.

We make a portion of our mailing list available to reputable third parties that offer products we believe may interest you. If you prefer that we not exchange your name with third parties, or if you wish to clarify or modify your communication preferences, please visit us at www.ReaderService.com/consumerschoice or write to us at Harlequin Reader Service Preference Service, P.O. Box 9062, Buffalo, NY 14269. Include your complete name and address.

*Next month, follow Louise Allen's SCANDAL'S VIRGIN
as she leaves a trail of broken hearts across London's
ballrooms, and discover the only man who can heal her
own shattered dreams…*

Now he carried Laura to the bed and set her carefully on
her feet beside it before returning to the door. His hand
hovered over the key. "I will lock the world out, not you in."

"Leave it, I trust you." She smiled faintly at his raised
eyebrow. "In this, at least."

"Why, Laura? Why have you come to me?" Propose to
her now, or afterward? Afterward, instinct told him. Do not
complicate this moment. In passion, in the aftermath of
passion, surely he would see the truth in her.

She half turned from him and ran her fingers pensively
over the old chintz bedcover, tracing the twining flowers
and stems that some long-dead lady of the house had
embroidered. The curve of her neck, the elegant line from
bare shoulder to ear, was exposed to him, pearl-pale in the
lamplight. Between her breasts was a shadowy, mysterious
valley where a gold chain glinted.

"It has been a long time," she said finally, without looking up. "You think me loose, but there has not been anyone
since…since before Alice was born. And there is this thing
between us. This desire. I feel cold inside almost all the
time. Flirting and laughing is no longer enough. And with
you there is heat, even if there is nothing else but dislike
and suspicion."

Avery had not expected this frankness, this simple confession of need. His body stirred, eager, but he did not
move. She spoke of nothing but desire, dislike, mistrust.
Could he ever replace that with even the basic tolerance
marriage would require? He probed a little, testing how
open she would be. "You know you are fertile. Why take
such a risk again?"

Laura did look up then. The brown eyes that could look
so cold seemed pansy-soft in the lamplight. "We were
young and foolish. We were to marry, so what did it matter?
And Piers was inexperienced. You, I think, are both experienced and not inclined to be careless."

Avery could argue that all the care in the world was
sometimes not enough, but somehow his prized self-control
was slipping away, sand through his fingers. Tomorrow he
would take that huge risk with his life and his heart and
with Alice's love. Tomorrow he would disregard all the
lessons of his own parents' disastrous marriage.

Tonight he would lie with this woman who was ruining
his sleep, haunting those dreams he could snatch from a few
hours of slumber.

Don't miss
SCANDAL'S VIRGIN
Available from Harlequin® Historical
June 2014

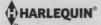

HARLEQUIN®

HISTORICAL

Where love is timeless

COMING IN JUNE 2014

Scars of Betrayal

by

Sophia James

Cassandra Northrup had believed Nathaniel dead…until now.
Once, she had loved him, given herself to him in
the hidden depths of the snow-covered Pyrenees.
But then she had betrayed him….

Relief at the sight of Nathaniel turns to darkest shame as Cassie
sees the hate in his eyes. Years have passed and their physical scars
have faded, but the pain runs deeper than ever. Yet passion can be
born out of betrayal—and as desire crackles between them once
more, will Cassie reveal the secret she's long kept hidden?

Available wherever books and ebooks are sold.